LITTLE BLACK GIRL LOST 2

ALSO BY
Keith Lee Johnson

Little Black Girl Lost
Fate's Redemption
Pretenses
Sugar & Spice : A Novel

LITTLE BLACK GIRL LOST 2

KEITH LEE JOHNSON

www.urbanbooks.net

Urban Books
74 Andrews Avenue
Wheatley Heights, NY 11798

ISBN 1-893196-39-9

First Printing February 2006
Printed in the United States of America

10 9 8 7 6

Submit Wholesale Orders to:
Kensington Publishing Corp.
C/O Penguin Group (USA) Inc.
Attention: Order Processing
405 Murray Hill Parkway
East Rutherford, NJ 07073-2316
Phone: 1-800-526-0275
Fax: 1-800-227-960

Acknowledgements

To Him, who is able to do considerably more than I can ask or think, I give You thanks.

Special thanks to my darling mother and my aunt Darlene for reading all my books.

To Martha Weber, thanks for all your insights and questions. Were it not for all the questions you asked, the novel would be incomplete.

Special thanks to Carl Weber for answering all my calls in a timely manner, for returning ever message in a matter of minutes, and for being a true professional in this tough literary game.

To my man, Phillip Thomas Duck, author of *Playing with Destiny* and *Grown & Sexy,* in stores April 2006, thanks for all the laughs you provide and the invaluable wisdom.

To my good friend, Kendra Norman Bellamy, author of *Because of Grace* and *More than Grace,* in stores April 2006, thanks for your sensitive listening ear and all the Godly advice in my time of need.

Thanks to Brandi Brown of Toledo, Ohio's Mix 95.7 for all the air time.

Special thanks to Tabitha, manager of Borders Bookstore in Toledo, Ohio. Thanks for always looking out for me from the beginning. I won't forget you.

To Martina Tee C. Royal of RAWSISTAZ Book Club, and to Robilyn Heath of Girlfriends Reading Circle, I haven't forgotten either of you and all that you two have done to further my literary career.

To all my coworkers who have bought and read every single book, I can't thank you enough and I appreciate each of you.

To all my fans, thanks for all the emails, and thanks so much for buying and reading *Little Black Girl Lost* and making it a Black Expressions Best Seller for over 8 months. Thanks for all the reviews and talking about this book. I hope you enjoy *Little Black Girl Lost II.* I personally think it's better than book one, but I wrote it, what do you expect me to say? LOL! I crack myself up! LOL!

Book One

The End

Napoleon's Bayou
New Orleans
August 1953

TWO ITALIANS swaggered into the Bayou, a nightclub in the French Quarter, firing menacing stares at everyone who looked their way, threatening them all with their eyes. Both men were dressed in very expensive dark suits, ties, and fedoras—gangster attire. As they made their way through the crowd of Negroes who were dancing to the rhythm of a live band, an aisle parted as if Moses had lifted his staff over the Red Sea. Their names were Chicago Sam and Vincenzo Milano.

Sam was a reputed Mob Boss and had a seat on the Syndicate's Commission, the board of directors of gangsterdom. He held the power of life and death—a god to all those who feared his unpredictable and merciless wrath. Vincenzo, better known as Vinnie in

Mob circles, was his lieutenant, available twenty-four hours a day to do whatever Sam needed him to do. They had just left the immaculate home of John Stefano, the Boss of New Orleans.

Stefano called Sam because he needed his permission to whack Napoleon, who was under Sam's umbrella of protection. Normally, Sam would have just whacked Napoleon himself, but he was a man of his word and owed Napoleon because he had taken the manslaughter wrap for Vinnie, did hard time in an Illinois federal prison. Vinnie had beaten a man to death in a Chicago suburban bar over a minor offense. In return for doing the time, Napoleon was promised the Colored section of New Orleans, which was originally promised to Vinnie.

Stefano lost serious money when Napoleon killed Richard Goode, which caused a riot. Stefano wanted Sam to straighten Napoleon out; he wanted him to make sure Napoleon knew and understood that he was hanging on by a very thin thread.

Sam and Vinnie approached Napoleon, who was standing as he waited patiently for them to make their way over to his table. Sam and Napoleon smiled when they greeted each other with a kiss. But Napoleon only shook hands with Vinnie Milano; both men were stone-faced. Vinnie tried to have Napoleon whacked in prison, but, Bubbles, a Negro, saved his life and had been his right hand man ever since.

I'm gonna kill you, you dago bastard, Napoleon thought, while forcing a smile as he stared into Vinnie's eyes.

"Vinnie, how's it hangin'?"

"It's hangin' to my fuckin' knees," Vinnie replied. "And you?"

"To the fuckin' floor—draggin'."

Sam barked, "That's why we're here. Your fuckin' dick, Napoleon."

Bubbles watched the exchange between Vinnie and Napoleon from a distance and then walked over and spoke respectfully to Sam and Vinnie.

They all sat down at Napoleon's table and Sam said, "You really fucked up this time. I mean you really blew it with Stefano. It's a good thing for you I'm on your side. You got the fuckin' FBI lookin' into our business because you decided that a nigger bitch is more important than business." Sam looked at Bubbles for a reaction, but he didn't reveal his emotion. He just listened stoically.

"Stefano wants you dead, but I said no," Sam continued. "Everybody deserves a second chance, I told him. I gave him my word that I'd talk to you, and I have. We're taking the next plane outta here, Napoleon. But remember . . . you're only here because John Stefano owes me and I owed you. You fuck up again and you're on your own."

"Thanks, Sam," Napoleon said. "I guess we're even now."

"Don't guess, Napoleon," Sam hissed. "I won't warn you again. Vinnie, let's get outta this dump."

Vinnie could hardly contain the glee that rose from deep within, but he managed to keep it on a short leash, and only grinned slightly when they stood up. The smile alone was evidence that this wasn't the end of it as far as Napoleon was concerned. He knew they were planning to come back when the heat was off, but by then, Napoleon planned to own New Orleans.

The moment Sam and Vinnie left the Bayou, Bubbles turned to Napoleon and shot a white-hot stare at him. He knew this day would come the night Napoleon met Johnnie Wise, the stunning sixteen-year-old beauty who looked to be in her late twenties. Everything that happened after that was inevitable, and it was all Napoleon's fault. The moment Napoleon decided to kill Richard Goode to gain favor with Johnnie, Bubbles knew it would all come crashing down on both of them.

Richard Goode, the former Grand Wizard of the Ku Klux Klan had murdered Marguerite, Johnnie's mother, because she was attempting to blackmail him by threatening to expose his long-time relationship with a known black prostitute. Sheriff Tate had witnessed the murder, but talked Johnnie out of pressing charges because Whites wouldn't convict a white man for killing a black prostitute.

In Bubbles' mind, he and Napoleon were dead men, and nothing was going to change that. Not now. Not after seeing Chicago Sam in a nigger joint. It was already settled. It was just a matter of time.

Napoleon watched Sam and Vinnie as they got into a car, then said, "Get the chessboard, old friend, and bring it into my office."

"The chessboard? Are you fuckin' crazy, man? Chess? We gotta take them muthafuckas out—both of 'em. If we don't, we're through."

Napoleon looked at Bubbles. "Relax. Get the board and bring it into my office." Then he left without another word.

Minutes later, Bubbles walked into the office with the chessboard and pieces. Still angry, he said, "Didn't I tell you this shit was gon' happen? I told you not to get involved with Johnnie. And if you did, Chicago was gon' come down here and take everybody out. Didn't I tell you that?"

Unmoved by Sam and Vinnie's arrival, Napoleon's intrinsic cool seemed to radiate and fill the office like a blast of cold air had encapsulated him in a huge block of arctic ice. He looked at Bubbles. "Set the board up."

Puzzled, Bubbles frowned. He stared at Napoleon for a second or two, wondering if he understood the gravity of the situation. "What's going on in that devious mind of yours?"

"Business. What else?"

Bubbles emptied the pieces onto the board and they set them up and prepared to play. "Why are we playing games, man? You know we gotta take 'em out. Tell me you understand that much—please."

"We're gonna kill Vinnie. That's for sure. But we don't have to kill Sam. Besides, if we killed him without the permission of the Commission, it all comes crashing down. And there's no way they're going to give permission. Besides, Sam is a great earner and has too many highly placed government connections. Right now, Stefano and Sam could take us out and nobody would give a fuck.

"Killing Richard Goode, the racist dog that he was, caused the riot. I was glad to do it, even if it did cause a riot. I don't give a fuck. But ya gotta understand these fuckin' dagos; it's about the money. They could care less about the riot as long as their prostitution, gambling, protection, and drug businesses aren't affected. If the Feds weren't here taking their pictures, you'd have cause for concern. But believe me, nothing, and I mean nothing's gonna happen right now."

Bubbles shook his head. "Chicago's serious, Napoleon. And we're playing games?"

"They're playing a game too—the game of death. But they don't have the acumen to fuck with a superior player like me. See, I set all of this up."

"That's bullshit. You gon' sit there and tell me you knew there was gonna be a riot and Chicago was going to come down here?"

"No. I knew he would be coming for other reasons, reasons I can't discuss with you now. The riot was unexpected, but a blessing in disguise."

Bubbles shook his head again. "Explain that shit, man."

Napoleon looked at the chessboard. "What am I looking at?"

"A chessboard."

"That's what you see, but I see life and death, situations and opportunities. You follow me?"

Bubbles frowned. "No."

"Chess is a game, but consider the pieces, consider the situations. It's a turf war, is it not? You have your side of the board, which can be construed as territory, right?"

Bubbles thought for a moment. "Right."

"You're the king, and you have people who do your bidding. Some are expendable pawns, nothing more. But even the pawn can kill the king, can he not? The trick is to set up situations to get the king in trouble. To do that, you've got to think ten, twenty moves ahead of the other king. That way, he's surprised when you kill him, right?"

Bubbles smiled as if he now understood the game of death. "Right! Right!"

"Now . . . old friend, tell me, which piece is the most powerful?"

"The queen."

"Why do you believe that?"

"Because of how she can move around the board."

Napoleon looked into Bubbles' eyes. "You're still thinking about the game of chess. I'm talking about the game of death. The queen is indeed the most powerful piece, but not for the reasons you think. She's powerful because she is of the female persuasion."

Bubbles frowned again.

Napoleon laughed. "She's got a pussy, man. And the pussy will get you killed. That's why Chicago came in here. Didn't he say, 'you decided that a nigger bitch is more important than business'?"

"Yeah . . . so?"

"They think I'm weak, man. And as long as they believe that, I'm in control. We're playing chess because you're gonna be running the Colored section when I move uptown. You're gonna have to learn to use people as easily as you move the pieces on this board. Why? Listen, and believe me when I tell you, they all wanna be the king. Every last one of them. Remember that. Some will be pawns, others will be knights, and still others will be bishops. But the king must control everything and everyone, especially his queen. Never the other way around, or you die. That's how the game of death is played. Understand?"

"I'm starting to."

"Two things you gotta know. Know your enemies, and know who your snitches are. You'll always have both. For example, how did Stefano find out about me and Johnnie?"

"Somebody talked. But who?"

"Exactly! And I know who. The snitch did just what a snitch does . . . waited until after the riots to tell Stefano for maximum damage."

"Let's whack the muthafucka now!"

"No, no, no. Don't you see? When you know who the snitch is, you can use him to give information to the other kings. No, we don't kill the snitch yet. We use the bastard until he's of no more use. Then we get rid of 'im. Understand?"

"Who is it, man?"

"You don't need to know that right now; maybe never. Just know that all traders think their king is stupid. That's what you want him to believe and you do everything to keep him believing that. The snitch thinks he's a fuckin' genius compared to the king, so he goes on his merry way, believing the king doesn't know shit, especially if the king would endanger his whole operation over the queen."

"So, the thing with you and Johnnie . . . it's not about the pussy?"

Napoleon laughed from his belly. "Well, in this case, it is. But when you warned me that night, the night I met her, I got the idea to take Stefano out."

"And Johnnie?"

"As I said, I'm keepin' her. At least for a while. I never came so fuckin' hard in my life."

"What about her boyfriend, Lucas? He works for us, but he's an expendable pawn and you're going to kill him, right?"

"Can't kill 'im and keep Johnnie. No fuckin' way. But I have a plan, and believe me, this whole thing is gonna make you rich in the end, old friend."

While Bubbles didn't say anything in Lucas' defense, he was glad he didn't have to kill him. He liked Lucas, but the millions that would be coming his way when Napoleon took over New Orleans were too much to ignore. If it ever became necessary to kill Lucas to get the money Napoleon promised him, he wouldn't like it, but he would do it.

Little Black Girl Lost 2

Part One

Paradise Lost

"The heart is deceitful above all and desperately wicked." Johnnie thought he was talking to her as he spoke, like he was standing right next to her, speaking directly in her ear. "Some of us are so self-righteous that it's going to take a lifetime to discover the truth of this verse so that we might be truly saved."

Reverend Staples
Little Black Girl Lost

Chapter 1

"You can't change what you are."

A THUNDERSTORM swept through New Orleans. Lightening flashed suddenly in Johnnie's bedroom window. The howling wind and rolling thunder seemed to be directly over her Ashland Estates home. It had been raining all night, but Johnnie slept soundly for the first time since the night she watched George Grant, affectionately known as Bubbles, murder Richard Goode. Goode was paying Johnnie's mother, Marguerite, to commit kinky sex acts. He later, under the threat of blackmail, ruthlessly beat her to within an inch of her life and then put a bullet in her brain.

From time to time, images of that night flooded Johnnie's mind. She could still hear Goode's final words to her as she watched from Marguerite's powder blue Oldsmobile. She had watched Bubbles and the teenaged football player she loved, Lucas Matthews, beat Goode savagely with a pistol and brass knuckles.

"You're just like her!" Goode had screamed, referring to Marguerite's trade. He could see Johnnie's silhouette in the moonlight. You're a good for nothin' black nigger whore too! Don't forget that! You can't change what you are!"

But Johnnie hadn't forgotten. How could she? She couldn't because there was a certain measure of truth in his words. The house she lived in, the furniture and appliances in it, and the ever-growing stock portfolio served as constant reminders too—all provided by Earl Shamus, the insurance man who had paid Marguerite a thousand dollars to bed her over a year ago. Earl even set her up with his friend and stockbroker, Martin Winters, who she later bedded to learn how the stock market worked.

On Christmas Eve, Earl, who had tried to procure her when she was twelve, dragged her into her mother's bedroom and savagely plundered her sensitive and unblemished fruit like a conquering Moor. When he finished, after he'd pumped her the last time, after spilling his unwanted seed in her, he withdrew himself, got dressed, and placed a five-dollar bill on her pillow. The money helped ease Earl's conscience, but it inadvertently taught Johnnie that the fruit she possessed was of great value. And with her newly found carnal knowledge, she began the slippery slide down the path of prostitution.

The senseless murder of Reverend Staples on the stairs of the library as he pled with the volatile mob to come their senses was also a constant image in her young and still impressionable mind. Staples, who was wearing his clergy garb the night of the riot, had tried to reason with them, begging them not to burn down the library and the school. He was pelted with racial invectives and shot in the head for his bravery.

So many people had died that night, black and white alike. Women and children fell in the middle of the street, dead because she had to have her brand of justice for her mother's murder. It was the kind of justice a Negro couldn't get in a courtroom, but Johnnie's beauty was able to procure with relative ease.

And so no, she could never forget, as all of this reminded Johnnie of how she acquired her small fortune. But deep in her heart, having been a born again Christian for nearly five years, she knew that just as Richard Goode had his day of reckoning, she would have hers too.

Johnnie found herself constantly fighting back tears because everything in her life had gone wrong the previous year. Her mother was murdered, and her precious virginity was auctioned. After being plundered at fifteen by a grown man who should have known better and a mother who sanctioned it all, Johnnie eventually submitted to the weekly humiliation day after day, month after month, and learned the value of her body and how to subdue men with it.

She sold her body to Earl Shamus for money, to Napoleon Bentley to save her boyfriend's life, and to Martin Winters for knowledge of how the stock market worked. Earl Shamus and Martin Winters were a not so pleasant memory, but Napoleon Bentley was another story altogether.

Chapter 2

I want it now!

JOHNNIE OPENED her eyes, turned on the light, and looked at the clock on her nightstand. It was nearly 6:00. Sadie, her next door neighbor and best friend, would be coming over for breakfast before they drove to the Garden District, where they worked as maids for the affluent aristocracy of New Orleans. Although Johnnie had plenty of money and didn't have to work, today would be her first day. She was excited because not only was this her first job, she would be working for the Beauregards, her white relatives. She'd wanted to meet them for years.

Marguerite had told Johnnie she was related to them because Nathaniel Beauregard was Marguerite's father by blood. He had been having an affair with Josephine Baptiste, Marguerite's mother, who was also a prostitute. When Johnnie was a little girl, before she knew she was a Negro, and the overt ramifications of being of that persuasion, she never understood how she could have such rich relatives, who lived in an expensive neighborhood, while she and her mother lived in run-down Sable Parish.

Johnnie wanted to tell Sadie about the conflict that raged within her, but she'd promised Sadie she wouldn't sleep with Napoleon Bentley. If she told Sadie about the sexual liaison, she would have to admit to everything, including admitting how she felt about Napoleon and how he skillfully awakened her young body a little over a week ago, and gave her the kind of orgasm that caused her to faint from its consuming power. The night at the chic Bel Glades hotel was becoming a constant fixture in her mind, and she fantasized about Napoleon daily. No one had made love to Johnnie the way Napoleon had.

Napoleon Bentley was a ruthless gangster, and that made the allure even more tantalizing. The memory of him lapping at her secret place for what seemed like an eternity and the raw sex between them bombarded her mind like a vampire's ravenous hunger; an insane hunger that would never know satisfaction. Her own words echoed in her mind; the words she said to him, literally begging to have her walls filled with his thick tool, plowing uncharted territory. *Stick it in me now! I want it now!*

Nevertheless, she was in love with her boyfriend, Lucas Matthews, who had come to her rescue when classmates accosted her on the way home from school one day. The crowd was led by Billy Logan, who'd had a crush on Johnnie before learning of her dalliance with Earl Shamus.

Deeply hurt by this knowledge, Billy called her a whore and suggested that she was not only having relations with a white man, she was performing fellatio too. It was one thing to be called a whore, but to have everyone know the intimate details of her "business" transactions were more than she could bear, and she wept.

In Johnnie's time of utter desperation, high school football star, Lucas Matthews, who was tall, powerfully built and ruggedly handsome, had a well-deserved and legendary reputation for kicking ass and taking names. It had been rumored that he had even whipped a few men. When he came to her rescue that day, when he whipped Billy Logan, when he made him apologize on his knees, she fell deeply in love with him on the spot because he respected her even though he too had heard the same stories as everyone else.

Lucas was so enamored by her beauty that he sacrificed his pride for her, letting her continue the "relationship" with Earl Shamus because she promised to stop as soon as it was financially feasible. But later, he realized that Johnnie had been unfaithful to him, and had allowed Napoleon Bentley to bed her. Lucas found a note written by Napoleon in her purse when he innocently looked inside to see what women kept in them. The note mentioned that by having sex with Napoleon, Johnnie had saved Lucas' life because Napoleon had threatened to kill him. It wasn't until Lucas saw the amorous look on Johnnie's face when she looked at Napoleon the night they killed Richard Goode that he realized she enjoyed the erotic romp.

Now the contradiction of loving Lucas and the desire to have sex with Napoleon confused her. Johnnie didn't understand how she could love Lucas yet want to be with Napoleon—and she hated Napoleon. What bothered her most was his nonchalant attitude toward her the day after she had sex with him.

She'd opened her long, well-toned, elegant legs to him, let him enter her voluptuous body with no resistance, let him pump her hard and steady until she couldn't help herself and pumped hard too. And then, Napoleon telling her it wasn't as great as he'd hoped it would be, humiliated her, and made her feel somehow less than the woman she thought she'd become over the course of a very tumultuous and unpredictable year.

After a few more minutes of soul-searching, she finally got out of bed and showered. As the water rained down on her, she thought about Lucas Matthews and how even though she'd had sex with another man to save his life, she adored him because he was the only one who cared about her. The fact that he'd slept with Marla Bentley, Napoleon's sexy wife, meant nothing to her. After all, she had been busy herself, accommodating four different men. More important, she slept with Napoleon because he had blackmailed her. He knew about the secret affair with Martin Winters, her former stockbroker—Lucas didn't, and she wanted to keep it that way.

I'm going to convince Lucas to trust me again. I'm never going to betray him again. I'll just give him all he can handle until he realizes how much I love him. And then, we'll get married, start a family, and move to San Francisco with my brother, Benny, and his wife, Brenda. I have plenty of money. But first, I have to get to know my white relatives.

Then she went downstairs and prepared breakfast.

Chapter 3

"No. Not this time, Sadie."

THE KITCHEN was too quiet for Sadie. She knew something was bothering her friend and she was concerned about it. They had become instant friends the day they met, when Johnnie brought Marguerite to Ashland Estates to look at her new home. Sadie greeted them and welcomed them to the neighborhood. Later, over coffee, Sadie told Johnnie how she became a kept woman for Santino Mancini, the father of her children, when her dream was to become a Broadway choreographer. After that story, after learning they were both in similar situations, they became eternal friends.

Sadie watched Johnnie eat her breakfast like an automaton, trapped in the maze of her own thoughts, putting forkfuls of food in her mouth, chewing slowing, swallowing, and repeating this again and again. Vacant, absent, far away eyes stared at Sadie, but nobody was home.

What's wrong? Is she still blaming herself for the riot?

Sadie said, "Johnnie?"

Silence.

"Johnnie?"

"Huh," Johnnie said, sounding like the sixteen-year-old girl she was.

"What's wrong, girl? What's bothering you?"

"Oh. Well, you know this is my first day at my new job. Thanks for talking to Ethel for me."

"No problem. So what did you think of Ethel?"

Johnnie laughed a little. "She's pretty much like you said. She thinks she the queen of England."

"What about Eric, her whorish husband? Did you meet him yet?"

"Oh, yeah, I almost forgot about that," Johnnie said, a little more excited. I'm going to meet my grandfather, Nathaniel Beauregard. Eric is supposed to be bringing him to New Orleans. As a matter of fact, they should be there when I get there this morning. I can't wait to meet him. I wonder if he'll recognize me. I recognized him the moment I saw his picture in the library yesterday."

"That's great. I'm happy for you. But you're not going to tell them who you are, right?

"I might. I'm blood just like they is."

"Just like they are," Sadie corrected. "Johnnie, tell me you're not seriously contemplating disrupting that family, are you?"

"Depends."

"Johnnie, listen, don't do that. We just had a race riot and we're still trying to rebuild. The Beauregards are one of New Orleans' oldest and proudest families.

They might kill you to keep their dirty laundry in the closet."

An ocean of silence filled the room.

"Johnnie, be sensible about this. Don't—"

"Okay, Sadie. I won't say anything. I just want to get to know them. Is that so wrong?"

"I understand, but be careful, okay? Now, is something else going on? You and Lucas okay?"

Johnnie finished the last of her food, put her fork down, and looked at Sadie. "We're havin' some problems right now."

"What did he do?"

"Nothing," Johnnie replied, clearing her dishes.

"Nothing? Girl, please. He's a man. And as a man, he's automatically into some shit—constantly. What? You two got into it about something?"

"Yep." *But I can't tell you it was about me going to bed with Napoleon.*

"Are you going to tell me about it?"

"No. Not this time, Sadie. We got some things to discuss. As a matter of fact, I'ma call him right now." She went over to the counter and picked up the phone and dialed Lucas' apartment. "We haven't talked since those crackers came here to burn our homes."

Actually, they hadn't spoken since the night Lucas saw how Johnnie looked at Napoleon, like she wanted him to enter her folds again, like she wouldn't mind doing it with him on a regular basis, like he had sexed her all night and again when the sun rose. Lucas was so hurt by that particular betrayal that he slapped her and suggested that she was a whore after all.

Chapter 4

"You're not fooling me, girl."

"Hello," Lucas said, fully awake and vibrant.

"Hey, baby! I'm glad I didn't wake you."

Lucas' reply was suddenly less than enthusiastic. "Hey."

"What's wrong?"

"Don't play dumb, Johnnie. You know what the deal is. You fucked Napoleon and you enjoyed that shit. You think I'ma forget that in one fuckin' week? And I don't wanna hear that shit about you doing it to save my life either. You shoulda came to me with that shit, but you didn't, did you? You just opened yo' legs, didn't you? The same legs you said was mine, and let him do it to you, so don't expect me to forget that shit overnight. It was bad enough that you was givin' it up to Earl. Now it's Napoleon. Who else been up in it?"

Johnnie ignored the question. There was no way she was ever going to tell him that Martin Winters had sampled her merchandise too. She wanted to tell him the whole truth, but knew that would only make matters worse. If she confessed, her relationship with Lucas would be a memory, and she wasn't about to let that happen. So, she decided to ignore the accusing question.

"I asked you if we could put it behind us. Can we?"

Lucas barked, "And I said I would think about it, didn't I?"

"Well, will you at least come by when I get off work? I'll make you dinner and we can talk then, okay?"

A bridge of silence filled the phone line.

"Lucas. I know you heard me. Are you coming or not?"

"Yeah, I'll be there."

Johnnie beamed. In her mind, it was all over. Once she fed him, talked some real sense to him, explained everything, she was going to bed him. There was no way he was going to turn her down either. She would see to it. "I'll see you then. Bye!"

She turned around and looked at Sadie. Deep, abiding joy surfaced and she smiled, which lifted the fog that previously saturated the kitchen.

"Girl, you must really love that boy. Your whole countenance is like a beam of light shining through a window."

"I do," Johnnie said, still smiling. She collected the rest of their plates, rinsed them off, and put them in the sink. "He's coming over for dinner."

"Don't hurt the man."

"Huh? What do you mean?"

"You're not fooling me, girl. I know you want him to come by so you can get him upstairs. That's how we do when we did something wrong, because we know they're not going to turn us down. It's our power over them."

Johnnie laughed. "Well, don't come over borrowing anything tonight. Come on. Let's go so I won't have to hear Ethel's mouth."

Chapter 5

"I swear this is definitely the last time."

LUCAS hung up the phone and looked down at Marla Bentley, who was between his legs, pleasuring him the entire time he was on the phone with Johnnie. Then he relaxed and let his head find a comfortable position on the pillow. They were in bed talking before the phone rang, but when Marla realized Lucas was talking to Johnnie, she made her way down to his toes and sucked them, which made him hard. As she listened to Lucas talk about her husband and his girlfriend having sex, hearing the anger in his voice, she made her way up his legs and lapped at his sack until silenced filled the room.

Then when he spoke to Johnnie again, her tongue roamed the base of his long tool and climbed ever upward until he quieted himself again. Once there, her tongue danced an incredible minuet, one that made him agree to anything Johnnie asked just so he could get off the phone and bask in the erotic prance. The dance was so stimulating that he found himself groaning a synchronized cadence in a pace she set, until he gripped the sheets as if he were strangling them.

When Marla came up for some much-needed oxygen, she looked into Lucas' face. His eyes were closed. She could tell he was still in the blissful moment she provided. A smile came forth. She was pleased that the work she put in was quite satisfying for them both. She curled up next to him and then pulled the cover over them, as it was a bit chilly in Lucas' bedroom that morning.

"Can Johnnie make you feel that good?"

Lucas opened his eyes, turned his head, and made eye contact with her. "You know we gotta stop this shit, Marla. You know Johnnie has my heart and she always will, so ain't no point in competin' with her. You don't stand a chance against her."

"Yeah, but can she make you come like that? Yes or no?"

Lucas stared at her for a long moment and turned away from her. "What difference does it make, Marla? This is the last time you come here, hear? Don't come back. This is it. I'm through with you, so leave me be."

Marla grabbed his shoulder and pulled hard until he rolled over. "Leave you be? Ha! That's a laugh. I'll be back again, and you know what, Lucas? You'll let me in again. And you'll keep letting me for a long, a very long time, because you know your little girlfriend is nothing but a child. I'm a woman, and I know you know the difference, don't you?" She didn't wait for an answer. "The truth is you've never felt anything remotely close to what I give you, have you? And you never will."

Lucas would never admit it, but she was right. As much as he wanted to stop entering her body and thrashing around, he couldn't. Sex with Marla was getting better, not worse. He was far from having enough. He was seriously whipped, but the strange thing was, his feelings for Johnnie hadn't changed. He knew he had to stop; he wanted to stop, but the sex kept calling his name like wine to a wino, and it was equally intoxicating. He answered every time. And just like Marla said, the next time she came over in the middle of the night, he would let her in and then swear that was the last time—again.

"Where does Napoleon think you were all night, Marla? He doesn't care where you spend your nights?"

"Home, I guess."

"You guess? Are you tryin' to get me killed?"

"Don't worry. He called me and told me he wasn't coming home last night. He said he was staying at the Bayou, but that means he was staying with a woman last night."

Filled with jealousy, Lucas whipped his head to the left to see her face. "Tell me the truth. Was he with Johnnie last night?"

"Ask her where he was."

"All right, I will," he said with resolve. "I'll find out tonight."

"Just know that when you ask her, you better have a good reason for asking. And be prepared when she asks you if I was with you tonight."

"Damn!"

Marla laughed. "What's wrong?"

"I'm no good at lying."

"Well, I gotta get going, Lucas. You want some more before I go or you want me to just get out now?"

Lucas stared at the ceiling mindlessly. As much as he wanted to scream, “No! Get the hell outta here and don’t come back!” He couldn’t, so he remained quiet, trying to suddenly find a measure of discipline, which would rectify everything.

Marla swung her feet onto the floor, found her black panties and was in the process of sliding them up her legs.

“Yes,” Lucas said.

She turned around, her panties halfway up her legs. “Yes what?” Marla said, teasing him.

“You know,” Lucas said and looked away as if he were reluctantly giving in to his insane addiction.

“No, I want to hear the words, so when you tell me not to come back, you’ll know you wanted me to come back.”

Lucas pulled the cover back for her so she could get in. Marla furrowed her brow, waiting for the words she needed to hear before pulling her panties back down.

“I want you to stay, but I swear this is definitely the last time.”

Chapter 6

"And they let a Negro in? Way back when?"

MORGAN THOMAS, the Beauregards' butler, opened the back door for Johnnie, who was nearly forty-five minutes early. He introduced himself and they shook hands. Morgan was fifty-two years old, tall, solidly built, with coal black skin, but no gray hair. He looked to be about thirty-six. His face still showed traces of bruises from the beating he took from an angry mob during the riot. His left eye was black, and there was visible swelling on his cheekbones. He and his wife of thirty years were sitting in the Sepia theatre when the mob swarmed in like locusts during the middle of the pie-throwing antics of a Three Stooges reel.

Out of nowhere, Whites attacked and beat him, his wife, and the rest of the moviegoers like they were runaway slaves. He fought back, but in the end, there were too many of them and the element of surprise made the attack incredibly effective. Fortunately, he and his wife survived that deadly night with only a few bruises that would heal and leave no trace of ever existing.

Morgan believed God had intervened because when they eventually left the theatre the day after the riot, they saw Negro men, women, and children hanging on light poles, their naked bodies still smoldering from having been burned alive. The smell of their charred carcasses would be forever seared into his conscious being. It was a miracle that his wife wasn't raped like so many of the other colored women and little girls.

"You're early," Morgan said.

"Ethel made it clear she wanted me here on time, so I left early."

Morgan laughed. "Yeah, that's Ethel." Then he mocked her. "Y'all must really learn to get here on time."

Johnnie laughed with him.

Morgan said, "Did she show you around yesterday? Do you know your duties?"

"Yes. She explained everything before I left."

"Sorry I wasn't here to meet you when you arrived. Ethel called me after you left and told me how much she liked you, but she was embarrassed because I wasn't here to open the door. She probably felt common opening her own door. But she made it damn clear she wanted me here today when you arrived."

"Common, huh?"

"Yeah, girl. You'll find out soon enough that rich white folks' biggest fear is to appear to others as common. That's why they do everything they can to ensure that Negroes and poor Whites feel beholden to them, dependent. The more dependent you feel, the more aristocratic they feel."

"You went to college, didn't you, Mr. Thomas?"

Morgan laughed a little. "Yes. How could you tell?"

"You talk like my next door neighbor."

"Oh, you mean Sadie? Nice lady. Smart too. She told me she was going to see if you wanted to work here."

"So, did you graduate? Sounds like you did."

"Yeah. Got a degree in education. I started out as a teacher. It was my dream to educate the Negro. The lack of education and fear keeps us in our 'place.' You know what I mean."

Johnnie nodded. "How come you not teachin'? You talk good."

"I met a fine woman some thirty years ago and fell in love. Fell so hard for her that I had to marry her. Had to. She was the crème de la crème. Still is. And she's just as pretty today as she was when I met her. Knows how to love a man; makes me feel good about being a man, which makes me love her all the more. Teaching doesn't pay much, and when you have a beautiful wife, you better be able to provide for her—*well.* If not, another man will. I wasn't about to let another man have my Michelle. I quit teaching and accepted Mr. Beauregard's offer of being a butler. Pays more money and we own our own place about two or three blocks from you at the coroner of Pride and Dignity streets."

"So, we're neighbors, huh?"

"Yeah, girl! You live on Vision, right?

"Yes. Nice house too. I love it and I'm glad them white folks didn't burn our property down like they wanted to."

"Did anybody ever tell you why the streets in Ashland Estates are named after important attributes and fruits of the Spirit?"

Johnnie frowned. "No. It never even crossed my mind to ask, Mr. Thomas. Tell me, please."

"Let me give you a little history on Ashland Estates. Thirty years ago, the Tresvant family bought the whole area. I don't know if you know this, but the Tresvants are the descendants of Negroes who owned slaves. When Walker Tresvant, Sr., died, Walker Tresvant, Jr., who was educated at Harvard, got the idea of building our own Parish."

"Harvard? That's that fancy school up north, right?"

Morgan laughed. "Yes. You can call it that."

"And they let a Negro in? Way back when?"

"Listen girl, a Negro can do anything he wants to do in America if he has the money. Look at Madame CJ Walker. She lived right across the street from the Rockefellers in a $250,000 mansion designed by Woodson Tandy—a Negro architect. And this was in 1917." He beamed with pride. "Shows you what a Negro can do if he puts his mind to it. But anyway, Walker Tresvant, Jr., wanted the Negro to have his own home, in his own neighborhood, among his own people. And he wanted our posterity to know who they were and what they had on the inside of them. So, he named a lot of the streets: Freedom, Vision, Pride, Dignity, Love Your Neighbor, Fidelity, Peace, Charity, Obedience, et cetera. He knew at some point, when a people got prosperous, they would forget from whence they came. He thought the street names would serve as a reminder that we are a proud people."

"Hmm, I'm gonna remember what you told me, Mr. Thomas. I promise."

"Good. And pass it on to your children and your grandchildren, so that they know and understand and aspire to great things, never . . . ever settling for second best."

"I will."

"Well, I have to get to work. The Beauregards will be up in a little while and they'll want breakfast. I'm late waking up Katherine. She's going to be upset because the Shreveport Beauregards came in last night and she has to cook more food than usual, so let me go and wake her up. I'll talk with you later if I get a chance."

"Okay, Mr. Thomas. It was nice meeting you," Johnnie said, careful to use proper diction around the educator she'd just met.

Morgan went out one door and Johnnie went out the other. She was going to start cleaning in the library so she could look up all the words Morgan used. She had to know what *posterity* meant—it sounded so fancy. She liked the way he spoke to her; the words rolled off his tongue with ease and sounded good in her ears.

She opened the French doors and walked in. Immediately, she heard the sounds of intimacy. Someone was having sex in the library.

Chapter 7

"Oh, hi, Lucas. How have you been?"

LUCAS HEARD a horn blow and looked out the window of his apartment. He saw the cab Marla had called to take her back to her Rivera Heights mansion. Across the street, he saw his neighbors looking out of their windows too.

Shit! I shoulda got her ass outta here over an hour ago. Now look at this shit. My damn neighbors are watching to see who gets in the cab. Did they see her come in the building last night? I wonder if they know she came to my apartment. What difference does it make? Nobody knows what Napoleon's wife looks like in this neighborhood. She never goes to the Bayou. But still, this is fucked up.

"Is that my cab?" Marla called out from the bathroom. She was putting on the finishing touches of her makeup.

"Yeah. Come on. You gotta go."

Marla heard the fear and desperation in his voice and laughed as she came into his living room. "Nervous, Lucas? You should have kicked me out when you could have. Now everybody's going to see the pretty white woman leaving your apartment building in broad daylight."

"This is over now, Marla. Don't you come back here, and don't call me either. It's over!"

"Sure it is, Lucas," she mocked. "See you later, lover."

"No, you won't. Now, get the hell outta here please."

Lucas cracked the door of his apartment and peeked out, hoping no one would be in the hall. He knew he should have told her no and made her leave, but he had to get his last piece. After all, he wasn't going to see her again. He looked to the left and then to the right. Seeing no one, he said, "Okay. Go."

"What . . . no kiss good-bye?"

Lucas grabbed her by the arm and pushed her into the hallway and closed the door. Then he hurried back to the window to see if his neighbors were still watching. Only the lady who lived directly across from him was still looking out her window, as if she was the neighborhood spy. Suddenly, she looked at him and waved. Lucas got the feeling that she was waving to let him know she knew his secret.

Shit!

He waved back, attempting to appear like any other neighbor who wanted to know who the cab was for. The woman looked down to the street again. Lucas did too. They both saw Marla come out of his apartment building and get into the cab. The woman looked at Lucas again. He looked at her. She pointed at Marla and then pointed at Lucas. Lucas shook his head. The woman curled her lips and nodded. Then she closed her curtains.

Fuck!

Lucas went into the bathroom and took a quick shower. He was running late. He was supposed to have breakfast with Napoleon and Bubbles before he started his rounds.

About twenty minutes later, he walked into the Bayou. Napoleon and Bubbles were already eating and talking in whispered tones, but he still managed to hear Chicago Sam and Vinnie Milano's names and something about when they'd come back to New Orleans. On his way over to the table, Napoleon and Bubbles stopped talking suddenly and looked at him disapprovingly. He sat down.

"Sorry I'm late. I overslept."

Bubbles shot him a menacing stare and said, "Don't make it a habit. This is business. We expect you to be here on time and ready take care of business—every day!"

"Okay, but I—"

"I don't give a fuck if a bitch is suckin' yo' dick! You understand? And I don't care if you about to bust a nut. If you see you gon' be late, snatch yo' dick outta that bitch's mouth and get yo' ass in here on time. You got that shit?"

Just as Bubbles finished ripping him to shreds, Marla Bentley came out of the kitchen and sat at the table with them. She smiled deviously and said, "Oh, hi, Lucas. How have you been?"

Chapter 8

"Y'all must be the new maid."

JOHNNIE GASPED and stood perfectly still, barely breathing as she watched a man enter a woman, who was on the table, where Johnnie planned to study at some point in the future. Now, looking at them, seeing him pumping her hard and fast, seeing him hold an ankle in each hand, making a wide V, hearing the woman's stifled sighs as she tried to quell them, Johnnie knew this visual would invade her mind every time she opened a book at the table. But still, she watched, unable to turn from the live pornographic scene in the library.

The man was white and so was the woman. His boxers were down to his knees. The woman's gown was pushed up beyond her waist. Suddenly, the woman saw Johnnie and gasped loudly. Johnnie could see her face and she could see Johnnie's.

"Beau," the woman said in a hushed tone. "There's somebody in here."

Beau, still pumping, craned his neck to see who it was. When he saw the woman staring at them, he said, "Y'all must be the new maid. I'll meet y'all proper later, okay, honey? Now leave us alone for a bit longer, will ya, darlin'? I'll be done directly." Then he looked down at the woman and continued his powerful thrusts.

Their words awakened Johnnie, but she was still stunned as she backed out of the library, gently closed the French doors, and went back into the kitchen, where she saw a black woman standing over a large, flat stove, cracking eggs into a huge mixing bowl. The woman was tall and looked as if she easily weighed over one hundred and seventy-five pounds, but she was far from fat. In fact, she was put together quite nicely, but not nearly as nice as Johnnie.

She turned around to toss the eggshells into the garbage pail and gasped when she saw Johnnie standing there. She placed her hand over her heart as if she were having an attack, and took in deep breaths.

"Girl, you near 'bout scared me half to death," she said.

"That's twice today," Johnnie managed to say.

"What do you mean by that?"

Johnnie offered her hand to avoid the question. "You must be Katherine. I'm Johnnie, the new maid."

"Yeah, I know. I'm Katherine," she said, taking her hand. "I'm running late with breakfast, so don't just stand there lookin' all pretty. Help me."

Katherine had been teased a lot when she was a child by black and white children alike. She had often heard her mother apologize for her size, saying, "Kathy's just big-boned is all." She wasn't pretty and she wasn't ugly, but she knew what men liked, and she wasn't it. Katherine was the kind of woman that pretty friends, when attempting to find her a date, described as "nice" to potential suitors, meaning that she was presentable, but don't get your hopes up.

Katherine was bigger than the boys she liked when she was a teenager, and now she was bigger than the average man. Men found her to be quite intimidating, even when they found her attractive. When she learned that people were afraid of her, and she learned this early in life, she began to see it as an asset, not a liability, using it to intimidate beautiful girls like Johnnie, who always had the boys and the men of any race sniffing her scent.

"What do you want me to do?"

"Stir the grits. Watch the bacon and the sausage. Y'all know how to do that? Pretty thing like you shouldn't have to be no maid."

Johnnie stood there watching the woman as she kneaded the biscuit dough, wondering what she meant by that comment. *I guess she thinks it's okay for pretty women to sell what they got to get ahead.*

"Well, whatcha waitin' for? The grits won't stir and the bacon won't turn without your help."

Johnnie went to the stove, peeked over the huge pot, and then stirred the grits. She wanted to ask a thousand questions, but was afraid to. She soon realized that Katherine was in charge of the kitchen and everything in it, even the people, just a few moments after meeting her.

Katherine grabbed a rolling pin, put some flour on it, and thinned out the biscuit dough. "Y'all don't talk much, huh?"

I talk plenty. "How long you been workin' for the Beauregards?"

"Pretty much all my life. I grew up with Ethel. My mama raised us both and because of that, I've had it made ever since. I've got my own apartment over the garage, my own phone, my own car, everything. Plus a salary."

"Well, how come Ethel didn't have you take over after Betty Jean left?"

"I'm a cook, not a maid," Katherine said with pride. "I don't clean up behind others. I clean up what I mess up, and that's the kitchen only."

Johnnie rolled her eyes. *Hmmm, so Katherine is what they call a high and mighty Negro. She thinks she's white.* "I think the grits are ready, Katherine."

"I'll be the judge of that. Let me see," she said, and looked inside the pot. "Yeah, they're ready." She looked at the clock: 7:58 A.M. "They should be coming downstairs any moment. They love my food."

"Smells good, Katherine," Johnnie said, offering a sincere compliment.

"Well, it's for the Beauregards first," Katherine snapped. "When they finish, you can have what's left if you want."

"No thanks. I cooked breakfast for me and Sadie before I came to work today. I'm full."

"Pretty girl like you? Cook? Hmpf."

Johnnie frowned. "What does being pretty have to do with cooking?"

"Most are used to a man takin' care of 'em. If a pretty woman even looks at a stove, the house is liable to burn down."

"I'm a good cook and I'm pretty too," Johnnie said, feeling the need to defend herself. "If you want, you can come to dinner one day this week and have dinner with me and Sadie."

"Hmpf. Please. You think the Beauregards can go a day without my cooking for 'em? Besides, I don't like Sadie. Never will."

"Why?"

"Your friend is an adulteress. Didn't you know? She's sleeping with Santino Mancini. Got kids by a married man."

"Katherine!" Ethel said, nearly shouting. "I've told you time and again, I will not have that kinda talk in my house."

"Yes, Mrs. Beauregard."

"Good morning, Johnnie," Ethel said, changing her tone. "I'm so glad y'all could make it to work on time today."

"Yes, ma'am. I got in at about 7:15."

"Good. Good. I love to help Negroes. Shows you can train anybody."

Chapter 9

Outta town? Hell naw!

WHEN LUCAS saw Marla come in, acting and speaking as if she hadn't been in his apartment all night, committing the very acts Bubbles described, his heart thundered in his chest. *Oh, shit!* He was staring at her but didn't realize it, unable to respond to her cheerful greeting in the presence of Napoleon and Bubbles, who were looking at him, amazed at the look on his face.

Why the hell didn't you tell me you were coming here? All you had to say was, 'I'm going to the Bayou.' So, that's what she meant about seeing me later. Fuck! This bitch is crazy! But why is she here? What possible reason could she have showing up today, after we were in bed all night?

Seeing the look in his eyes, Marla quickly decided to bail him out. She had gotten the reaction she hoped for. She wanted him to know that their relationship wasn't quite over and that she was in charge because Napoleon was her husband. She said, "Surprised to see me in the Bayou, huh?"

Picking up on the hint, Lucas cleared his throat. "Uh, yeah, yeah. How did you get here? Did you finally decide to drive again?"

"I decided to take a cab here so you wouldn't have to drive all the way out to the house. I have some errands to run and I'm wondering if you wouldn't mind driving me like you did last time. Remember?"

Lucas looked at Napoleon, who by this time was eating again. He looked at Bubbles, and he too was looking at his plate while he ate. *What the hell is goin' on?*

He said, "Well, actually, I got a lot to do today, Mrs. Bentley."

"Now, Lucas, I thought I told you to call me Marla."

"Bubbles," Napoleon interrupted, "put someone else on his rounds today. Lucas, my man, I can count on you to help me out again, can't I?"

"Well . . . I—"

"Good, it's all settled."

Lucas looked at Bubbles, who was smiling broadly. "We got a big surprise for you, kid. Big surprise! You're gonna love it."

A big surprise, huh? Marla showing up in the Bayou ain't surprise enough?

"Yeah, Lucas," Napoleon said. "You'll love it. But we need to have a chat when you return. There are some things you definitely need to know about, okay?"

Excited, Lucas asked, "What things?"

"When you return, I'll spell it out for you."

Lucas looked at Marla. "How long we gon' be gone?"

"I'm not sure. Why? You got a hot date with that pretty girlfriend of yours?"

Now, you know damn well that I'm supposed to have dinner with Johnnie tonight.

"Well, yeah. I'm supposed to have dinner at her place later this evenin'. I need to let her know I'll be late, so she won't worry."

Napoleon said, "I understand. Pretty girl like that, you gotta keep 'em happy or they'll find another man."

Like you, muthafucka? Lucas thought. *Ya threaten my life just so you could fuck my woman. Then gon' sit up there and act like you care?*

"Give her a call and let her know you may be a bit late tonight," Bubbles said. "I'm sure she won't mind. In fact, she'll miss you all the more. Like they say, absence makes the heart grow fonder."

Marla said, "Yeah, but too much absence makes a woman wonder. Isn't that right, honey?"

"That's right," Napoleon agreed.

"She's working in the Garden District. I don't know the number," Lucas said. "I don't know where the house is either."

"Who does she work for?" Marla asked.

"The Beauregards."

Marla looked at Napoleon and rolled her eyes. "She's working for the Queen Bee. I know where they live. We can stop by on our way out of town."

Outta town? Hell naw! I'm supposed to stop by my girl's job with you? We tryin' tuh put our thing back on the right track. What's Johnnie gon' say when I tell her I'ma be late because I'm outta town with a woman she knows I done fucked—several times? Shit!

"Well, where I gotta drive you to, Marla?"

"Shreveport."

Shreveport! That's nearly five fucking hours from here. Ten hours round trip! And knowin' you, this is just a way to get me alone.

"That's a five-hour drive. When are we leaving, Marla?" Lucas asked.

"Right after you have some nutritious breakfast. A growing boy like you needs his nourishment to keep his strength up. I'll make you a plate and bring it out."

With that, Marla left them and returned to the kitchen. Lucas forced himself not to look at her plump ass as she walked away from the table. He looked at Napoleon and Bubbles, who were devouring their food like there was no tomorrow.

Chapter 10

"I think now is a good time for introductions."

THE BEAUREGARDS were sitting in the dining room, waiting to be served breakfast. Eric, the son of Nathaniel, was sitting at the head of the table with his adoring wife, Ethel, who was seated next to him on the right. Beau Beauregard, Eric's favorite son, sat next to him on the left. His wife, Gina, and their three children sat next to him. Blue Beauregard, Ethel's favorite son, sat next to her. His wife, Piper, and their two children sat next to him. At the other end of the table, opposite Eric, sat his father, Nathaniel Beauregard—Johnnie's grandfather.

Nathaniel sat in a wheelchair, quietly zoned out. He'd been the victim of a recent stroke, which turned an otherwise vibrant grandfather into a totally dependent invalid. He couldn't speak and he had no motor functions. Fortunately, he could hear and communicate by blinking his eyes when asked yes or no questions; one blink for yes and two blinks for no.

He felt so useless being confined to a wheelchair, having to be waited on hand and foot, unable to utter a single word when he was once known as a great orator. His mood was sullen, no sign of happiness in his dark eyes.

Now, when Johnnie walked into the dining room to help Katherine serve them breakfast, Nathaniel's eyes lit up. He was positively glowing, beaming for the first time since a stroke had taken his life away. He recognized her immediately, as she looked just like Josephine Baptiste, the woman he'd loved over three decades ago. His sharp mind came alive again, his eyes filled with joy. He tried to speak to her, but he was still a prisoner in his own mind. But he could smile, and smile he did.

Johnnie was carrying a breakfast plate stacked high with fluffy, golden brown pancakes and a large silver sauce cup filled to the brim with maple syrup, and set them on the table. As she turned to leave, in her periphery, she saw him, her grandfather; a man she had only known by name in passing. Suddenly, she was nervous. *Will he know who I am?* When she returned with two more breakfast plates on which sat delicious smelling eggs, bacon and sausage, she stole a peek at Nathaniel, whose penetrating gaze made her uncomfortable.

Johnnie left and returned a third time with a huge bowl of buttery grits and set them on the table. However, this time, she felt a different set of probing eyes following her around the room, watching her ever move. Although she was accustomed to men leering at her vivacious curves as if they were in a trance, this was different. It felt like someone was transmitting a repeating message: Look over here. Almost as if someone was turning it, her head swiveled to the left and she saw him, the man who was in the library having sex less than an hour ago.

The man made no attempt to look anywhere other than right into Johnnie's dark brown eyes. A crooked smiled emerged, evidence of wicked thoughts running around in his lust-driven heart. While it was true, the man was a passion slave, he wasn't thinking of bedding Johnnie. The man was wondering how long it would take her to put it together. And when she did, how would she respond? At any moment, she could realize a truth that only he and the woman knew. So, he waited with great anticipation for the crystallizing epiphany to occur.

Something inside Johnnie's mind began a slow but persistent prodding to look at the woman seated next to the man who stared at her unrelentingly. She did. Her eyes followed the prodding and looked into the face of the woman on his left, who was busy filling her son's plate with pancakes and scolding the other two, who were hitting each other. Instantly, she knew that was his wife, but it wasn't the woman he was having sex with earlier that morning. She gasped just a little when the realization materialized. She looked at the man again, who was now smiling devilishly at what must have been going through her head at that pivotal moment.

With his eyes, he told Johnnie to look at the woman sitting next to the man across the table from him. She did and gasped again. The woman was sitting next to a man she presumed was his brother because the resemblance between the two men was uncanny. The woman made eye contact with Johnnie and the desperation in her eyes begged Johnnie to keep their sordid secret, which was the opposite of what the man's face said. He didn't seem to care who knew.

"Johnnie!" Katherine called out from the kitchen. "What's takin' you so long? Come and get the juice and milk!"

"Johnnie is it?" the man said, still grinning. "I think now is a good time for introductions. I'm Beau Beauregard. This is my wife, Gina, and our three children, Joshua, Faith, and John. And the man across from me is my brother, Blue Beauregard, the preacher. That's his wife, Piper, and their daughters, Hope and Charity."

"I'm Eric Beauregard, father of Beau and Blue. And the man at the other end of the table is my father, Nathaniel Beauregard III."

"She sure is a pretty thang, ain't she, Daddy?" Beau said. "We kinda met this mornin', didn't we, Johnnie?"

"You kinda met?" Ethel asked. She didn't bother to correct his English, as Beau was always defiant and had his own way of doing things. The more she tried to correct him, the more he rebelled.

"Mama, I had to relieve myself about an hour ago, and I was in a powerful hurry. But we saw each other, didn't we, darlin'?"

"Yes, sir," Johnnie said and lowered her eyes.

Chapter 11

"Pride."

What are they up to? Is Napoleon planning to spend the day with Johnnie while I'm driving Marla to Shreveport? Hmm. Is Johnnie gon' let him do it to her again? I saw how she was lookin' at him. I know she enjoyed it. I could tell. But then she asked me to come by tonight for dinner. She musta invited me over later to cover it all up. I bet she knows all about me driving Marla to Shreveport. I'ma straighten this shit out as soon as we leave. If she wants him, fine. I'll let her ass go. And just for that, I'm fuckin' Marla again.

"Lucas," Marla began, "snap out of it."

Lucas blinked his eyes a couple of times, awakening from his thoughts about Napoleon and Johnnie. Rage filled his mind. The idea of her and him, together again, doing God knows what and her loving it, was too unthinkable.

"Hey, kid," Bubbles said. "You all right? The lady's talking to you."

"Huh? I was thinking about a couple of things."

"We can see that, kid," Bubbles said. "What's wrong?"

You know what's wrong! You were the one that warned me about Marla in the first fuckin' place. And you have the nerve to ask me what's wrong when Napoleon's getting me out of town for nearly ten hours? What's he gon' be doin' while I'm with his wife; especially since he knows I done been with her? And Marla's in on it. She has to be. Why else are we goin' all the way to Shreveport when we can get just about anything she needs right here in New Orleans? If she just wants to leave town, why can't we go to Baton Rouge, which is less than an hour and a half away, depending on how fast she wants to get there.

"I'm okay, man. I just got a few things on my mind."

"Okay, when you finish eatin', I need to talk to you about some business."

"I'm finished. Let's talk."

"I'll be in the car when you finish, Lucas," Marla said and left.

Napoleon said, "I gotta go to the can. I'll be right back."

Lucas waited for Napoleon to leave and said, "What's on your mind, Bubbles?"

"Pride."

"Pride?"

"Yeah. See, sometimes shit happens. Sometimes a muthafucka can be warned about some shit comin' down and still stick his neck in a goddamn guillotine. But even though the criminal has committed a crime worthy of death, every now and then, the king grants amnesty." He paused for a second. "Do you understand that word, *amnesty*?"

Lucas shook his head.

"Amnesty is a pardon . . . clemency . . . a release from punishment." He paused again. "See, kid, you haven't done any time yet. You've never been caged like an animal. Me and Napoleon, we did some of the hardest time ever in prison, and words like *pardon*, *clemency*, and *amnesty* become a part of a man's vocabulary."

Lucas looked into his eyes. "So, why you tellin' me this?"

Bubbles stared at him for about thirty seconds before speaking. "The king is the king. Take King David for example. Ever heard of him?"

Lucas nodded.

"Then you know David saw a woman he had to have. Was he wrong? Hell yeah! Did he know he was wrong before he did it? Hell yeah, he knew that shit and did it anyway! And the consequences of committing adultery were death at that time. But God granted clemency. Now, some shit happened behind his deeds, but the king was not executed for his crime. Tell me, do you think he was grateful?"

"I wouldn't know."

"I didn't ask you what you know. I asked you what you think. Thinkin' and knowin' is two different things."

"I think the king shouldn't have fucked the woman. But because he did, he got what was coming to him. And didn't his son end up fucking the king's women behind that shit?"

"Yeah, but the king's son ended up dead over that shit. Clemency is not a license to continue committing crimes against the king. To stay outta jail, the pardoned must stop breaking the law. Do you understand me, kid?"

How come when you got somethin' tuh say, you always gotta talk in parables and shit instead of saying what you gotta say? That gets on my fuckin' nerves!

"Well, I—"

Bubbles cut him off. "Yes or no?"

Lucas stared at Bubbles for a long time before he said, "Yes."

"All right then."

"Bubbles, are you tellin' me that because—"

"No more questions, kid. You know the reason. Be smart."

Napoleon came back and sat down. He looked right into Lucas' eyes when he spoke. "Do you know who the king is, Lucas?"

Lucas nodded.

"Then you understand clemency, right?"

Lucas nodded again.

Bubbles intervened. "No, kid. The king needs to hear the words before you walk out that door."

"Yes, I understand clemency."

"All right then," Napoleon said and tossed him the keys to his car. "Now, Marla is waiting for you in my car. Be careful with my possessions. If you play your cards right, we'll let you in on the thing with our friends in Chicago. It's going to be huge, my man."

"You mean you guys have something going on with Chicago Sam and Vinnie Milano? I definitely want in on that."

"Like I said, kid, be smart," Bubbles said, warning Lucas one more time before he left with Marla.

"Okay, Bubbles. I'll be smart."

They all stood. Lucas turned and walked out the door. Napoleon and Bubbles went to the large picture window and watched him get into the front seat.

Napoleon said, "You warned him, he understood, and he's still going to fuck Marla." He smiled. "Human nature. You can count on it. I love this shit."

Chapter 12

They just jealous of you, girl.

"What's taking you so long in there?" Katherine snapped. "You're not in there to talk. You're in there to serve. I bet you was just showin' off. Yeah, that's what you was doin', showin' off."

"Showin' off?" Johnnie questioned with a frown. "What are you talkin' about? I wasn't showin' off. I was doin' what you told me to do. And then Beau Beauregard introduced his self to me. That's all."

"That's Mr. Beauregard to you. And you stay away from that man. He's married, and no colored wench need tuh be messin' up his marriage."

Under her breath, Johnnie said, "Hmpf, he don't act like he's married."

"What?"

"Nothing."

"You said something. What did you say?"

"Didn't you just say my job is to serve and not to talk? I came to get the milk and the orange juice."

"Fine, but when you go back in there, don't be showin' off, hear?"

Johnnie looked at her. "What are you talkin' about, Katherine?"

"You know what I mean. Ain't nobody in that room interested in anything you have to say just because you pretty. That's what's wrong with pretty women; they think somebody wants to talk to 'em when they don't."

At the moment, Johnnie heard her mother's voice echo in her mind. *They just jealous of you, girl. Women have always been jealous of us Baptiste girls 'cause we's pretty. They was jealous of my mama. They was jealous of me. And they sho' as hell gon' be jealous of you.* Johnnie laughed under her breath when she realized what was really going on.

"What are you laughin' about, girl?"

You, ya big buffalo. "Can I go and serve the Beauregards now?"

"You just make sure you don't be in there botherin' them good white Christians. You hear me, girl?"

Johnnie smiled. "What if they start botherin' me?"

Katherine was about to say something and Johnnie turned around and left her standing there, looking at a spot she no longer occupied.

"You little bitch," Katherine said, but Johnnie didn't hear her.

Seconds later, Johnnie poured orange juice and milk into each glass before setting the pitchers on the table. She felt Nathaniel's unrelenting stare again and looked at him. He was still smiling broadly. Everyone was eating except him. She frowned momentarily. Then it occurred to her that he couldn't feed himself, and they just left him there to fend for himself. She looked at Ethel, and even she wasn't paying attention to the old man. It angered Johnnie.

No wonder he's in that wheelchair. His own flesh and blood won't lift a finger to care for him.

She thought about asking for permission, but changed her mind. Nathaniel was her flesh and blood grandfather, the only relative she had in New Orleans as far as she knew. Benny, her brother, and Brenda, his wife, were back in San Francisco, where they lived. She looked at her grandfather again and her heart melted. She loved that old man without even knowing who he was. He was responsible for her being alive, and she wanted to know and care for him. She went over to where he was sitting and pulled up a chair and sat down at the table with the rest of the Beauregards.

"What on earth do you think you're doing, girl?" Ethel's voice boomed from the other end of the long table.

"I'm going to feed him," Johnnie said boldly without looking at Ethel.

"Bravo, Johnnie!" Beau said, clapping his hands. "Stand your ground. The old man's got to eat too."

When Katherine heard this, she went to the dining room entrance and looked in. "Johnnie! What did I just tell you?"

"I say we let Grandpa decide if she should stay," Beau offered. "Grandpa, do you want her to feed you or do you want one of us to feed you?"

Nathaniel synchronously blinked both eyes once and smiled again.

"That settles it," Beau said.

You damn right that settles it, Katherine thought. *She's gotta go. You don't come up in my house and take over like you a blood relative, sittin' at the table like you belong there. You just a nigga wench with no good breedin'. If anybody oughta be sittin' at the table with white folks, it oughta be me. I'ma get rid of that little bitch. I'm the queen up in here!*

Chapter 13

"You expect me to believe that?"

LUCAS opened the driver's side door and got into Napoleon's Chevy. He started the car, put it in first gear, and pulled away from the curb after checking his mirrors. He drove down Bourbon Street, passing a host of bars, restaurants, and burlesque establishments in complete silence. The car seemed to be driving itself as Lucas' mind was on other things.

The king, huh? Right! I should be grateful for clemency? That's a laugh. Like he's not planning to bed Johnnie while I'm in fuckin' Shreveport. Right! If he can have Johnnie whenever he wants, I can have Marla whenever I want. It's only fair. I'll stop fuckin' Marla when he stops fuckin' Johnnie. How 'bout that, Mr. King? That's clemency—my style, anyway. You know what? Fuck it. I'm through with Johnnie. He can have her if he wants her that bad. I'ma go by the Beauregards and tell her it's over.

He looked in the rearview mirror. Marla was smiling at him.

"How do I get to the Beauregards? I wanna talk to Johnnie for a minute."

"You know how to get to the Garden District, right?"

"Yeah."

"The address is 1619 Harmony Street. But don't you want to take me home first so I can freshen up?"

Lucas shot a hot gaze at her reflection. "Why didn't you tell me you was goin' to the Bayou, Marla? You tryin' tuh get us caught?"

"Caught? We're through, remember? There's nothing between us anymore. You threw me out of your apartment this morning and told me not to come back, so what difference does it make to you where I go and when I go there? Are we through or not?"

Lucas cut his eyes to the rearview again. "Not just yet."

"Hmpf. What changed your mind?"

"Napoleon."

"Uh-huh. So, you finally believe he's not your friend, huh?"

Marla had told him this bit of information months ago, but he didn't believe her because Napoleon had given him a job, bought him new clothes, and promised to give Johnnie the justice she deserved.

"You know he knows about us, don't you?" Lucas asked rhetorically. "He probably knows you were with me last night too."

"What makes you think that?"

"I just talked to Bubbles and he was givin' me some bullshit about Napoleon being the king and how the king has granted me clemency. But I'm not supposed to see you again. Yet he can see Johnnie again. What kinda shit is that?"

"What makes you think he's seeing Johnnie again?"

"Ain't that shit obvious? Damn! He's sending me on another goddamned errand to get me away so he can have Johnnie again. And what's fucked up is they think I'm too stupid to figure out what's going on."

"Hmmm, so you think we're going to Shreveport to give him the day with Johnnie?"

"Don't play stupid, Marla. You in on the shit too, and you know it."

"No, I'm not."

"Yes, you are, and I can prove it."

Marla looked into the rearview and calmly said, "I'm listening. Let's hear your theory."

"Huh?"

"Your educated guess," she said patiently.

"Why didn't you say that in the first fuckin' place? I'm not stupid, Marla."

"I know. I'm sorry, okay? Now, tell me why you think I'm in on my husband's scheme to get your girlfriend."

"Because we goin' all the way to Shreveport. That's ten hours, depending on how fast I drive." He looked at his watch: 9:25. "We probably won't be back before 9:30 tonight, dependin' on how much shoppin' you gotta do."

"Lucas, I'm not going to Shreveport to shop. I'm going to pick out a new car. Napoleon knows the owner of the dealership, and I'm going to pick out the new car."

"You expect me to believe that? Why wouldn't he pick out his own car?"

"I always pick the car I ride in, Lucas. Even before we met you."

"Uh-huh. So, you asked if I would drive you this time?"

"Yeah. He's not going to do it. Especially since it's a ten-hour trip. I used to drive up there and pick up the cars, but after the accident, someone had to drive me so I could pick out the car I want to ride in."

"Hmm, so he's not goin' to be seeing Johnnie while we're gone?"

"That I don't know. But I know this trip doesn't have anything to do with getting you out of town—well, not on his part, anyway. I prepared a picnic basket before I came by your place last night. We can stop and have a bite to eat."

"Right, so one of them crackers can lynch my black ass for having lunch with a white woman. No thanks."

"Then we'll eat in the car. As long as I'm in the backseat, we won't have a problem."

"You hope."

Chapter 14

"Marla Bentley? Here? To see me?"

AFTER FEEDING her grandfather, Johnnie started her cleaning duties. The first room she wanted to clean was the library—specifically the table where Beau and Piper were doing naughty things earlier that morning. She entered the library with a bucket of soap and water, a few rags, and some furniture polish. She tossed a rag into the warm water, pulled it out, and squeezed the residual liquid over the table and scrubbed the table, spending most of her energy in the spot where Piper's flesh and probably her bodily fluid had been. As she scrubbed, Johnnie began to frown as if she could see them doing it in her mind's eye. How nasty it seemed to her to do it right there on the table when anyone could and did walk in on them.

Beau and Piper are doin' it and they're married to different people. She shook her head. *And Piper is married to Beau's brother. I don't know which is worse, Beau doing it to his brother's wife, or his brother's wife lettin' her husband's brother do it to her.*

Suddenly, the words of Billy Logan echoed in her mind. *She a whore! And she comes from a long line of whores!* He had screamed these words to her in front of a crowd of school kids while they were on their way home from school.

How many whores are in the family? Let's see, Grandmama Josephine was seeing Granddad and nobody else until she got pregnant with my mama. So, I might as well count Granddad too. He was married at the time he was seeing Grandmama. My mama makes three. Benny makes four; he had sex with Sadie when he was in town a few weeks ago. Eric and Beau make six. Six whores. The men and the women. If you count me, that makes seven. And seven is symbolic of perfection. Does that make us perfect whores? I wonder if—

"Johnnie," Ethel called out.

She turned around and saw Ethel and Katherine standing in the doorway. Katherine had her hands on her sizable hips, looking like she was ready to strangle Johnnie.

Ethel said, "Johnnie, I know this is your first day and all, but you've been a Negro all your life. You had to know that it was inappropriate to sit down at a table with Whites."

Just as Johnnie was about to respond, the doorbell chimed.

Looking at the floor like Negroes were told to do when addressing a white person, innocently, she said, "Yes, ma'am, it was very inappropriate and downright disrespectful of me to feed Mr. Beauregard too. When I saw him there, waitin' to eat while everybody else shoveled Katherine's delicious food in their mouths, I felt sorry for the man. But next time that poor man is starvin', I'm gonna let him starve too. I mean, that's the proper thing to do in a white family, right?"

Ethel realized that Johnnie had told her how trifling she was for not feeding a blood relative who was incapable of feeding himself and said, "Well, now, you did do the right thing, Johnnie. And Grandpa did want you to feed him. Come to think of it, I've never seen him happier, even before the stroke. He must really like you. I'll tell you what. Tomorrow, if he wants you to feed him again, you can. How about that? You can sit at the table with us white folks and everything."

Johnnie looked at Katherine, who was seething. She looked like, if it were possible, steam could come out of her ears. Although she wanted to, Johnnie didn't dare smile, let alone laugh. But she got immense pleasure from turning the tables on both of them.

Hmpf! Katherine don't know who she messin' with. I'll run her right outta her kitchen if she keeps this up.

Morgan Thomas came to the door and said, "Excuse me, Mrs. Beauregard. There's a Mrs. Marla Bentley at the door and she's—"

Ethel's eyes lit up. "Marla Bentley? Here? To see me?"

"No, ma'am. She's here to see Johnnie."

Chapter 15

"Hey, Lucas my ass!"

MARLA BENTLEY entered the library and looked at Johnnie, who appeared to be very apprehensive at that moment. Marla took a couple of steps toward Johnnie when Ethel sang, "Mrs. Bentley. It's so good to finally meet you. And where is that charming husband of yours? You two really must come to dinner sometime."

"Excuse me one second, Mrs. Beauregard," Marla said and stepped away from her to Johnnie. The two women examined each other briefly with jealous eyes. "Lucas is outside waiting for you. He needs to speak with you."

Ethel felt a bit shunned by Marla's need to speak with her hired help before speaking to the Southern woman of the house and became surly. She looked at Johnnie and began wondering how she knew Marla Bentley on a personal level. Ethel had heard about Napoleon Bentley and his reputation. She wanted to have the Bentleys over for dinner just so she could innocently ask leading questions about the Mafia that she'd heard about. She wondered if he was anything like Al Capone since he was from Chicago.

Without a word, Johnnie quickly walked out of the library, leaving them there as she blew through them. Katherine followed her through the foyer. She had to see what was going on. Who did this little heifer think she was, coming in her kitchen, taking over and sitting at the table with the Beauregards? And now getting visitors? And all of this on her first day of work? This was outrageous behavior for a white woman, and Johnnie was black, so that made her actions totally unacceptable. She had to go.

Lucas was leaning against Napoleon's car when Johnnie saw him. She was so excited that he came by to see her that she walked right out the front door like she lived there, forgetting that Negroes always used the back door, never the front. Johnnie was absolutely glowing as she walked down the stairs and down the sidewalk to see what he wanted. However, as she got closer, she could see that he was angry about something.

What could've happened? I hope he's still coming to dinner.

"Hey, Lucas! Is everything—"

"Hey, Lucas my ass! We through!"

"What? Why? What did I do, huh?" Johnnie said. Her heart broke a little more with each word. They were supposed to meet tonight, and now that was out of the question. She had no idea what had happened to change his mind.

Lucas frowned before speaking. "What did you do? You know what you did."

"I thought we was gon' talk about that tonight."

"I did too. But you had other plans, didn't you?"

"Huh? What are you talking about?"

"You know what I'm talking about, Johnnie. You're meeting Napoleon today while I'm outta town."

"What? Did he tell you that?"

"No, but when he had me and Bubbles following the Grand Wizard around all night, he didn't tell me he was gon' be fuckin' you that night either."

Johnnie felt like someone had thrown a javelin at her and it sunk deep into her heart. Tears formed in her eyes and dropped. "Don't you understand, Lucas? What could I do? Let him kill you?"

"Maybe you shoulda. Maybe you shoulda let him put a gun to my head, look me right in the eye, and blow the brains right outta my head. That's how I feel right now. You wanna stand up there and cry . . . you ain't the only one hurt in this."

"I'm sorry I hurt you so bad, Lucas," Johnnie said as tears continued to form and tumble out of her eyes one after another. "I need you to listen to my side of the story, okay? Please, can you do that? You used to love me, Lucas. I know you don't now, and I know we through, but if we gon' be through, I want you to at least know the truth so I can clear my conscience about all of this."

"I never said I didn't love you."

"So, you still love me after all of this?"

Silence filled the air.

When Lucas said that, Johnnie knew she had a chance to salvage the relationship. She needed to get him alone, say whatever he needed to hear, and get her man back. She knew she would have to lie, and whatever lies she conjured up in her desperate mind would have to be credible.

"I get off work at about Noon. Come by my house when you get off work, okay? I'ma tell you everything, okay? I can explain it all to you, okay? And I'm not gon' try to talk you into stayin' with me either. I just want you to know the truth."

And with that, the lying had begun anew. She wasn't going to tell him the truth. How could she? Napoleon had found about Martin Winters, Johnnie's former stockbroker and part-time lover, and threatened to tell Lucas unless she opened her legs to him. By the time Napoleon finished with her, she realized that sex with him was the best she ever had. She wasn't going to tell Lucas that. What made matters worse was that she wanted Napoleon to do what he did to her again and again and again—it was that good. But she would never, ever tell Lucas these truths. Denial and magnificent lies would be the order of the day from now on.

"I won't be able to come by tonight. That's another reason I came by."

"Why not?"

"I told you I gotta go outta town."

"Where you goin'? And when you comin' back?"

"I'm leavin' as soon as Marla comes out."

Chapter 16

"So, you enjoy yo' self for the last time."

ALL THE EXCITEMENT made Johnnie momentarily forget that Marla had come inside the Beauregard mansion to get her. She was so happy Lucas came by that she didn't even think to ask why Marla had come with him.

And why did Marla have that look on her face, like she had something to hide?

She looked deep into Lucas' eyes. "Are you still seein' Marla?"

"Nope!" he said without hesitation, as if he knew the question was coming. "But now that you done decided to see Napoleon again, hey, I might as well."

"I told you I wasn't seein' him. How come you don't believe me?"

Lucas kind of laughed. "You got a lotta nerve askin' me that."

"Well, fine. We gon' straighten this out when you come back. And where you goin' anyway?"

"Shreveport."

"Marla goin'?"

"Uh-huh."

"Napoleon and Bubbles goin' too?" she asked desperately.

"Nope."

"So, y'all goin' by y'all self?"

Lucas nodded.

"Umm. Y'all still fuckin'."

"No we ain't."

"That wasn't a question, Lucas. That was a statement of fact. You make sure you bring yo' ass by my house when you get back, and I don't care what time it is. We gon' get this shit straight—tonight. This gon' be yo' last piece. I hope you enjoy it."

"So, you sayin' it's okay to do it one more time?"

"You get yo' last piece and we even, Lucas. And if Napoleon find out, I'm not openin' my legs again to save you. You got that?"

"So, you still want me to come by, knowing I done been with her, huh? What you gon' do, kill me in my sleep?"

"You know what? I don't know what she's doing to you that you can't give it up, but whatever it is, I can do it better. And if I don't know how to do what she's doin', I'll learn, and I'll get good at it, and I'll give it to you better than she ever has, and I don't care what it is. I'ma do it too. She ain't gon' take my man from me. So, you enjoy yo' self for the last time. After that, we even and you mine."

"Okay, Johnnie. I'll be by tonight, and we gon' talk this shit out."

"Okay, Lucas. I gotta get back to work now."

Just as she turned to go back into the house, Johnnie saw Marla coming down the stairs. She turned back around, walked up to Lucas and forcefully kissed him on the lips. Then she looked at Marla to make sure she understood that this was war.

Chapter 17

"Negroes could never hate Whites . . . not after all we've done for them."

AS THE TWO WOMEN crossed paths, they eyed each other, looking for any weakness they could exploit. Their heads turned as they passed; yet they continued the stare-down. Finally, they both stopped walking and eyed each other like they were about to come to blows right there in the Beauregards' front yard. They stood there, staring, neither one backing down. Ethel, Katherine, and Morgan crowded the front door, watching it all.

"Mrs. Bentley," Lucas called out. "We better get on the road if you wanna get to Shreveport at a reasonable time."

"Okay," Marla said, still looking at Johnnie. She lowered her voice so that only Johnnie could hear. "Just so you know, I fucked him last night, and I'll be fucking him tonight before we come back. Think about that all day."

In an equally quiet tone, Johnnie said, "I'll be fuckin' him tonight too. I'll be fuckin' him tomorrow, the next day, and the day after that and the day after that. You think about that all day."

And with that, both women turned around and went their separate ways. Johnnie was about to walk back into the house, using the front door, but when she reached the steps and was about to climb them, she looked up at Katherine, Ethel, and Morgan. All of them had seen the show and were wondering what was going on.

Johnnie looked at Ethel and said, "I'm sorry, Mrs. Beauregard. I guess I forgot my place again. I'll go around to the back."

By the time Johnnie made it around to the back door, Ethel was there, waiting for her. "Johnnie, as much as I like you and need a maid to keep this place clean, if you walk out that front door again like you're a white woman, I'll fire you on the spot. You've already caused a ruckus by sitting at the dining table and feeding Grandpa. You've angered Katherine and she wants to get rid of you. Then you have a problem with a guest in my home, staring at a white woman like you're equals. What were you two talking about?"

Johnnie looked at her for a brief moment then looked at the floor. "Just sayin' hello, ma'am."

"Hmpf. It looked more like a catfight to me. How do you know Mrs. Bentley anyway? We've been trying to get the Bentleys to come over for years, but that husband of hers seems to love spending his time with the Negroes more than he does with his own kind."

"My boyfriend works for Napoleon, and I sang in his nightclub about a month ago."

"Napoleon? I heard he lets Negroes call him by his first name. That kind of thing is going to make Negroes wonder why he's so different from the rest of his race."

Johnnie looked Ethel in the eye again and said, "Maybe that's why Coloreds love him. Do Coloreds love the Beauregards the same way . . . the way they love Napoleon?" After saying this, she diverted her eyes to the floor again.

"Are you saying that Negroes hate Whites?"

"I don't know, ma'am. I just know they love Napoleon."

"Negroes could never hate Whites . . . not after all we've done for them. We took them out of a hedonistic Africa, brought them to a Christian nation, and gave them Christian names, and taught them a Christian language. How can the Negro hate us for doing good to him? That's preposterous."

Johnnie said, "You went to college, didn't you, Mrs. Beauregard?"

Whenever people used big words in a conversation with her, if she didn't like them, she always asked if they went to college as a way to get smart and to make them realize that it wasn't necessary to use words they knew she probably didn't understand. To use them was counterproductive.

Ethel laughed from her belly. "Yes, I did. Now, back to work."

I swear I don't understand how these white folks can go to college for years and still be stupid as hell, wondering why Coloreds hate 'em. Coloreds hate you for the very reason you think we should love you, you stupid bitch!

"Okay, Mrs. Beauregard, I'll finish the library first. I wanna look up that word you just used so I can learn how to talk white—I mean right."

"Good for you, Johnnie."

Chapter 18

"What'll it be, sir?"

"Would you like a sandwich, Lucas?" Marla asked.

Silence saturated the car.

"Oh, so you're not talking to me now, huh? I wonder why."

Lucas didn't respond.

"If you don't answer me, I swear to God I'll climb over the seat and ride up front with you the rest of the way."

After hearing the threat, Lucas cut his eyes to the rearview mirror. They had been on the road for nearly two hours and Lucas hadn't said a word. No matter how many times Marla tried to be pleasant, he never acknowledged her.

"You'd do that?" Lucas asked, still looking in the mirror.

Marla placed both hands on the front seat and pulled herself forward. Lucas couldn't believe she was actually going to climb over the seat. When he saw her foot coming over the seat, he jerked the car to the left and then to the right. The car's sudden movements threw Marla back into her seat. She laughed uproariously, like she was high on bourbon.

"You're going to talk to me, Lucas. If you're angry with me, say so. I can take it. I won't start crying like a little girl."

Lucas looked at her through the rearview, his anger visible. He knew that was a swipe at Johnnie, and he didn't appreciate it. "You want me to talk to you? You want me to get mad? You want me to tell you the truth? Fine! I wanna know what happened between you and Johnnie. What the hell did you say to her?"

"The truth?"

Lucas stared at her reflection. "What did you say exactly?"

"Exactly?"

"Yep."

"Word for word?"

"Word for fuckin' word."

"Syllable for syllable?"

When Marla saw the look on Lucas' face, she laughed uncontrollably for about thirty seconds, which infuriated him, and that made it even funnier to her. Lucas saw a sign that read: MOBIL GAS STATION, ¼ MILE AHEAD. He looked at the gas gauge. The needle was nearing the E.

"I'ma pull into this fillin' station and get some gas. I gotta go to the bathroom too. When we get back on the road, I wanna know what you told her, okay?"

"I have to go too. And when we get back on the road, I want you to talk to me and eat this food I made for you, and then I'll tell you what I said to Johnnie."

"Word for word?"

"Word for fuckin' word," Marla said, mocking him.

Lucas smiled. "Okay then."

He pulled into the Mobil station and parked next to the red-and-white pump. A black man wearing a red-and-white uniform came out of the station and approached the driver's side window.

"What'll it be, sir?"

Chapter 19

"You interested in makin' some real money?"

LUCAS LOOKED at the man's nametag. PRESTON was written inside a patch sewn onto his shirt just above the left-side pocket.

"What'll it be, sir?" Preston repeated

"Fill it up," Lucas said, and smiled. No one had ever called him sir. It made him feel like a man even though he was only eighteen. "Is this your station, man?"

"No, sir. The owner had to go home to see about his sick wife. He left me in charge, though."

"Excuse me, Preston," Marla said, "but where's your restroom?"

"White folks on the right side, ma'am."

"Thank you," Marla said and got out of the car and walked to the restroom.

"Damn!" Preston nearly shouted. "She's pretty. Too bad she's white. I'd like to fuck her—three times, at least! Damn! And you drive her around?"

Lucas swelled with pride all of a sudden, not only because he had been with her, but she'd done special favors for him too. Everything in him wanted to scream, "Man, I been up in that!" But he just smiled.

"I see you smilin', man. So, did she offer you some or what?"

"Naw, man. She's a nice lady."

"I'll bet she is. You ain't gotta admit it, but I know you been up in that—all the way up in it too." He laughed. "You be careful, man. Them crackers'll kill yo' ass over that shit. At the very least they'll cut yo' dick off. And what good is a nigga without it?"

"If I was doin' it with her, I would be careful, but I'm not."

"That's smart, man. Never ever admit to fuckin' a white woman, no matter what! I don't care if somebody catches you on the down-stroke. Deny that shit while they stringin' yo' ass up, ya hear?"

"I'll remember that," Lucas said and got out of the car. "I gotta go to the bathroom."

Preston said, "It's on the wrong side of the building."

"Huh?"

"The left side, man. White is right, so they go to the right. Niggas is wrong, so they go to the left. Understand?"

Lucas laughed. "Okay, I get it."

"Hey, man," Preston said, "you interested in making some real money?"

"Yeah. How?"

"I'll be in the bathroom in a second and I'll tell you. It's a little dangerous, but it's worth it. A nigga can make some real money—money he can use to buy his own land, start his own business, live like the white folks. You interested?"

"Hell yeah."

"Here comes the white lady. I'll be in there in a second."

Chapter 20

What's funny about it?"

THE TIRES SCREAMED when Johnnie pulled her car away from the curb, which was parked a couple of houses away from the Beauregard mansion. It was 12:00 P.M. and she and Sadie were done for the day. Johnnie's anger was still inflamed. She was angry with Napoleon for putting thoughts into Lucas' mind of her sleeping with him later that day, knowing that wasn't going to happen.

She sped down the street, weaving in and out of traffic, unable to get the conversations she'd had with Lucas and Marla out of her head. She couldn't wait to get to the Bayou to give Napoleon a piece of her mind. He had a lot of nerve sending Lucas off to Shreveport with Marla, knowing full well that they had been together; especially since he was the one who told her about the affair in the first place, just so he could be with Johnnie himself.

"You okay?" Sadie asked hesitantly.

"Yeah," Johnnie fumed.

"Why are you driving so fast?"

"I'm mad, Sadie."

"About?"

"Nothin'."

Sadie stared at her for a long time. "Is it about what happened with Marla Bentley in the Beauregards' front yard?"

Johnnie looked at her briefly, wondering how she found out so quickly. She would have told her at some point, but not today. "No."

Skeptical, Sadie said, "It didn't have anything to do with Marla Bentley?" Silence. "So, it did have something to do with Marla Bentley?" Silence. "What happened, Johnnie?"

"Nothin'."

"Nothing, huh? Well, why are you so upset? Something had to have happened. Did you and Lucas have words? That was him that drove her over to the Beauregards', right? At least tell me that much."

"Yeah. That was him."

"So, what did he say? I know he had to have said something. Did he break up with you or what?"

"Yep."

"Umm. Okay. Now we're getting somewhere. Why did he break it off?"

"'Cause he's stupid, that's why!"

"He found another woman, huh?"

Johnnie looked at Sadie. Tears formed. "You can say that."

"Do you know the woman? Did he tell you her name? Is it somebody that works for Napoleon? What?"

"No, it's not somebody who works for Napoleon."

"Hmm." Sadie stared at her. She thought for a moment and said, "Let me ask you this. Is something going on between Marla and Lucas?" Silence. "Oh, shit! Lucas fucked Marla?" Silence. "You mean to tell me he's stupid enough to not only get involved with a white woman, but he's brazen enough to fuck the wife of Napoleon Bentley? Oh, shit. Napoleon is going to kill him over this if he finds out."

"Napoleon already knows about it," Johnnie blurted out.

"What? He knows about it and he's letting him drive his wife around in his car? What the hell is going on?"

"It's complicated."

"It's complicated? What's that supposed to—" Sadie stopped in mid-sentence. All of a sudden, it came to her all at once. "Did you do it with Napoleon?" Silence. "Oh, shit! Didn't I beg you not to do that, Johnnie? Damn! When did this happen?"

"The day before they killed the preacher."

"And Lucas found out about it?"

"Yep."

"Shit. So, now he's fucking Marla?" Sadie asked, shaking her head. "This would be funny as hell if it wasn't so dangerous."

"Actually, he did it with Marla first. Remember that day that Napoleon came over and I asked you to give us some privacy?"

"Yeah."

"Well, I didn't tell you this, but he told me about Marla and Lucas then. And when that didn't work, he blackmailed me and threatened to tell Lucas about Martin Winters. That's the whole truth, but I didn't tell you that because I didn't want you to think bad of Lucas. He was wrong, but so was I."

Sadie said, "You might as well tell me what happened with Marla now that the cat's outta the bag."

Shaking her head as if she couldn't believe what she was about to say, Johnnie said, "If you think that's crazy, Napoleon sent Marla and Lucas to Shreveport for the day."

"What?"

"Yep. Sho' did."

"But you just said he knows they've been intimate, didn't you?"

"Yep."

"Let me ask you something. Are you—"

"No!"

"Why would he send them away—together—knowing they are seeing each other?"

"That's what I'ma find out."

Chapter 21

"Don't make me slap the shit outta you!"

JOHNNIE STORMED INTO Napoleon's Bayou like a raging tempest at about 12:20. She nearly caused an accident, driving at speeds she was too inexperienced to handle. There could be only one reason for sending Lucas and Marla away together for the day, she deduced, and that was so he could bed her again to save Lucas' life.

Even though she told Lucas she wouldn't do it to save him again, deep down inside, in her innermost being, in her precious heart, she knew she would. She would still do anything for Lucas because he was the only one who really cared for her. The fact that he was so upset with her earlier proved that—in her mind, anyway. Besides, if Napoleon wanted her again, she could barter with him, using the sex she wanted from him as a bargaining chip. This was the perfect excuse to open her legs to Napoleon again, and she could pretend that she was only doing it to save Lucas. But right now, he needed to be told off, and that's exactly what she was going to do.

She saw Simon Young, better known as Fort Knox, the emcee who had lost all of his teeth in barroom brawls and replaced them with gold. He was sitting at the piano, playing a familiar tune that she couldn't quite remember at the moment, probably because her mind was full of fiery heat that would only dissipate when she saw Napoleon. She fast-walked over to the piano. "Where's Napoleon?"

"He's in the office with Bubbles," Fort Knox said. "Sit down for a minute and let's sing a song together, pretty lady."

"Another time," Johnnie said and stormed off toward the office. She knew she should knock, but she didn't. She turned the doorknob and walked in like she owned the place. She saw Napoleon and Bubbles playing a game of chess.

Napoleon looked up when he heard the door open. When he saw her, he smiled and whispered to Bubbles, "What did I tell you? I bet she just got off work too. Didn't even bother to go home. Watch this." He stood up. "Hello, Johnnie. How have you been?"

Johnnie rushed over to him and slapped him as hard as she could. Bubbles stood up and grabbed her.

"Hey, hey, hey, little lady," Bubbles said. "What's the problem?"

"Let me go, Bubbles!" Johnnie said, struggling to get at Napoleon, her chest heaving rapidly as she sucked in huge amounts of oxygen.

"I'll let you go when you calm yo' ass down. You don't run up on Napoleon like that—I don't give a fuck what the problem is. Now, I'ma let you go and you gon' get yo' shit together and I mean now. You got that?"

Johnnie stared at Napoleon, still fuming.

Bubbles had her by the shoulders, looking at the fury in her eyes. He shook her a little to get her attention. “Don’t make me slap the shit outta you! Now, you calm yo’ ass down—right—fuckin’—now.”

When she heard that, her senses returned to her. “Why, Napoleon?”

“Before you say another muthafuckin’ word,” Bubbles went on, “don’t you ever come through that door without knocking. If we wanna talk to you, we’ll let you in. Now, I like you, Johnnie, but this is business. And don’t think for a second that I won’t kill you as easy as I killed the preacher. You understand?”

Humbled, Johnnie nodded.

“Now,” Bubbles continued, “what’s got yo’ goat?”

“You know what I did to save Lucas’ life?” Johnnie asked Bubbles, looking into his eyes.

“Yeah, I know.”

“Then you know Marla and Lucas—”

“Yeah, I know.”

“After what I did, I wanna know why he sent them to Shreveport together, Bubbles.”

Bubbles let her go and said, “Sit down.”

Chapter 22

"You called that perfectly, man."

IF LOOKS COULD KILL, Napoleon would have been vaporized the way Johnnie was staring at him. Somewhat calm now, she sat in the seat Bubbles previously occupied and looked at Napoleon, who was seated again. "I'm never having sex with you again, Napoleon," she said with venom.

"Listen, little girl," Napoleon began. "I thought I made myself clear. I'm not interested in fucking you again. It wasn't worth the trouble the first goddamn time. I tried to be nice and let your young ass down easy, and then you run up in my place of business talking about the same shit I told you about two fuckin' weeks ago. Now, if Lucas is dumb enough to fuck Marla again, that's his ass."

"I'm not no little girl. I'm a woman. And if you didn't enjoy it, you got a problem, not me. Maybe you funny or somethin'," Johnnie said, defending herself.

However, deep down, Johnnie felt like something was wrong with her. She didn't even consider something being wrong with Napoleon. Men couldn't keep their hands off her, and yet here he was telling her it wasn't worth the trouble. Johnnie knew that if she opened her legs, there wasn't a man alive who wouldn't stand in a ten-mile line to get his chance to pump her. Yet Napoleon thought it wasn't worth the trouble? That had her mind in serious knots.

"Well, why did you send him to Shreveport with her then? You know they gon' do it, don't you?"

"Look, I don't owe you an explanation. I have my reasons."

"So, you hoping they do it, huh? For what? You don't want me no more. Why are you putting Lucas in that situation?"

"You think Lucas is that weak? He can't be trusted or what? For all I know, Marla wasn't that great for him either. As a matter of fact, Marla is a terrible lover. That's why I go to black women when I wanna get seriously fucked. They know how to put a man to sleep. But you too damned young right now. Maybe in a few years you'll have learned how to screw a man right. Besides, I'm sure Lucas wouldn't want to disappoint a pretty thing like you even though you're a terrible lover too. I mean, if I can turn you down because it wasn't all that great, he can turn Marla down for the same reasons, don't you think?"

After those words, Johnnie's young mind twisted even more. Not only had Napoleon told her she was terrible in bed, but he didn't even want her anymore, and planted a seed of doubt about Lucas being weak and stupid in the process.

Feeling the need to defend Lucas, Johnnie said, “Lucas is just as strong as you.”

“I suppose that’s why you came in here screaming at me—because he’s so strong?” He stared into her brown eyes intensely and said, “Listen, I’m busy. I don’t have time for this silly shit. I’m a businessman. Bubbles, get her outta my sight.”

Johnnie was about to say something when Bubbles grabbed her by the arm. “Unt-uh. Don’t say another word. Let’s go.” Then he escorted her to the front door. “And Johnnie, let that be yo’ last time comin’ up in here, accusing Napoleon of anything. You got that?” He shoved her out the door.

Napoleon came out of the office, and he and Bubbles stood at the picture window, watching Johnnie get into her car, much like they watched Lucas earlier that morning. About thirty seconds later, they saw Johnnie and Sadie get out of the car and walk around it. Sadie got in on the driver’s side, and Johnnie got in the passenger’s seat.

Bubbles reached into his pocket and pulled out a wad of money. He flipped it open and took out a five and handed it to Napoleon to pay off the bet on whether Johnnie would come to the Bayou that day in an uproar. Then he said, “You called that perfectly, man. That was flawless. And that shit you said to her is going to bother her for a long, long time.” He laughed a little. “Look at this. She can’t even drive.”

“Yeah, I know,” Napoleon said, laughing. “I can’t wait to fuck her young ass again. Next time, she’s going to go out of her way to be great in bed. Did you hear that bullshit about being a woman?”

“Uh-huh.”

"Now she's gotta wrap her mind around me being strong enough to leave her alone and Lucas being too weak to leave Marla alone."

"Is that shit you said about Marla being terrible in bed true?"

Napoleon looked at Bubbles and said, "Marla is going to have Lucas' nose so wide open he's going to make taking his woman a piece of cake. Patience is all we need now." He put his arm around Bubbles and said "Come, old friend. Let's plan the New Orleans coup."

Chapter 23

"He was gon' do it anyway, Sadie."

"Maybe I better drive," Sadie said when she saw how angry Johnnie still was. Judging by the expression on her face, Sadie believed that her friend hadn't gotten anywhere with Napoleon. And if she drove to Ashland Estates as recklessly as she'd driven to the French Quarter, Sadie thought they might not make it in one piece.

"Yeah, you better," Johnnie said.

Both women exited the car and walked around the front of it, totally unaware that Napoleon and Bubbles were watching with great interest.

"So, what happened?" Sadie asked, and pulled away from the curb.

"I slapped him," Johnnie said with righteous indignation.

"Napoleon?"

"Yep!"

"And he let you get away with that?"

"What could he do?" Johnnie said. "And I told him I wasn't going to open my legs again no matter what."

"Did he say why he sent Marla and Lucas to Shreveport together?"

"Yeah. So that me and him could be together one last time. That's when I slapped the taste outta his mouth."

"And he didn't do anything? He just let you slap him?"

"Yeah, he did something. He got on his knees and begged for some. And when I told him no, he tried to put his face in my stuff, talking about let me just taste it then."

Sadie laughed from her belly. "Then what happened?"

"We got tuh strugglin' up in there 'cause he kept tryin' tuh put his face all up my dress, sayin', 'Just a taste, just a taste. I ain't gotta put it in.' Then he started sayin' I had the best pussy he ever had. I knew he was lyin', with all the women he done been with. There's no way a sixteen-year-old black girl is going to satisfy a man like that. He just wanted some more, just like you told me he would, Sadie. Then I broke free and ran outta there." Johnnie hated lying, but there was no way she was going to tell Sadie what really happened in Napoleon's office.

"Well, I'm glad he didn't try to rape you."

"He tried, but thank God I got outta there before he could get his pants down."

"Yeah, that was definitely God's intervention. So, uh, what's going to happen with you and Lucas?"

"We gon' work it out when he get back in town tonight."

"You think him and Marla might stop someplace on the way back?"

"I'm sure of it, Sadie. I told him to get his last piece and we even after this."

"So, you told him it was okay?"

"He was gon' do it anyway, Sadie. Tellin' him to get his last piece lets him know I know and he can't bring up Napoleon again. And what did it cost me? Nothing. Not really. I did it with Napoleon and he found out. Now it's out in the open. I don't have to feel guilty. And when he gets back, we gon' get back together and I'ma be so good to him, he's gon' leave Marla alone for good. I've got money, a house, a car, everything. If I want to, we can leave New Orleans right now—today. And if it wasn't for my sweet granddad who needs me right now, me and Lucas would leave New Orleans tonight."

"Sounds like you've got it all figured out. I hope it works out for you two."

"It will, Sadie. I'ma make sure of it tonight."

"Well, tell me this: Are you sure you're through with Napoleon? Women say he's irresistible."

"Not to me. Lucas is the only man that can satisfy me. When I did it with Napoleon, it was just something I had to do—nothing more. He put it in, pump for about two minutes, and he was through, just like the rest of them cracker men. But Lucas knows how to do it right."

"I see. Okay. I'm glad you didn't swoon over him like most black women do. You definitely have your wits about you. I wish I had been smarter when I was your age. I wouldn't be in this mess with Santino Mancini."

"Oh, that reminds me. You know Katherine don't like you, right?" Johnnie said, glad she had a chance to change the subject.

"I know she doesn't."

"Do you know why?"

"Yep. But she has lots of nerve, Johnnie. She was giving it up to Beau Beauregard for years. And if he wanted some today, you'd need a vise to close her legs."

Johnnie laughed for the first time since they got off work. "You definitely right about that. She does have a lotta nerve. She was telling me you were an adulteress because of your situation with Santino."

"I figured she would tell you that. I didn't mention it because I didn't want to turn you against her before you even started working there. She's a mess, and you have to work with her."

"I know. She already tried to get me fired on the first day."

Sadie shook her head. "What a bitch! She needs to find a man to put it on her. That's her problem. I bet if Beau gave her some like he used to when he came to town, she'd be all right for a week. She thinks nobody knows, but we do. We just pretend we don't, like they did during the slave days."

"Guess what else? I caught Beau doin' it with his brother's wife in the library this morning. Right there on the table where I'm supposed to do my reading. I cleaned that table real good before I left today, though."

"On the table?"

"On—the—table. And then he didn't stop when he saw me looking at 'em. He told me he would meet me proper later and kept right at it like I never even walked into the room."

"What did Piper say when she saw you? You know she's a pastor's wife, don't you?"

"Not much. She just kept on moanin' like what he was givin' her was the best thing on earth."

Part Two

The Wiles of the Devil

Chapter 24

"I've got some money saved up."

LUCAS PULLED into the Chevrolet dealership and parked Napoleon's car in an open space. He got out and opened the door for Marla Bentley. She was wearing dark sunglasses, a cantaloupe sleeveless dress and matching open-toe leather sandals.

Marla laughed a little and said, "Watch how the men fall all over themselves when they see me coming."

Lucas got back in the car and watched Marla as she made her way to the entrance. Sure enough, five men came out of the dealership to greet her, just as she said they would. Marla looked back over her shoulder and smiled.

Once Marla and the men were inside the office, Lucas got out of the car and decided to take a look around, admiring all the beautiful, shining new cars. He was particularly drawn to a 1954 white convertible Corvette with burgundy leather interior. The hubcaps were silver with burgundy material that stood out next to the white walls, which was just outside the burgundy inner wall.

He wanted to sit in it, start the engine, turn on the AM radio and go for a nice long drive. He pictured Johnnie sitting next to him as they drove to the drive-in theater in Baroque Parish and a smile emerged. He looked around to see if anyone was watching. A white man in a suit and tie was coming toward him.

The man said, "You cain't afford that car, boy. Hell, I cain't even afford that car. This is the kinda car that'll make a man think about sellin' his wife just so he can dream about a beauty like this. Yessiree Bob, you can dream about it, but that's about it."

"I'm gonna have one of these babies real, real soon," Lucas said, thinking about the offer that Preston had made him three hours earlier.

The station attendant's name was Preston Leonard Truman, and he offered Lucas the sweetest deal any Negro looking to make some quick money could imagine. Preston had a Harlem connection that supplied him with more weed than he could sell on his own. He told Lucas he would cut him in on the deal for thirty percent of what he sold. He also told Lucas that if he was a good earner, he'd take a smaller percentage.

When Preston told him he was making fifty dollars a week selling to customers at the filling station and musical groups that happened past, Lucas saw a marvelous opportunity to make some quick money. He was going to invest his money in the stock market just like Johnnie did. And if it worked out like he knew it would, they'd have enough money between them to leave New Orleans for good.

Lucas wanted to go out to the coast—to San Francisco, where a man with some dollars in his pockets had a real chance to make a life for himself. He thought that if San Francisco was good enough for Benny, Johnnie's pugilist brother, it would be good enough for them too. Plus, he knew he was living on borrowed time messing around with Marla Bentley.

"Boy, this car costs $3523." The man laughed a little. "It'll be ten years before you can afford this car. The good thing is, she's an instant classic. Only three hundred of these sweet so-and-so's rolled off the assembly line up there in Flint, Michigan."

"You say $3523?" In his mind, Lucas calculated the number of months it would take to pay cash for it. Even though he wasn't a good reader and did poorly in school, he was good with numbers. Napoleon was paying him $50 a week and he thought he could easily sell $150 a week to the bands that came to town and played at the Bayou—maybe more. He was getting to know them all personally. They would trust him and buy from him, he thought. Getting high was what the musicians did, like it was a religion or something. The way they frequently shot whatever it was they shot in their arms, if he could get a hold of some, he could buy the Corvette sooner. "I'll be back in about four months or less to get one of these."

The man laughed even harder, and said, "You gon' rob a bank, boy?"

"No, sir."

"Then how are you gonna get that kinda money? I just told you I cain't even afford this car, and I'm white."

"I've got some money saved up," Lucas said. "Been savin' for years. But it'll take a while to get the rest."

The man's laughter was replaced by a sober gaze. Then he laughed again. "Boy, you almost had me. Ya almost had me." Then he laughed again.

"Lucas," Marla called out. "Help me pick out a car, okay?"

Chapter 25

"I know, baby. I know."

THE 1954 CHEVROLET zoomed down the dark road exceeding eighty miles per hour. After they traded in the old car for the new convertible, Marla shopped for several hours before they finally got back on the road at about 6:30. They had been on the road for just over three hours and Lucas wanted to get back to New Orleans as soon as he could.

Excited, he couldn't wait to tell Johnnie about the great deal Preston Truman had thrown in his lap. His ship had finally come in, and he was feeling great. This was the opportunity he had hoped would come his way. He made up his mind to concentrate on selling as much marijuana as he could and to invest as much as he could so that they could move on with their lives—that is if Johnnie was through with Napoleon.

"Lucas," Marla said from the backseat. "Pull over so we can put the top back up. I'm freezing. Aren't you cold?"

"Breeze feels good to me," he said, pulling over to the side of the quiet road.

He stopped the car and they got out and pulled the white canvas top to the front and locked it into place. They got back into the car. Lucas was about to turn the ignition key when Marla leaned forward. In a breathy whisper, she said, "You still wanna know what I told your girlfriend this morning?" Then she leaned back and looked at him through the rearview.

"Yeah," Lucas said and turned his body toward her, resting his arm on the back of his seat.

"Word for word?" Marla asked, pulling her panties down while he watched, straining to see her exposed vagina.

"Word for word," he said, his eyes deep into her crotch.

"I told her I fucked you last night and that I was going to fuck you tonight on the way home."

"What!" Lucas said, surprised. Then it came to him. Johnnie had told him to get his last piece. *Hmm, so that's why she said that. She already knew about everything.*

"So, are you still through with me?" Marla asked, looking deep into his eyes as if she could see what was in his heart.

"Yeah," Lucas said, still staring between her legs.

"So, you don't want one last time before we get back to town?"

"One last time? You gon' leave me alone if I do it?"

"No. It feels so good. Why should I, when you know you want it too? Don't I make you feel good, Lucas? Don't you love what I do for you? Can you really just give it up all of a sudden?" Silence. "Come to Mama, Lucas. Nobody'll know. We haven't seen a car for at least an hour. It's just you, the crickets, and me all alone on a dark road. And you can tell yourself this is the last time if you need to."

Why can't I say no to her? Shit! I need my ass whipped but good. Damn! Johnnie loves me and I love her. I need to leave this bitch alone before she gets us both killed. And what if Johnnie was tellin' the truth? What if she wasn't gonna see him again today? But she did fuck Napoleon behind my back, didn't she? For all I know, she could've fucked other men too. Yep, I bet she did fuck somebody I don't even know about. How can I trust her?

Life is so damned complicated. I love her and I hate her. How we gon' straighten this shit out so we can move forward? We gotta get outta New Orleans. That's the only way. I gotta seriously hustle that weed so we can go. I'm not gon' live off no woman. Fuck that. I'ma man. But since Johnnie gave me permission, I'ma fuck this bitch one last time. Then I'm through with it. After this, it's me and Johnnie for sure. I mean it for real this time.

Lucas' eyes shifted from Marla's crotch to her eyes. "This is the last time, Marla."

"I know, baby. I know." Marla laughed. His struggle to leave her alone tickled her. "Come get it. It's already warm."

Lucas looked into the empty night to see if anyone was around. Then he climbed over the seat.

Chapter 26

Come on, baby. Let's go."

JOHNNIE WAS ASLEEP. She had dozed off for a moment in her car, which was parked near the entrance of Napoleon's Bayou. When Lucas didn't come by her place in what she thought was a reasonable amount of time, she went to the Bayou looking for Napoleon's car, which was usually parked near the entrance. She was determined to talk to him that night, and wasn't about to let him give her the lateness-of-the-hour excuse, so she decided to wait for him at the Bayou for as long as it took.

She heard a car door slam shut and opened her eyes. She saw Lucas opening the door for Marla and blew the horn to get their attention before getting out of her car.

"Lucas!" she shouted, and began the short trek over to him. "How was your trip?" She looked at Marla, who was wearing a satisfied grin. "I see your trip was pleasurable, Mrs. Bentley."

"Just as I told you it would be this morning at the Beauregards' home. You do remember what I said, don't you?"

"I do. And you remember what I said too, I'm sure." Johnnie turned to Lucas. "Come on, baby. Let's go."

At that time, Napoleon and Bubbles came out of the Bayou.

"I see you've made it back. I trust it went well, my dear," Napoleon said to Marla.

"It was an arduous journey to Shreveport, but we were able to find a new car," Marla said.

"Is this it?" Napoleon asked rhetorically. "How do you like it, Lucas? You did pick it out, didn't you?"

"Yes, I picked it. It's a great car. I thought you'd love it."

"I do. It's a great car and it's all yours, my friend."

Excited, Lucas said, "You kiddin', Napoleon! For real?"

"Yeah. I told you I had a surprise for you when you came back. I have plenty of cars. The whole trip was for you. That was the surprise, kid!"

Lucas looked at Johnnie, who was stunned by the news too. Then he said, "Napoleon, it's a great car, but I can't take it, man." *Not after fuckin' your wife on the way home. That's goin' too damn far. How am I supposed to accept a gift like this from you now? How come you didn't tell me that shit before I left? I wouldn't have fucked her. And what's this friend shit? You fucked Johnnie and I ain't forgot that shit, muthafucka!*

"Sure you can, Lucas," Napoleon said. "Remember what Bubbles discussed with you this morning about clemency?"

Lucas nodded.

"Good. Now, let's all get over to Walter Brickman's for some burgers and fries and malts. They're one of the few shops that have opened back up since the riots."

"Napoleon," Johnnie interrupted, "me and Lucas have plans. Can we do this some other time?"

"I insist. It won't take long. I promise," Napoleon offered without even looking at her. "Bubbles has some things he has to discuss with Lucas. And you too. Let's go."

Chapter 27

"I wanna hear you say you understand, kid . . ."

TWENTY MINUTES LATER, four cars stopped in front of Walter Brickman's Malt Shop. After they finished their meal, they each had plans of their own, which was why everyone drove their own vehicles to the late night restaurant. Even though it was late, Walter Brickman's was full of people. After the riots, people needed to get out of their homes and entertain themselves, which was why reopening the restaurants and the Sepia Theatre was a high priority.

Bubbles saw Lee Shepard, the pompous vixen Dennis Edwards was seeing before Denise, his wife, put a stop to it. Dennis was the Parish tailor who lived right across the street from Johnnie. Bubbles walked over to Lee's table, sat down, and spoke to her quietly. She had been waiting for him. Tonight would be their first date. They met during the reception at Johnnie's house after Marguerite's funeral. The subsequent riots and the curfew made it impossible to see each other, so they chatted on the phone regularly.

Lucas and Johnnie sat at one booth, and Napoleon and Marla sat at another. Although Johnnie was anxious to talk to Lucas, she had a plan. Instead of telling him about Napoleon in Walter Brickman's, she told him about her first day at work, and what it felt like to finally meet her grandfather. A few minutes later, Bubbles came over and slid into the seat across from them. They ordered cheeseburgers, fries, and Coca-Cola.

Bubbles said, "Listen, kid. You too, Johnnie. I'ma make this shit real quick because Lee Shepard is waitin' for me and I know we gon' have a good time tonight. Now, as both of you know, some shit went down that was not cool. People fucked up on both sides. Y'all know what I mean?" Johnnie and Lucas lowered their eyes and nodded. "Good, good. What happened, happened. Ain't no goin' back to change that shit either, right?" They nodded again. "The important thing to remember is that people made decisions for whatever reasons.

"But all that shit is in the past now. I know Napoleon . . . been knowin' him for years, and this is the closet thing you're gonna get to an apology. We gotta keep our shit together. We got other shit goin' on with the Chicago people that y'all don't know about. We cain't afford to let this bullshit get us all killed. Lucas, do you like the car?"

"Yeah, man, but—"

"Ain't no fuckin' buts, kid. That car was generous as hell, especially considerin' what's been goin' on, don't you think?"

Lucas nodded.

"What are you, eighteen now?"

"Yep."

"And you drivin' a brand spankin' new Chevy. Brand fuckin' new, man. And guess what else?"

"What?" Lucas said.

"We're givin' you a raise in pay. You makin' fifty a week, right?"

"Right."

"We're doubling it to one hundred a week. Now, that's gotta put a smile on ya face. Brand new car, money in ya pocket, nice apartment, and a beautiful woman. What else do you need, kid?"

Lucas smiled from ear to ear. *I'ma get that Corvette sooner than I thought. With a hundred a week, I can buy more weed and sell it quicker. This is gonna be great. Me and Johnnie are gonna finally get outta here and I won't have to worry about Marla Bentley messin' with me either.*

"Nothing, Bubbles. I don't need nothin' else. You're right, man. What happened, happened. I have everything I need."

"Good, good. Now, there's one catch."

"What's that?"

"No drugs of any kind, kid."

Lucas furrowed his brow, surprised that Bubbles and Napoleon would bring this up now, but he dismissed it almost immediately because of the raise in pay and the brand new car he was just given.

"At some point," Bubbles continued, "we figured somebody's gonna approach you about some fast money, okay? That'll get everybody pinched. Stay away from the shit. We've taken good care of you, man. We want you to eventually do runs to Harlem. Lots of temptation in that city. A man can make a fortune on the side, but if you get caught, you go to prison for a long, long time. And when a man's lookin' at that kinda time, he's liable to shoot his mouth off and take down the whole damned thing. We won't allow that. Understand?"

Lucas nodded, knowing full well that he was still going to sell the weed no matter what. It was too good a deal to pass up. He was going to get himself and Johnnie away from New Orleans as soon as he could. If selling a little weed against the king's orders was what it would take, he would just have to be very careful, he thought.

"Don't worry, Bubbles," Johnnie said. "He won't be doing anything like that."

Bubbles kept his eyes on Lucas, ignoring Johnnie's words as if she never said them. "I wanna hear you say you understand, kid, 'cause if you violate the rules, it'll cost you your life."

"I understand," Lucas said.

Bubbles stared into Lucas' eyes for what seemed like five minutes. Then he said, "I hope so, kid." Then he got up and went back to Lee Shepard's table.

Chapter 28

"You have all of me . . ."

LUCAS AND JOHNNIE parked their cars in her garage, closed the garage door, and entered the kitchen. Johnnie was ready to tell Lucas what he needed to hear. It would all be a lie, of course, but what he didn't know wouldn't hurt him, she told herself. The strange thing was she had been taught never to lie at the Holiness church she used to attend, where she led most of the songs as a member of the choir on Sunday mornings. But all of that seemed like decades ago now.

From time to time, Johnnie still wondered how she ended up in this situation. How did she go from being a good, church-going Christian to a whore, an adulteress, and an accessory to murder? What was lying to save a highly valued relationship compared to selling yourself for money? What was lying compared to adultery? What was lying compared to cold-blooded, calculated murder? But still, her conscience was pricked. She'd made some terrible choices, and she was ready to change some things.

However, sex wasn't one of them. She needed it. It was her ally, her weapon of choice in the war she was about to wage against Marla Bentley to keep her man. Besides, if God could forgive her of prostitution and murder, certainly He could forgive fornication, couldn't He? After all, it wasn't adultery and it wasn't murder, the two worst sins, she told herself.

It's God's fault anyway. He knew my mother was going to sell my virginity to Earl Shamus and He didn't lift a finger to stop it. Only Lucas cared enough to at least fight for me. I was a good girl. I AM A GOOD GIRL! And since God knew all about it and didn't help me out, He knew I was going to make these choices because He didn't help me. I know fornication is wrong, but I'm not gon' lose Lucas. And if I have to give it to him three times a day to keep him away from Marla Bentley, that's exactly what I'm going to do. Mama told me right; that's what men want. If I don't give it to him, I'm forcing him to get it from her.

"Sit down, Lucas. It's time for me to tell you what happened, okay?"

They both sat at the kitchen table and stared at each other for a few seconds then looked away. They were both ashamed, probably for the first time since they made the decision to sleep with other people. Before this moment, they hadn't really dealt with their betrayal. Now it was all going to come out, and the idea of that was daunting for them both. But Lucas felt even worse because he had just been with Marla, and now he wanted to be with Johnnie in spite of her having been with Napoleon. He felt completely powerless to control his sexual appetite, and the constant erections he got from seeing Johnnie no matter what the circumstances were.

After a long silence, Johnnie finally said, "Lucas, I know you think I just dropped my panties for Napoleon, but that's not how it happened. Before I go any further, are you sure you wanna know absolutely everything?"

"Yep. Word for word. I want the truth. You enjoyed it with him, didn't you?"

"It's not that simple. You said you wanted to know everything, so I'ma tell you, okay?" Lucas nodded. "You remember that day when I told you about Earl's wife comin' over here accusin' me of wantin' her husband?"

"Yeah, I remember."

"Well, what I didn't tell you is that Napoleon was already here."

"Before Earl's wife came over?"

"Yep. He came over to tell me that he found out about you and Marla. And when I told him that it was probably Marla's fault, he was surprised that I didn't get all upset about it. That's when I knew he was tryin' tuh get some from me. I told him I wasn't the least bit interested and to get the hell outta my house. That's when he threatened to kill you if I didn't give him some. I couldn't let him kill you, Lucas. I just couldn't. Don't you understand that?"

"Did you enjoy it?" Lucas asked, avoiding the question, staring at her intensely.

"No."

"Yes, you did, Johnnie. I saw you! I saw how you looked at him that night we killed the preacher! You enjoyed it and you wanted him to stick it in you again, didn't you?"

"No, I didn't, Lucas. That's not what I wanted that night when you saw me looking at him, however it may have looked."

"Then why was you looking like you wanted him to fuck you again?"

"Lucas, what were we about to do that night?"

"Kill Richard Goode," Lucas said forcefully.

"Don't I have the right to be happy about that? Don't I have the right to look with admiration at the man who was going to give me the justice I deserved? Before that night, who did Sheriff Tate arrest? Huh? Who?"

Reluctantly, Lucas bowed his head and mumbled, "Nobody."

"That's right, nobody. And when the Klan found out we killed Richard Goode, what did they do? They came in here to kill anybody they could, didn't they? But they didn't care about justice for a poor black whore, did they? Kill a black woman and it means nothing. Kill a murdering preacher who has to have his brown sugar and they wanna kill us all.

"So yeah, Lucas, I looked at Napoleon with admiration, but that's all it was— admiration! Now, you tell me; didn't I have a right to be glad we were finally going to kill him? Didn't he deserve to die that night after the way he beat my mother like that? You saw her, Lucas. My mother was the prettiest woman in the Parish. Everybody knows it. And how did she look, Lucas? How did she look before Fletcher fixed her back up again to bury her?"

Lucas believed her and he felt so foolish. A considerable load was lifted from his wide, football-player shoulders. He needed to know he was the only man that could make her feel good in bed. He needed to believe that he was the only "real" lover she had ever had. He needed to believe that no white man could ever measure up to a black man in the bedroom. He needed to believe that he was still the only man she wanted inside her—no one else, just him, forever and ever. He looked Johnnie in the eye and said, almost pleadingly, "So, you didn't enjoy it?"

"Hell naw. I didn't even have a chance to enjoy it. Don't repeat this to anybody, but Napoleon took me to this fancy hotel, like it was going to be the greatest thing in the world."

"What hotel?"

"The Bel Glades."

"Ain't that where Earl used to work?"

"Yep. He took me to the top floor in this real fancy room and everything. He had flowers everywhere and all kinds of food. Now, I ain't gon' lie. The food was good. But then, when it came time to do my *duty* to save *your* life, he put it in and it was over thirty seconds later. It was like I hadn't done anything at all." She paused and bowed her head in pseudo contrition. "Are you going to hold those thirty seconds against me, Lucas?"

"Thirty seconds? Is that all?" Lucas repeated, almost laughing.

"If that," Johnnie said, feeling like all the lies were working. "So, are we okay now? I told you everything. Are we okay?"

"But Napoleon's got this reputation with lots of black women that say how great he is. And you're saying thirty seconds?"

"Lucas, Napoleon is a mobster. What else could they say? If it got out that he was a terrible lover, what do you think he'd do?"

"Probably kill whoever put it on the wire."

"That's right, and that's why neither one of us can ever let it get out, just like all those other black women that claim he's great in bed. We gotta keep it to ourselves, right?"

"Right," Lucas said. "Ain't no sense in gettin' killed now after what you had to do for that cracker."

"Okay, now, tell me about you and Marla. And I wanna know everything."

"Why?"

"Because I love you, and if you need something she's doing, I'ma do it too. I'm not gon' lose you, not after what I had to do to keep you alive, so tell me everything—all of it."

"You sure you wanna know?" Lucas asked.

"I'm definitely sure," Johnnie said, remembering the seed that Napoleon planted in her young mind. "I need to know what it is about her that makes you so weak. I need to know why you can't seem to leave her alone."

"Hey!" Lucas shouted. "I'm not weak, and I can leave her alone. She keeps comin' after me. I never go after her. *Never*!"

"You are weak, Lucas," Johnnie offered respectfully. "You just don't know it. You're like a drunk that thinks he can stop anytime he wants, yet he never chooses to stop, baby."

"Well, I can stop, Johnnie. I ain't like no drunk! I'm a man!"

Johnnie kinda laughed. "Listen to you. You can stop, but you haven't. But okay. Lucas. You say you can stop. Tell me this: Why haven't you stopped?" She paused and let the question sink in a bit. Lucas stared at her for a long time and then he looked away. "Oh, so you don't wanna give it up? You have the nerve to question me about Napoleon? And I don't wanna hear that shit about women are supposed to understand, either. If that's the case, *you* should understand too. If you can't understand as a man, don't expect me to understand as a woman."

"But didn't you ask me to understand what you was doin' with Earl?"

"And you know why, Lucas, don't you? You know I had to keep doing it with Earl so I could make enough money to get on my feet. You knew that, right?"

"Well, if you want me to face the truth, you need to face the truth too. The truth is you loved the money he was givin' you more than you loved me. That's the truth, Johnnie. And I proved I loved you by puttin' up with it. Now, you tell me what man would put up with another man stickin' his dick into his woman. But I did it, didn't I? And you call *me* weak? It takes more strength than you think to do that shit. I did it because I love you. Don't that count for nothin'?"

"So, you put up with another man doin' it to me because you love me? Is that the truth, Lucas?"

Lucas lowered his head. "Yep."

"How did it make you feel, knowin' I was doin' this for money?"

"I don't know . . . weak . . . hurt . . . powerless, I guess."

"That's exactly how I felt when I had to do it, not for money, but to keep my man alive—the only man who ever meant anything to me. When I did it for money, I had to at least get something out of it. Wouldn't it have been worse to have done it all for nothing? No house, no clothes, no money, nothing? Look around you, baby. Look where I live." She paused. "I'm not proud of how I got all of this, but I'm glad I got something for what they did to me."

"Who?"

"My mother and Earl Shamus. They did it to me, and I turned lemons into lemonade. I've got money and the knowledge of how to get more. I'm through selling myself. I no longer have to. I'll never do that again. I'm yours, baby. You have all of me, don't you know that?"

Lucas didn't respond. He just stared at the floor.

Chapter 29

"Now . . . come on upstairs . . ."

"Look at me, Lucas," Johnnie demanded. "Look at this face of mine. Have you ever seen anything as beautiful? Look at the color of my skin. Have you ever seen anything quite like it?" She unbuttoned her blouse, took it off, and tossed it on the floor. Then she reached around back and unhooked her bra and slid each arm out of it and showed him her large breasts. Lifting one in each hand, she said, "Have you seen anything like these? Are Marla's breasts anything like these? Are her nipples as sweet as mine are? Can they fill your entire mouth and give you the same pleasure?"

Lucas' mind was being filled with all kinds of erotic desires as he listened to Johnnie talk about her beauty in a way that he had never heard. His erection was alive again, and he wanted to enter her recklessly and thrust himself inside her at that moment. It didn't matter who she had let enter her private place before or after their first sexual experience together. All he could see was her pretty face and her thick, exquisite breasts and the large nipples that stared at him like they were in a hypnotic trance.

Johnnie saw the lust in his eyes and continued the show. Reaching around back again, she unsnapped and unzipped her skirt, letting it fall to the kitchen floor, right next to her blouse and bra. All she had on were black panties and pumps. Lucas shook his head like he was at a feast full of delicious food and he was the only guest. His mouth watered and he swallowed hard. It took every bit of strength he had not to throw Johnnie on the floor, enter her, and pump her hard until he released his scions.

"Look at these legs, Lucas." Johnnie continued the tantalizing entertainment. "Have you ever seen anything like these? Long, beautiful, and the color of brown sugar." Then she slowly pulled her panties down, bending her knees until she was nearly in a stoop position. She rose slowly, watching his wanton eyes roam all over her incredible body like a Moor looking over the southern peninsula of Europe as the word *conquer* filled his mind. "Look at my stuff. Have you ever seen anything like it? And it's all yours. All you see before you is yours, baby."

After hearing that, Lucas stood up and fast-walked over to a naked Johnnie, who was still in high heels. She put her hand out like a traffic cop and stopped his forward momentum. She let him stare for a moment, let him get even harder, before saying, "You gon' get it tonight, but not before you get her scent off you. I'm not gon' let you stick it in me with her still on you. And don't bother denying it. Marla already told me you did it to her. Now . . . come on upstairs," she said, taking his hand and leading the way, "so I can bathe you and get all of her off you so we can start all over."

Chapter 30

"Remember that day I spent the night?"

JOHNNIE UNBUTTONED LUCAS' shirt slowly, one button at a time, while the tub filled with soapy water. Then she rubbed her hands across his thick, muscular chest as she pushed the shirt over his wide shoulders. She wanted to start at his chest and kiss all the way down to his rippling abdomen. She wanted to lap and suck his dark nipples, which she knew would drive him crazy, but she smelled Marla's perfume on his skin. There was no way she was going to put her lips on him while she could still smell Napoleon's wife on her man.

Lucas stretched his neck downward to kiss her. She let him. She had intended the kiss to be a quick brush of the lips, but it felt good when their mouths touched, better than she wanted it to feel, and as they kissed deeper, she unbuckled his belt, unsnapped and unzipped his pants, and let them fall to the floor. She massaged him through his underwear, and he kissed her harder and deeper. She felt a familiar twitching in her private place that made her wet, and backed off. He grabbed her arms with his powerful hands, pulled her back to him, and forced her to kiss him again. She felt herself getting weak, and she was about to give in when she smelled Marla's perfume again and pushed him away.

"Come on." Lucas offered an incredibly desperate plea and swallowed hard. His rod stood out like a javelin and was stiffer than a brick. He needed to enter her and receive the indescribable pleasure she gave him.

"No, Lucas," Johnnie said softly. "Not while I can still smell her on you."

Lucas kicked off his pants, snatched down his underwear, and got into the tub, which was still filling with water. He sat down, and the lower half of his body was completely submerged, but his thick tool was long, and half of it was not in the water, pointing toward the North Pole.

"You gon' get in here wit' me?"

"I told you I don't want her on me. When you get her off you, she'll still be in the water. I'll let her touch my hands as I wash you, but that's about it."

Johnnie turned the cold and hot water knobs until the water stopped splashing into the tub. Then she went over to the linen closet, which was only a few feet away, and grabbed face and body towels that were pink with navy roses in the center. On the way back to the tub, she stopped at the sink and grabbed a bar of soap. "How does the water feel, baby?"

"Good. You gon' wash me?"

"Mm-hmm. And I want you to tell me about you and Marla. How did it all start?"

Lucas thought for a moment, remembering every detail of that first encounter that blew his mind. "You not gon' get mad?"

"No."

"You promise?"

"I promise."

"Swear you won't get mad."

Johnnie stared at him for a few seconds and thought about all the lies she told him. She felt guilty because she knew Lucas was about to tell all. She cast aside her guilt and said, "I swear, baby. I won't get mad at you no matter what, okay? Now, tell me everything."

Lucas diverted his eyes to the water and lowered his head, like he was embarrassed to tell the woman he loved about the sex he'd had with another woman. Even though she'd asked for the play by play, still, to look her in the face and tell her how he and Marla began the affair was unthinkable. While he could tell her what he had done, he knew he would have to find something else in the room to focus his eyes on as he told her his difficult truth.

"Remember that day I spent the night? The first time we did it? The night Dennis Edwards and his wife got into it and we watched from your bedroom window?"

"Mm-hmm," Johnnie said as she lathered the face towel with soap. "Lean forward, baby. I'ma do ya back first."

Lucas leaned forward, feeling a little more at ease with telling her, yet still apprehensive. "Remember when you dropped me off at Napoleon's?"

"Yeah," Johnnie said as she scrubbed his back. "I love your back, Lucas. It's so thick and muscular."

Lucas smiled. The sound of her voice, the sweetness that poured out of her, the words that seemed to come from deep within made him feel like he was the most important thing in her life. He relaxed a little more. "Well, Napoleon took me to his house, and that's where I met Marla. She's pretty." He stopped for a second and looked at her to get her reaction.

"Yeah, she's pretty, Lucas," Johnnie agreed and put him at ease.

"Well, you know we had been out the previous night and I didn't have no clean clothes. Napoleon told me to take a shower and put on some of his. He told us he had some errands to run and that he would be back in a couple of hours. Marla asked me if I wanted to take a swim after I showered. I said, 'yeah.' Then when I came out to the pool, she had on this bathin' suit that looked real nice on her." He looked at Johnnie. She was calm—no sign of anger.

"Go on," she said, and twisted the towel tightly, which rained down water on his back, removing the soap. "I'm not mad, Lucas, if that's what you're worried about."

"Okay. To make a long story short, we was playin' around in the pool when Napoleon walked in."

"What did he say when he saw y'all?"

"He got mad at Marla."

"He did, huh?"

"Yeah. He started screaming at her about having me ready by the time he got back."

"He didn't say anything about you two being in the pool messin' around?"

"We wasn't messin' around."

"Yes, you were. But go ahead."

Lucas sucked his teeth. "So anyway, when Napoleon got finished tellin' her off, he told her to get my clothes and that he would be in the car waiting, listening to the Yankees. We went to the bedroom to get the clothes, and the next thing I know, she had me on the bed. I tried to stop her. I did."

"Lucas?"

"Huh?"

"As big as you are, you mean to tell me you couldn't stop her?"

"I tried to stop her but she pulled my swimmin' trunks down and started . . . you know."

"She sucked it?"

He hesitated. "Yep."

"And you liked it?"

A thick fog of silence filled the room.

"And you liked it?" Johnnie repeated. "Tell me the truth."

He couldn't bring himself to answer, so he simply nodded his head.

"And that's why you can't let her go?"

He nodded again.

"Hmm, okay, is that all she does different from me?"

"Yep. You mad?"

"No. Let me ask you something."

"Okay."

"If I did that for you, do you think you could leave her alone then?"

"Johnnie, good girls don't do that. You a good girl."

"So, you don't want me to do it?"

Thick silence again.

"Lucas . . . look at me." He looked at her. "Do you want me to do that to you? Yes or no?" He turned away from her and nodded again. "Okay, I'll do it."

Lucas whipped his head around. He had to see her face. Was she really willing to do that? "For real?"

"Yeah."

Then he frowned and said, "Hey, have you ever done that before?"

"No," she lied without hesitation. "But I'ma learn how so we can stay together, okay?" She thought for a moment. "Did you do the same thing to her?"

"Nope."

"She didn't ask you to?"

"Nope."

"Okay," Johnnie said and finished bathing him.

Chapter 31

"I can still do it, though."

LUCAS WAS NAKED, out of the tub, and Johnnie was standing behind him, drying his back. She had lied again, and now she had to pretend like she didn't know how to pleasure a man with her mouth. With Earl Shamus, her former lover and benefactor, she discovered she had a real gift.

Every time Earl did something especially nice, he wanted her to give him oral pleasure, and at some point, she began to enjoy the act, becoming a skilled practitioner, which was something she had to hide from Lucas, at least for a while. At least until she could make it look like he was the first man she'd ever done this to. After all, Lucas thought so much of her—still—after all he knew about her, still believing and calling her a "good girl." When enough time had passed, she was going to really show him just what she could do with her mouth.

Johnnie continued drying his shoulders, his legs, his chest, and his feet. Then she looked up at him—his javelin stiff. He was looking down at her. She said, "You want me to do it?"

"Uh-huh."

When she finished drying his toes, she looked at his tool, which was throbbing at regular intervals, needing immediate attention. She took him into her mouth and Lucas moaned loudly. "Ooooh, yes. Just like that." She looked at him. His eyes were closed, but the look on his face let her know that she was doing something he really enjoyed. She focused on his tool, taking her time, pretending she didn't know what she was doing.

It didn't seem to matter how she did it because Lucas was nearly insane with pleasure. His moans filled the bathroom as he could not control them. "Ooooh, shit." His face twisted, bent, and contorted. With each stroke she applied, his moaning grew louder and louder, like he was in a state of absolute bliss, like the pleasure she gave him was incredible, like he wanted her to go on and on and on, pleasuring him without end. And pleasure him she did, careful not to get too involved, keeping the deception real and believable.

Then she felt his seed rushing forward. She stopped and grabbed the base and applied pressure, which stopped his scions from splashing all over the floor. She picked up the towel she'd dried him with and wrapped it around his thick tool, and then let his seed spill into the towel. Lucas' knees got weak when his seed left his body as if they were miniature rockets, blasting off into space. His lips quivered like he was suddenly in a cold environment. He was still hard.

"Did I do it right?" she asked innocently.

With his eyes still closed, still obviously enjoying the moment, he said, "Mm-hmm."

She stood up and kissed him on the lips, still holding his tool in the towel, slightly pulling and releasing him, getting all of his seed in the towel. "You ready for some more, baby?"

"Mm-hmm," he said and followed her into the bedroom like he was her puppy.

"Get in the bed. I gotta get a condom."

Lucas crawled under the covers and waited for her to put the condom on him. He watched her, unable to believe that his Johnnie, his beautiful Johnnie, his good girl had given him oral pleasure. He loved her even more than before because she loved him enough to do something that he thought good girls didn't do. Now he knew he was definitely through with Marla. What could she do for him that Johnnie couldn't do? And besides, who was going to kill him for having sex with his own girlfriend?

Johnnie crawled into bed and lay on top of Lucas. "I love you." Then she kissed his neck and nibbled his ears. Lucas moaned. "You like that?"

"Yeah."

She took a nipple in her mouth and sucked and licked while she massaged his balls. She kissed his lips and a strange thing happened. Napoleon Bentley invaded her mind. Surprised, she opened her eyes and the image disappeared. She was uncomfortable all of a sudden. Why was Napoleon invading her mind? How dare he interrupt her intimacy with Lucas? Who did he think he was, trespassing, breaking and entering, as it were, into the one place she didn't have to share with anyone? Only God had a right to enter her mind at will.

"What's wrong?" Lucas asked when he felt her body tense all of a sudden.

"Nothing."

"Why did you stop?"

Johnnie felt guilty and lied yet again when she said, "I just thought about my mother."

"Oh, I'm sorry," he said. "Are you okay?"

"I can still do it, though."

"You can?"

"Yeah."

Johnnie, still on top of him but crouching, positioned his tool to her opening and slid down until she had all of him, which was considerable. She wasn't ready for this part yet because whenever she closed her eyes, Napoleon would magically appear, making it impossible to enjoy Lucas. But she was determined to give him what he needed to prevent him from running to Marla. She thought that if she kept her eyes open, which took away from her pleasure, she could rid herself of Napoleon's image, and it worked.

She rode Lucas like he was a stallion, sliding, twisting, grinding, and pumping him for over an hour. Every time she felt him about to release, she used her well-developed muscles and grabbed the base, squeezing him tightly until he regained control. Then she rode him some more as their loud, erotic sighs bounced off the walls, the ceiling, and the floor and made their way out of the open window and into the quiet neighborhood. The headboard bumped, the bedsprings creaked, adding to their guttural yearning, and it went on and on and on.

Chapter 32

"Just a few months, okay?"

A QUIET STILLNESS filled Johnnie's bedroom as their erratic breathing slowed and their minds became tranquil. Lucas pulled Johnnie close and wrapped his massive arm around her as her head lay on his chest. He was happier than he'd ever been in his short life. Not even the cheers students, parents, and faculty members offered after he scored a touchdown for his former high school football team bridged the chasm in his heart after his father died and left him with nothing but an extraordinary body, speed, balance, and enviable power. He was happy because he knew his beautiful girlfriend really loved him, and would do anything for him. She had just proven this—in his mind anyway.

Lucas was ready to straighten out his life. But first, he needed more money. Johnnie had gotten plenty of money on her own without help from him, and he felt the need to get his own money without her help. However, he would defer to her advice on stocks because she had quickly acquired a small fortune. The extra fifty a week that Napoleon was going to pay him would help too.

"Johnnie," he whispered.

"Huh?"

"I'ma tell you somethin', but it's just between you and me, okay?"

"Okay."

"I met a guy today. He offered me a sweet, sweet deal. Lots of money on the table and I know I can make it work if I hustle."

In a quiet, physically drained voice, she asked, "What kinda deal?"

"Sellin' weed to the musicians at the Bayou and at the other juke joints in the quarter. I can invest like you did and make some real money too."

Johnnie raised her head off his chest and looked him in the face. "Are you crazy?"

"What?"

"Bubbles just told you not to get involved with drugs. Why would you risk everything to make a few extra dollars?"

Lucas looked at her and frowned. "I can't believe you don't understand. How much money do you have, Johnnie?"

"What difference does it make? I have enough for both of us. Whatever you need, I'll get it for you. You don't need to be riskin' yo' life to make that kinda money."

"That kinda money? How you gon' say that to me when you done got rich makin' that kinda money? You wanted me to let you do what you had to do to get rich. Now that it's my turn to get a little money of my own, you don't want me to do it? I don't 'preciate that shit, either. A black man gotta make his money any way he can. I wanna get married and move outta New Orleans. Maybe move to San Francisco so you can be near ya brotha."

Johnnie beamed. "You wanna marry me?"

"Yeah, girl. I love you. I really do."

She kissed him. "I love you more than you'll ever know."

"If you love me, try and understand. I gotta make this money. It's easy money. I know I can make it work. Then we can move to San Francisco together as husband and wife."

"We can do that now, Lucas. I got the money. Just let me stay here for a few more months so I can get to know my grandfather. Just a few months, okay?"

"In a few months, I can have some serious cash. I want you to help me invest it in the stock market like you did with your money."

"Lucas, please . . . don't go against Bubbles and Napoleon. Please don't."

"Johnnie," he said firmly, "I'ma do this. I'ma make some real money and get the hell outta here. I want you with me on this. I can do it with you or without you, but I'ma do this. I've done everything you ask me to do. Its time for you to ante up now."

"But Lucas—"

"Yes or no, Johnnie."

Silence.

"Yes or no!"

In the precious few seconds Lucas had given her to think about what he had already made up his mind to do, Johnnie decided to go along to get along. In her mind, she owed him. He'd been there for her, now it was time for her to be there for him. And she would be there, all the way. Besides, if it worked, they would have more money to invest. When the idea of money filled her mind, she found it easy to agree.

"Yes. But we gotta be real careful, baby. You got a plan?"

Grateful she was behind his big venture, he kissed her tenderly. "Yeah, I got a plan. I done thought this shit out already."

"Let's hear it."

"Well, I told you about the musicians at the Bayou and in the Quarter, right?"

"Right, but, Lucas, that's a bad move. Don't do anything in Napoleon's backyard. You'll be caught inside of a week because them people pay protection money to Napoleon. They owe him, and they'll turn you in just to scurry favor with him. In fact, you can count on people in the Quarter being his spies, watchin' your every move, reporting everything to him."

Lucas thought for a brief moment. "You know what . . . you right. See, that's why I need you to be with me on this. I cain't think of everything."

Almost immediately, Johnnie's mind was bombarded with ways to help him sell marijuana, but she knew he needed to come up with the idea, so she decided to guide him to the most obvious market with very little risk. "You should stick with people you already know, people you know that smoke weed already. Do you know any people like that?"

Lucas thought for a few moments before saying, "I could get some of the guys I played ball with to sell some on the college campuses. Yeah, yeah, that's going to make me a nice little fortune. During football, basketball, baseball, and track, the sky's the limit. Ball players love to get high when they win and when they lose. That's a goddamned gold mine. I'm glad I thought of it."

Johnnie smiled, having given him the idea that could prove to not only line his pockets and keep him out of jail, but keep him busy driving and away from Marla Bentley too. She was proud of herself. "Now, that's a plan, baby. And I agree with you on that part about not being able to think of everything. So . . . maybe you should run your ideas through me first, and together we can come up with a good plan of action."

Lucas grinned from ear to ear. He had finally impressed her. This had been a great night for him. He'd met Preston Leonard Truman and made a deal, formulated a plan of action on his own, and reconciled with the woman he loved. Getting back together with her was the highlight of the day.

"You really think that's a good idea, Johnnie?"

"Yep. If you gon' do something like that, you always gotta have a plan. It's gotta be worth the risk if you get caught. So, when do you start?"

"This weekend. Oh, and I gotta show you the cars I'ma buy with my money."

"Cars? Why do you need more than one? Napoleon just gave you one. Don't spend your money, baby. Invest like you said."

"I was going to get this 1954 Corvette convertible I pictured driving you around in one day, but now that I have a new car, I guess I don't have to get it. But I gotta get at least one, though. It's a 1941 Chevy Special, two-door. Sweeter than sweet. I'ma have

Preston do some work on it and make it the fastest thing on the road, just in case I gotta move in a hurry. Might have to outrun the cops one of these days."

"Take me with you when you get it, so I can get you a good deal, okay?"

"You don't think I can get one on my own?"

"Not as good as I can. Men give me breaks they won't give you because they wanna fuck me. And as long as they want that, they'll do anything if they *think* they have a chance. The car is what, thirteen years old? You oughta be able to get it for a couple hundred. What did the dealer want for it?"

"Nine hundred ninety-nine dollars."

"A thousand dollars?" Johnnie nearly shouted. "And what were you going to offer him?"

"Just a couple hundred."

Johnnie laughed hard and from her belly. "You was huh? What was you really gon' offer? Seven hundred?"

Lucas laughed. "Six hundred, but I woulda paid seven hundred."

"When were you going to get the car?"

"This weekend. I've saved up some dough over the few months I've worked for Napoleon. I really want to get started on this thing. The sooner I get started, the sooner we can leave New Orleans and head out to the coast."

"Pick me up and we'll go together. Besides, you need someone to drive the other car. I'll make sure he doesn't rob you."

Chapter 33

"You can thank me later."

JOHNNIE KISSED Lucas good-bye and got out of his new car, the one Napoleon had given him the previous night. The two lovers stayed up all night, making love, talking, formulating a plan to make what Lucas called "real" money. She had to look out for him, she told herself. Who else would do it?

She looked into the open window of the car and said, "You're not going to go to your apartment, right?"

"Right."

"Okay," she said with a bright smile.

She turned and walked around to the back of the Beauregard mansion. Later, when she got off work, he would pick her up and they would head over to his apartment to get some of his clothes. He was going to stay with Johnnie for a few days because she didn't trust him to stay away from his seducer, Marla Bentley. While Lucas put up somewhat of an argument over this, he knew Johnnie was right, and agreed not to go home by himself, fearing Marla would be brazen enough to be there waiting for him.

It felt good to make love to Lucas again after all the madness in Baroque and Sable Parishes after the riot. She had won the affection of her man, reaffirmed their relationship, and now the only thing left for her in New Orleans was to learn about the white blood that coursed through her veins.

Morgan Thomas opened the back door for Johnnie and she walked in at 7:00 sharp, dressed in her gray-and-white maid's uniform, which fit her loosely, hiding her treasured assets from the eyes of covetous men who couldn't seem to take them off her.

"How ya doin' this morning, Johnnie?" Morgan asked.

"How you doin', Mr. Thomas?"

"Why are you here an hour early?"

"Couldn't sleep. I decided I might as well come to work and get started."

"Before you get too comfortable, Johnnie, do you mind getting Katherine up for me?"

"Yes, I do mind, Mr. Thomas. She tried to get me fired yesterday."

"Yeah, I heard about that," he said. "But Grandpa Nathaniel has taken a likin' to you too, I hear."

"Yeah, he has, it seems." She paused for a second, and then continued. "They didn't even think to feed the man yesterday. If it wasn't for me, the man would starve to death. Why do they treat him so badly?"

"I don't know. You'd think they'd be extra nice to him, seeing that he could die anytime now, the doctors say. His heart is on borrowed time. He could live a few more days or six months. The doctors don't know."

"What? For real? I gotta get to know him before he goes then," Johnnie said without thinking.

"Why do you care? You just met the man yesterday, didn't you?"

Johnnie realized she was on dangerous ground and said, "Caring about others is the Christian thing to do, Mr. Thomas. You disagree?"

"I guess not," he said. "You're a sweet girl. Okay, now, I've gotta run to the bathroom. Help me out and get Katherine up and at 'em. You can thank me later."

Then he walked out the door, leaving Johnnie standing there, watching his hind parts as he disappeared around a corner. Reluctantly, Johnnie opened the screen door, which led to the back porch, walked outside, and down the stairs.

Thank him later? For what? Waking up the Wicked Witch of the South? Why would I thank him for that when she tried to get me fired yesterday? I'll wake her up, though, because Mr. Thomas is a really nice man. But that Katherine is going to be hard to deal with. I guess I can deal with her for a few more months. Who knows? She could have been in a bad mood yesterday. She could've been on her cycle too. Katherine might be a nice lady.

Yeah, I've judged her too harshly. One day is definitely not enough time to be judging someone. I know I wouldn't like it if I started off on a bad note with someone. And if I was in the wrong, I'd want a chance to make it up to the person. I'll give her another chance. Everybody deserves a few chances in their life.

Chapter 34

"The Beauregards will want breakfast soon."

JOHNNIE WALKED across the courtyard, over to the six-car garage, and made her way up the white painted steps that led to Katherine's apartment, which was surrounded by trees with branches that stretched far into the heavens and kept the brutal rays of the sun from filling Katherine's dwelling with torturous unrelenting heat. After reaching the top of the stairs, Johnnie followed the balustrade that enclosed the walkway that led to Katherine's front door, which wasn't completely closed.

As she approached the door, she heard erotic sighs wafting through the cracked entry from within. Johnnie covered her mouth in an attempt to stifle her laughter, which was about to erupt. She pushed the door a little to get a quick peek. *I am so wrong for this, but I gotta see who Katherine is doin' it with. I'm just going to take a peek and then I'll leave.*

The door opened to the living room area of the apartment. Johnnie looked to the left and looked to the right. No one was in sight. She tiptoed into the residence, careful not to make a sound and alert the lovers to her furtive presence. The sound of them seemed to be coming from down the hallway right in front of her. She was about to stop and turn around and go back out the door, but it was like someone hidden was calling her name, watching her look around for them, knowing she would never guess where they were.

Her heart began to pound in her chest and she found it exhilarating. Step after step, she made her way down the hallway to the open door. The erotic sighs were loud now, the bedsprings screaming as if a ruthless maniac was torturing them. Johnnie had to know. She had to see. Who was it? She peeked in and saw two white butt cheeks raising and descending with speed and power.

It's Beau! And he's doin' it to Katherine? He was just doin' it to Piper yesterday in the library. Katherine got a lotta nerve talking about Sadie when she's doin' it with Beau again after all these years. I'ma get her off my back right now. Tryin' to get me fired my first day of work. I bet Piper don't know Beau is gettin' his brown sugar this morning. I'ma go in there and let her know I know what she's doing.

Johnnie walked in, laughing under her breath as she made her way over to the bed and peered over the man's back. Katherine's eyes were closed tight as she was on the verge of orgasm. Johnnie stood there, watching them pump each other like it would be their last time. And then, when Katherine's orgasm began, when she was at the peak of it, when she was howling loud and fiercely, Johnnie said, “Hi, Katherine. Mr. Thomas told me to come and wake you up. The Beauregards will want breakfast soon.”

Katherine’s eyes nearly bulged out of her head when she saw Johnnie staring at her. Frightened out of his wits, the man rolled off Katherine to see who had walked in on them. His eyes locked with Johnnie’s. They were both surprised to see each other. Johnnie’s mouth fell open when she realized it wasn’t Beau.

Chapter 35

Young and dumb as hell."

MARLA BENTLEY WAS NAKED and lying on his bed when Lucas entered his bedroom. At that pivotal moment, he knew he should have listened to Johnnie, who had told him not to go to his apartment until she got off work that afternoon. She was afraid that if he ran into Marla, he would get weak and give into his unabated lust. And now, here he was, right where he knew he shouldn't be, staring at delectable Marla Bentley, who knew his thoughts at that moment. She smiled and spread her legs wide so he could see all the way to New York City.

Lucas didn't just look; he stared, he gawked, he gazed hypnotically at her temple of love and felt himself weaken. He felt like a powerless slave, mastered by his innate desire to pillage her unprotected village and take prisoner all that lay before him, and do with it as he willed. It was there for the taking and he wanted it.

He wanted it because he shouldn't have it; especially after telling Johnnie and promising himself that he would never enter her body again. He swallowed hard.

"Come get it." Marla whispered a sensual command.

"Uh, I . . . I shouldn't. I . . . I . . . I mean I can't," he stammered in a subdued, weak manner. "I . . . I . . . I won't. I won't do it."

Marla laughed so hard that her jaws ached. The laughter went on for about thirty uninterrupted seconds.

As Lucas stood there, watching her double over, clenching her stomach, as he listened to the sound of her unquenchable giggling, anger began to rise. The longer she laughed, the angrier he became. All of a sudden, he found the resolve to keep his word to himself and his beautiful Johnnie.

With staunch resolve, he said, "I said no! And I mean no! Now, get dressed and get the hell outta my apartment and don't come back!"

Marla stopped laughing abruptly and said, "You're serious?"

"You goddamn right!" Lucas blared, having finally found the inner strength he needed.

"Hmm."

"Hmm, what?" Lucas asked.

"So, you spent the night with Johnnie, huh?"

"I sure did, and we did it all night long, too."

"Oh, that's it." Marla laughed. "If that's true, you can't get it up. It's not that you don't want to, you can't. And that's all there is to it. I'll wait a while. A young man like you should be able to go another round in a half an hour, I'm sure."

"Don't you get it, Marla?" He sighed. "Mrs. Bentley, I'm through. I love Johnnie and I'm not going to do this to her . . . I'm not going to do it to Napoleon. I'm not going to do it to myself. You got that? I'm finished with you! Now, please go, and don't come back."

"Napoleon? You're worried about Napoleon?"

"Not worried, but—"

"You mean to tell me you feel some twisted sense of loyalty to a man who sent you on an errand just so he could fuck your girlfriend? You're beholden to him?"

"Look, the man found out about us. He knew about it and threatened to kill me over it. He told Johnnie she had to do it to keep me alive. And the truth is it was only about a thirty-second thing. He put it in and came. That was it."

Marla laughed hard again. "Who told you that, Johnnie?"

"Yeah. We talked about it last night."

"And you believed her?"

"Yeah. And I told her the truth about us and how it all began with you suckin' me."

"I guess it's true then," Marla said, shaking her head and no longer laughing.

"What's true?"

"Young and dumb. Young and dumb as hell."

"Hey, I'm not dumb, okay?"

"If you believe that it was just a thirty-second thing between Napoleon and Johnnie, you're a fool. And not an ordinary fool, a colossal fool."

Chapter 36

"Do you want me to do it?"

ALREADY ANGRY because Marla Bentley laughed in his face, Lucas' anger had risen to a whole new level because now she had called him a fool to his face. To make matters worse, she was using words that were beyond his comprehension. He stared at her for a long minute before shouting, "I don't know what *colossal* means, but I'm nobody's fool, okay?" Then he paused and gathered himself. "But, uh, why would Johnnie lie to me about this when we agreed to be honest? I mean, I told her the truth. I told her everything. Why wouldn't she?"

"Because she's a woman, Lucas. Damn! I can't believe you would believe her lies."

"And I'm supposed to believe you? Over her? You outta yo' mind."

Marla rolled her eyes and shook her head. "Lucas, let me ask you something. And this is just a hypothetical, okay?"

"A what?"

Marla sighed deeply before saying, "Let's assume that what I'm about to say is the truth for argument's sake, okay?"

"Okay."

"What if it was more than thirty seconds, Lucas? How would you feel then?"

Lucas thought for a second or two. "Depends on how long it went on, I guess."

"How long would be too long?"

"One second is too long. Sticking it in at all is too goddamn long, to be honest about the shit. Why?"

Marla shook her head again. "What if I told you that I taught Napoleon everything he knows about making love to a woman? What if I told you that Napoleon could go over an hour without climaxing? How would you feel then, hypothetically speaking, of course?"

"An hour?" Lucas asked, and started pacing the room as he thought. *Did Johnnie lie to me about this? Why?*

"Don't torture yourself trying to figure out why she lied, baby," Marla said, cutting into his thoughts. "Do you wanna know why she lied, hypothetically speaking?"

Lucas turned around and faced her. *An hour? In my Johnnie? Pumping her over and over again? A whole hour? I don't know if I even wanna know why she lied.*

"Well, do you want to know? Are you man enough to hear the truth? No more hypotheticals. I'm talking about the truth now. Do you want to hear it or do you want to be willfully ignorant? It's bliss, they say."

"What's the truth?" Lucas said defiantly, like he had to defend his manhood.

Marla stood up, still naked and desirable, and looked directly into his eyes. "The truth is Napoleon doesn't have a reputation with women for nothing. The truth is he probably gave her the fuck of her young life. The kind of fuck that she will never, ever forget. I'm telling you Napoleon probably fucked Johnnie into a coma. Now, deal with that."

"Probably? You don't know," Lucas said desperately when the words of betrayal injured his believing heart. "Or were you there, watching?"

"I don't have to be there, Lucas. I know my husband, and I taught him everything he knows, from how to eat a woman right to lasting as long as he needs to last. The same things I'm willing to teach you. But one question remains, right? Do you know what the question is?"

"Why did she lie?"

"Exactly!"

"I don't know," Lucas lied and bowed his head.

"Sure you do. You know. She lied because if she told you the truth, you would never forgive her, and even if you did, you would never see her as you once saw her. Your mind would wonder if she enjoyed it, as it does now. I can see it in your eyes. Am I right?" She paused for an answer, but he didn't offer one. He turned around and began pacing again. "I can tell you, as a woman, a female of the species . . . she fucking loved it! Loved it, Lucas. That's why she couldn't tell you, and that's why she'll *never* tell you."

Lucas' head spun. What he'd just heard was the truth and he knew it. It was a truth that he'd known all along, but he wanted to believe his beautiful Johnnie. The sweet girl he had fought for and would do anything for had not only willingly given her body to another man, but also loved it beyond measure.

His mind went back to the night that she came home, when she lied about being with Earl Shamus that night. He began to wonder about it all now. He doubled over like he had been hit in the stomach with a sledgehammer. Tears formed in his deep, dark eyes, but he refused to let even one slide down his face.

Marla watched him for a moment, and when he stood tall again, went over to comfort him. She hugged him and whispered, "It's all right. I know it hurts." She pulled him tight and he responded. "You want me to take care of you now? You want me to take you to paradise? You want me to do it like you've never had it before, baby?"

A thick quiet consumed the moment of decision as Lucas thought, envisioning Napoleon inside his Johnnie, pumping her for over an hour. During the silence, he could hear Johnnie moaning, see her orgasmic blushes, and literally feel her body tremble as she climaxed powerfully. He felt his tears welling in the silent room as he contemplated Marla's tempting offer.

"Do you want me to do it?" Marla offered again, awakening him from the nightmare that plagued his consciousness.

Lucas was hard, and he wanted nothing more than to allow her to do exactly what she knew she was more than capable of doing. But the truth had sobered his erotically intoxicated mind. Evenly, calmly, he said, "No. I'm still through with you. I'm leaving. I have business to take care of. When I return, I want you gone. And Mrs. Bentley . . . don't come back." He took a few quick steps toward the door and stopped. He looked back at her and said, "And leave the key on the nightstand."

Chapter 37

I done learned my damn lesson.

DAILY COLLECTIONS were finished and Lucas went back to Johnnie's house in Ashland Estates to make a couple of long distance phone calls, one to Wendell Smalls, a junior, and the starting quarterback for the Grambling State Tigers. Smalls befriended Lucas when he was a senior and Lucas was a freshman at Sable Parish's Abraham Lincoln High School. Befriending Lucas turned out to be a great idea since the young running back was six-four, weighed two hundred pounds, and would often have to protect Smalls' blind side on passing plays.

The other phone call was to Herbert Shields, wide receiver for the Jackson State University Tigers. Shields left Abraham Lincoln the same year as Wendell Smalls. Both young men were intelligent and physically gifted—an incredible combination. Smalls and Shields held the quarterback/receiver record for touchdowns, having made it into the end zone an unparalleled ninety-two times. They both wanted to go to Grambling, but it didn't work out that way. Smalls and Shields worked with Lucas to keep him eligible for sports, but dyslexia made it impossible for him to get the kind of grades they were getting, let alone make the honor roll. Smalls and Shields were permanent members of that distinguished academic club.

When Lucas told Shields that Wendell Smalls agreed to sell marijuana at Grambling, he came on board with no resistance, believing it was a quick way to earn some spending money for dates. Plus, in their minds, it was a harmless crime. They agreed to meet the coming weekend when Lucas and Johnnie picked up his shiny new 1941 Chevy Special convertible.

But Lucas was still bothered by Johnnie's betrayal and her consistent lies about the affair with Napoleon Bentley. He wanted to slap the taste out of her mouth and would have if the vivid memory of him and Marla hadn't consumed his mind all morning. No matter how hard he tried, he couldn't justify having sex with Marla long before Johnnie had given herself to Napoleon. The truth was he had enjoyed Marla's forbidden fruit a number of times. In fact, he enjoyed it so much that he was powerless to stop himself.

At least she only did it once. Me, I kept fuckin' Marla every chance I got. I would've fucked her this morning, too, if she hadn't laughed at me. On the other hand, Johnnie loved me enough to lie to me, didn't she? She enjoyed it, but she didn't want to do it in the first place. If I hadn't been fuckin' Marla, this shit would have never happened. I done fucked myself up! Shit! Now that I know the truth, what am I going to do? Act like I don't know? Pretend?

How in the hell am I going to do that when that shit keeps playing like a fuckin' movie in my head? I know. I'ma do what Bubbles did when he warned me. He knew about me and Marla, but he never let on that he knew, did he? He talked around the shit. And that's what I'll do too. That way, we can try and move past this shit. I done learned my damn lesson. Quit fuckin' other women, maybe my woman won't fuck another man.

I guess what's really fucked up is Johnnie told me I could fuck Marla one more time to make up for what she did behind my back, didn't she? Yep, she did. All right then. The shit happened and there's nothing we can do to change it. Napoleon gave me a new car. I'll keep it as payment for fuckin' my woman, and I'ma get past this shit if I can. I still love Johnnie, and now I know she definitely loves me. I don't think I knew that shit until right now.

Finally, after reasoning it out and making the decision to stay with Johnnie, the tears that he'd held back for hours slid down his cheeks.

Chapter 38

"Excuse me?"

ERIC BEAUREGARD stared back at Johnnie, equally shocked, equally floored by the entrance of the uninvited guest who discovered him and his playmate in an incredibly compromising position. In the few seconds that passed, Eric began wondering why he didn't listen to his inner voice, which had told him not to go to Katherine's room that morning.

But he had to go, he'd told himself. He'd been in Shreveport for over two weeks, then Marshall Law had been declared due to the recent riot. He'd initially gone to Shreveport to get his father's affairs in order when he learned that Nathaniel didn't have long to live because of his heart condition.

"Now . . . now, just a minute," Eric Beauregard stammered. "Just a cotton pickin' minute, okay?"

Johnnie doubled over, no longer able to restrain her laughter. Tears ran down her cheeks. She shook her head and looked at Katherine. “Uhm, you want me to start breakfast?” Then she laughed again.

“Get out of here, Johnnie!” Katherine shouted. “I’ll deal with you later.”

Johnnie stopped laughing suddenly and was dead serious. “Excuse me? You’ll deal with me later? I got a news flash for you, Katherine. You’re going to tell Mrs. Beauregard that you weren’t feeling good yesterday and the last thing you want to see is Johnnie Wise fired because you had a bad day. And if you wanna keep your secret from getting out, you’re going to treat me with respect.

“As for you, Mr. Beauregard, shame on you. But since ya got caught fuckin’ the hired help who happens to be your wife’s best friend, you’re going to treat me like I’m a blood relative from this day forward. That means that if your father wants me to feed him at the family table, you’re going to be all for it. In fact, you’re going to lead the charge.” She paused and stared at them, still shaking her head. “Is it a deal, or do I tell Mrs. Beauregard what’s going on between you two?”

“I’m a white man, and I don’t havta make deals with niggers.” Katherine looked at him and frowned. “I don’t mean you, sweetie. You’re okay.”

“Okay, fine. I’ll just run over to the house and tell Mrs. Beauregard where you are.”

“Now, hold on,” Eric said. “Ain’t no need in gettin’ her all riled up. If you wanna feed my daddy, that’s fine with me, but don’t go shootin’ ya mouth off about me and Katherine. And the last thing I’ll ever do is treat you like family.”

"Okay," Johnnie said, thinking, *You're my Uncle Eric, my mother's brother, so I am family whether you like it or not.*

"Fine! Now get outta here so we can finish."

Without a word, Johnnie turned around and walked out of the room. As she made her way down the hallway, she heard the bedsprings howl again, along with Katherine's unfettered sighs.

Johnnie smiled as she walked down the stairs, realizing that Morgan Thomas knew all about their relationship and wanted her to know too. He was right.

I will thank him later! Now I don't have to worry about Katherine for the next few months—or Eric either, for that matter. She laughed out loud. *Our family sure loves to do it, black or white. We doin' it all the time and try to hide it all. I wonder how far back this thing goes. I wish Grandma was still alive. She might have some answers to all of this, like how she got involved with Nathaniel in the first place. I sure would like to know. What's messed up is the black and the white side of the family seems to be the same, but they live so much better than us. That ain't right!*

Just then, a still, small voice within her said, "Look up." She obeyed the voice and saw Morgan Thomas looking down at her from an upstairs window. He smiled and waved to her. To the left of him, in another window, she saw Ethel Beauregard watching her as she made her way back to the house.

I wonder if she knows all about Eric and Katherine. I bet she does and thinks she's too much of a Southern lady to say anything about it. Damn, our family is messed up!

Chapter 39

Plausible Deniability

ETHEL BEAUREGARD knew all about the ongoing affair that Eric was having with her best friend. They'd had separate bedrooms for years. Although she would never admit it, she actually approved of their nefarious erotic dalliance for several reasons. Ethel never developed a healthy sexual attitude. She never enjoyed the act, and only gave in to it after being relentlessly pressured by her husband. The first time she did it, on her wedding night, was a literal nightmare. The pain of him entering her never went away during the entire act. And her blood covered the sheets, which made her think she would bleed to death one day if she continued that kind of activity.

Every time they had sex, she bled far more than she should have. For whatever reason, her vagina remained tight, and when it was time to deliver her babies, they had to be taken via cesarean section.

Nevertheless, it was such a joy to be pregnant, because pregnancy gave her an excuse not to give into Eric's sexual advances, even though her doctor told her sex while being with child was perfectly all right.

Another reason she didn't mind Eric having sex with Katherine is that she believed it was better than the enormous scandal it would cause if he was having sex with good, Southern Christian white women when word got out. And word always got out when this happened. It was always the talk of the town. As a matter of fact, she took immense pleasure spreading the gossip about the latest so-called vestal virgin who was going to be given away at yet another pompous, ridiculously expensive wedding ceremony of the New Orleans aristocracy.

If Eric needed sexual companionship, fine. Get it from Katherine, who never really had a relationship with any man of her own. Katherine had been trained to serve the Beauregards from the time she could understand the words that came out of her mother's mouth. To Ethel, Katherine was the best alternative to widespread scandal, the kind of scandal she loved to hear about as long as it was about some other pretentious New Orleans family and not hers.

Ethel believed that if she looked the other way, if she pretended she didn't know, it never happened. That way, her secret of not being able to enjoy sex and Eric's lechery would remain a secret. At least that's what she told herself. Besides, white men having sex with black women was a centuries old tradition that respectable white women accepted. It wasn't even considered adultery, and therefore not a real reason to divorce one's husband.

It was no secret that rich white men had swarthy mistresses and whole families in Ashland Estates. The strange thing was, if a white man had another white family by a woman who was not his lawful wife, it would be grounds for divorce. But Negroes, well, they weren't real people. They were subhuman, and that made it okay.

From what she heard through the aristocratic grapevine, black women loved sex, so Eric got what he needed, and so did Katherine. It was a great arrangement for everyone involved, as long as no one ever talked about it.

That's what Eric was afraid of when Johnnie threatened to tell. If she ever told, if what everyone knew were ever voiced, it would destroy the family. Everybody knew and played their parts like actors in an elaborate play, seeing no evil, speaking no evil, hearing no evil, yet committing evil at will. It was comical.

Chapter 40

"Yes, sir, I sure do. I quit."

MORGAN THOMAS walked into the kitchen at about the same time Johnnie opened the back door. He smiled at her and said, "Well?"

Johnnie laughed again. "Thank you, Mr. Thomas."

"You're welcome."

"How long has this been goin' on?"

"Years."

"Years?"

"Yes, and—"

"Morgan!" Ethel's haughty voice called out from the staircase. She could hear them, and knew where the conversation was going.

Still looking at Johnnie, Morgan curled his lips and said, "Yes, Mrs. Beauregard."

"Come here, please."

Morgan, still looking at Johnnie, rolled his eyes, curled his lips, and then left the room. Then he immediately went to the bottom of the staircase. "Yes, ma'am."

From the top of the stairs, she looked down on him like she was a queen on a throne, holding life and limb in her delicate hands. "Don't you have something to do?"

"Yes, ma'am. I'll get right on it," Morgan replied and went on his way.

Ethel floated down the stairs with her head held high, like she was being carried on a cloud. Then she entered the kitchen and watched Johnnie, who had started breakfast.

"Johnnie, how are you this morning?"

"I'm fine, Mrs. Beauregard. How are you?"

"I'm feeling wonderful this morning. By the way, I saw you coming from Katherine's apartment. She's okay, isn't she?"

"Yes. She's feeling real good this morning, Mrs. Beauregard. Whatever was bothering her yesterday isn't bothering her today. It's as if something on her insides has changed her attitude."

"Hmm, double entendres."

"Huh?"

"Nothing. Did Katherine say it was okay to start breakfast? She thinks the kitchen is hers."

"I asked her if she wanted me to start cooking, but she never answered. I assumed it was okay."

"Never said a word, huh?"

"No, ma'am."

"Hmm, well, sometimes keeping quiet about things is a good idea. Do you know what I mean?"

"No, ma'am. What do you mean?"

"Ever heard the saying, what you don't know won't hurt you?"

"Yes, ma'am."

"Good. I'm going back upstairs. Let me know when breakfast is ready, okay?"

"Okay, but you don't want to know about—"

"Johnnie! I don't like gossip!"

"Mrs. Beauregard, I'm just trying to tell you that I'm supposed to feed Grandpa his food."

"Oh, okay." She thought for a moment. "Johnnie, don't call him Grandpa. That's a term only we Beauregards can use when addressing or speaking of him."

I know. Why do you think I'm using it?

"Yes, ma'am."

Ethel saw Eric coming from Katherine's apartment and said, "Let me know when breakfast is ready." Then she nearly fled from the kitchen and ran up the stairs.

Eric opened the back door and was on his way toward the stairs. He seemed to be in a big hurry.

"Feeling better, Mr. Beauregard?" Johnnie asked, unable to resist the urge to poke fun at the affair he was having.

Eric stopped in his tracks, turned around, and walked up to Johnnie. "Let's get something straight. You wanna feed my dad, fine. But don't forget for a second that you're a servant in this house. You be careful what you say and who you say it to. You got that?"

Johnnie diverted her eyes to the floor and said, "Yes, sir, I sure do. I quit. I'll do my duty today and that's it. I'm through."

"What?"

"You heard me. I quit!" Johnnie nearly shouted, looking him in the eyes disdainfully. She had met the infamous Beauregards and from what she could tell, they weren't any better than the Baptiste side of the family. She could easily quit because she didn't need the job in the first place. She had plenty of money.

"Now . . . now . . . no need to make rash decisions. Ethel needs you."

"So, you want me to stay? You want me to keep working for you?"

"Yes."

"Okay, but I'm a nice person. I like to be respected, don't you?"

Eric stared at her for a moment or two. "You just make sure you show the same respect you'd like to have, and we won't have a problem. And no more of this *I quit* talk, okay?"

Returning her eyes to the floor again, Johnnie said, "Okay, sir."

Chapter 41

"Okay, let's start over."

KATHERINE WALKED into the kitchen, looking like she wanted to kill Johnnie. She was breathing hard, and her face was twisted by the anger that raged within. At about the same time, Morgan Thomas walked back into the kitchen too. He smiled when he saw how angry Katherine was. He liked Johnnie and didn't want to see her mistreated by Ethel or Katherine, so he gave Johnnie the ammunition she needed to silence them both, if she wanted.

"Did you send her to my apartment?" Katherine whispered, knowing that Ethel often listened to them from the top of the staircase.

"Yeah, I sent her," Morgan replied. "What of it?"

"What the hell you doin' sendin' her to get me, Morgan?"

"Look, I don't work for you. I wake you as a courtesy. You got that?"

"Don't you ever send anybody to my apartment again," Katherine growled.

"Fine, get up on your own. Your secret's out anyway. Everybody knows about it."

Katherine put her hands on her hips and said, "You jealous, mister educated man? You want some? Is that it?"

"You ignorant bitch," Morgan shouted in a whispered voice. "I heard about you trying to have Johnnie dismissed. Don't do it again."

"Awww, that's precious, Mr. Thomas," Johnnie said, smiling. "That's one of the nicest things anyone ever did for me. Thanks for caring."

Katherine whirled around and faced Johnnie, her hands still on her hips. "Like mother like daughter!"

Confused, Johnnie said, "What do you mean?"

"Oh, I read that article in the *Raven* about Richard Goode and your sweet, departed whore of a mother and how she died. If you're not careful, you might be next."

Johnnie went into a quiet rage and was approaching Katherine to throw blows, but Morgan stepped between them and held her so close to his chest that she couldn't move.

In the distance, Johnnie could hear someone coming down the stairs. She was still being held by Morgan when she said, "If you ever mention my mother again, I'll slap the taste outta yo' mouth and tell everything I know about you and Eric. You don't believe me, you try me and see."

"Morgan," Katherine began in a calm voice. "Let her go so she can help me fix breakfast."

"You okay, Johnnie?" Morgan asked.

"Yeah, you can let me go, Mr. Thomas," Johnnie said. "But I got my own chores to do. Why should I help you with yours?"

Calmly, Katherine said, "'Cause I'm asking you to, that's why."

"So, you do have some manners, huh?" Johnnie asked.

"Are you going to help me or not?"

"All you had to do was be nice," Johnnie said. "I'd be happy to help you." She offered her hand as a sincere gesture. "Let's start over and try to be friends from now on, okay?"

"Are you going to keep certain things quiet?"

"Yes."

"You're never, ever going to throw them in my face?"

"No. And you're never going to mention my mother or how she died, are you?"

"No."

Johnnie extended her hand and Katherine took it. "Okay, let's start over. I'm Johnnie Wise, the new maid. Pleased to meet you."

Chapter 42

"Hell naw. That shit won't ever happen again."

LUCAS PARKED his newly purchased 1954 Chevy convertible in front of the Beauregard mansion and waited for Johnnie to come out so they could spend the rest of the day together. The car was white with rich burgundy leather inside. It had a mirror-like, high-gloss shine. The silver rims were surrounded by unblemished gangster whitewalls.

While Lucas waited for Johnnie to come out of the mansion, he listened to Helen Humes' "Million Dollar Secret" on the radio, which was apropos for the situation both he and Johnnie found themselves in for more than one reason. He switched the radio off rather than listen to his life play out in song, and thought about all the college students he could sell marijuana to, how much money he was going to make, and how quickly he would make it.

Then his thoughts shifted back to Johnnie and what he would tell her, how he would talk around the devastating subject of hers and Napoleon's sexual romp the way Bubbles had a few weeks ago, when he warned Lucas of the consequences of getting involved with Marla Bentley.

Never was it more clear to Lucas that he and Johnnie needed to get out of New Orleans before something terrible happened. He was lucky to be alive as it was, messing around with a white woman in the South, who was married to a made Mafioso. The strange thing was that he was only alive due to the generosity of the man he had betrayed.

The more he thought about it, the more he began to look within himself for his problems. Everything that happened with him and Johnnie had happened because of his inability to control his own lust, he reasoned. Even now, as he thought on these things, he knew he was still incredibly weak when it came to sexual desire. He shook his head.

I'm Samson and Marla is Delilah! Goddamned Delilah! I'm big, strong, and tough. I can handle just about any man in a fistfight, but pussy . . . that shit is potent. That shit be calling me all the damn time. I gotta learn how to stop myself. I gotta learn to put my woman first instead of a fresh piece whenever it's thrown my way. But who can do that shit when it be callin' a nigga? Especially when my dick be like a brick all the time! God is cruel, making men wanna fuck all the time and then when we do, we fuck up our lives. That shit don't seem right. God oughta—

"Hi Lucas," Johnnie said and got in the car.

"How was work?" Lucas asked and pulled away from the curb, making every effort to get his mind in a place where he could tell her what he knew without telling her what he knew.

"Interesting."

He looked at her and said, "Interesting, huh? Sounds like we both had interesting mornings."

"Oh, really? What happened to make your day interesting?" Johnnie asked, wondering who had the more difficult morning.

"You first."

"The white side of my family is no different than the black side."

"It's a little different because they got money, and money is everything, ain't it?" Lucas growled contentiously.

Johnnie looked at him and saw the scowl he was attempting to hide. "What's wrong? What happened today? Did you and Napoleon get into it or something?"

"I'll tell you about it later. Now, this money thing is gon' be a problem and I know it. When I have enough, we gon' blow this town together, right?"

"Uh, right," she said, frowning.

"Why you hesitatin'? You wanted to make some money, and you have. I wanna make some too, and when we have enough, we're leavin'—together . . . right?"

"Right, but why are you bringin' this up now, Lucas? Did anything happen this morning to put you in this kinda mood?"

"I said I'd tell you about my morning later. Now, get off of it!"

"Okay, okay. Ain't no need to get all mad."

"I'm not mad!"

"Okay, Lucas," Johnnie said with resignation.

"Now, I got some shit to run down to you, okay? So, just listen, all right? And don't ask me no damn questions either." He looked at her menacingly.

"Okay, I won't ask questions."

"I didn't lie to you about Marla. I told you what was what. The whole shebang. All right! The truth! But a man knows sometimes a woman can't tell the whole truth about some shit she done did."

Guilt rose in Johnnie and began to fill her mind with worry. *How did he find out?*

"If you talkin' about Napoleon, I told you—"

"Shut up, goddammit!"

Johnnie recoiled suddenly when Lucas yelled at her. He looked like a dangerous killer at the moment, like he could wring her neck with his thoughts alone. There was no doubt in her mind. She knew he knew her secret; he knew her intimate truth—her deep, abiding truth. He knew a truth that she wouldn't even admit to Sadie, that being that Napoleon Bentley had given her unimaginable pleasure.

She looked at Lucas, who was trying to maintain some measure of calm so that he could say what was on his mind. She wondered if he would beat her later. Was that next on his unpredictable agenda? Strangely, she felt as if she deserved it; she felt like a slut, like a whore, like she'd done something far worse than what he'd done, when in actuality, there was no difference. She was about to risk saying something when Lucas began speaking again.

"Now, listen to me." He paused and stared at her for a few perilous seconds to make sure she knew not to interrupt him again. "I know women do shit behind a man's back. Sometimes she feels she has to. Other times she don't." He looked at her to get a reaction, but Johnnie just looked at him, listening intensely. "When some shit done happened, and ain't nothin' a man can do to change it . . . it's best to let sleepin' dogs lie." He looked at her again. "You understand what I'm sayin' to you?"

"Yes," Johnnie said as anxiety sent an ice cold chill down her spine when she realized that he knew the truth about her and Napoleon. This was the only way he could deal with it. People dealt with the pain truth caused the best way they could, she deduced.

"Okay . . . now . . . when a man don't know some shit for sure, it's best he never know that shit for sure." He looked at her again, feeling like he was in complete control. "Some shit a woman gotta keep to herself when she loves a man, so that a man can cope with that shit." He looked at her again. "You know what I mean?"

"Yes."

"So, whatever the fuck happened in the past . . . stays in the past, right?"

"Right, baby," Johnnie beamed, realizing their relationship would survive her betrayal. "Right in the fuckin' past. That's where it's gon' stay all right."

"And that shit won't happen again either, right?"

"Hell naw. That shit won't ever happen again."

"I love you, girl," he said softly. "I love you enough to let some shit I don't know about, go."

"I know, baby. Thank you."

"All right then. Let's go to Walter Brickman's so we can tell each other about our interestin' days, okay?"

"Okay, baby," Johnnie said, and kissed him. "Let's go to Walter Brickman's and talk."

Chapter 43

Main Street Restored

WALTER BRICKMAN'S was one of Baroque Parish's glittering jewels. It was located on Main Street in a high traffic area right across the street from the Sepia Theatre, which was owned by a local Negro entrepreneur and millionaire named Walker Tresvant III, who also owned much of Main Street. Walter Brickman's was the hot spot for youthful teens who had plans to go to the theatre. They often came in and had burgers and fries and malts before their show began.

When Lucas turned onto Main Street, they were happy to see business was nearly back to normal. Well dressed Negro men and women walked the streets again, patronizing the many Negro owned and operated stores and shops. There were so many people on the street that day that Lucas had to park his new car several blocks away from Brickman's Malt Shop.

As they walked down the street, they occasionally stopped and window shopped for new clothes or shoes that neither of them needed. They walked farther down Main Street, approaching Michael and Beverly's Bakery and Sweets, inhaling deep doses of the scrumptious aroma the cookies, cakes, pies, and fresh beignets provided.

"Lucas," Johnnie began, "can we stop in and get a fresh beignet?"

"Yeah, baby, sure. No problem," Lucas replied with an almost unnoticeable grin.

This would be the first time since they became a couple that he would actually pay for something. It felt good, too. They entered the bakery and Johnnie told Beverly she wanted a beignet. Lucas pulled a wad of money out of his pocket and removed the rubber band.

He had one twenty wrapped around eighty ones—$100. It was a fortune to him, with plenty more on the way, that weekend, in fact. Lucas peeled off a dollar, smiling the entire time, proud as a peacock at that moment. "Keep the change," he said, full of himself.

Beverly offered a friendly smile and gave him back ninety-seven cents and said, "Son, keep your money. Put it in a bank or something for the hard times that will surely come. The fact that the lady is with you means you've already made a favorable impression on her. Don't be foolish with your money, hear?"

"Yes, ma'am," Lucas replied respectfully.

After that, Beverly went to the back of the bakery and got a hot beignet and brought it out to Johnnie. "Thanks for coming in, Johnnie," Beverly said.

Johnnie wasn't at all surprised that Beverly knew her name, because Lisa Cambridge had told her a few days ago that everybody knew she was behind the murder of former Klansmen, Richard Goode, and they all approved. Johnnie took in a deep breath before putting the beignet in her mouth. They left the bakery and continued on down the street.

With it being August, schools were still out, and Walter Brickman's was filled to near capacity when Lucas and Johnnie entered the restaurant. Walter, as he liked to be called, was into Negro cinema and entertainment paraphernalia. Pictures of Lena Horne, Dorothy Dandridge, Ethel Waters, Paul Robeson, Sammie Davis Jr., Sydney Poitier, Harry Belafonte, Cab Calloway, Louis Armstrong, Dizzy Gillespie, Abbey Lincoln, Diahann Carroll, Josephine Baker, Nat King Cole, the Nicholas Brothers, Bill Bojangles Robinson, and many others covered every wall, near every window and door.

The atmosphere was jovial; lots of schoolgirls giggling, plates scraping, loud talking, music, waitresses taking orders, and the cooks shouting to the waitresses, letting them know orders were ready for pick-up. But when Lucas and Johnnie walked in, a hush saturated the restaurant, and everyone stared at them like they were celebrities with the status of those that papered the walls of Walter Brickman's.

They had all heard the prevailing rumors of Johnnie having so much sway with Napoleon Bentley that she could have people killed. The same girls who once talked and laughed at Johnnie behind her back now saw her as someone to be admired and feared. After all, If Johnnie was friends with Napoleon, the kind of friend who would kill another white man for his crimes, she could have the same thing done to them. They all stopped talking about her—everybody except Billy Logan.

Chapter 44

"Get the hell outta here and don't ever come back!"

BILLY LOGAN was still enamored with Johnnie's beauty. Who could blame him? Not only was Johnnie very pretty, but she had an amazing figure too. A few months ago, he and a horde of other students followed Johnnie as she walked home from school, taunting her about the on going sexual liaison she was having with Earl Shamus, the white man who had paid a hefty sum to deflower her.

Prior to learning that Shamus was having his way with her regularly, Billy Logan wanted her to be his girlfriend, just like the rest of the boys who attended Abraham Lincoln High School. This revelation crushed him, and he led the other students as they taunted her mercilessly, saying, "She probably sucks his dick, don't you, whore? Don't you suck his dick?" But Lucas Matthews saw it and put a stop to it by beating Billy Logan to a pulp and making him apologize to Johnnie on his knees in front of the same crowd he'd led.

Another reason the restaurant was quiet was because they all knew Billy Logan was in the restroom. Less than five minutes ago, prior to Johnnie and Lucas' arrival, Billy had been running his mouth about what he was going to do to Lucas the next time he saw him. He'd told them it wasn't going to be like the first time. This time, he was going to beat Lucas to a pulp and make him like it. So, when Lucas and Johnnie walked in, the hush that saturated Walter Brickman's was actually the quiet before the storm.

The restroom was about fifteen feet behind Lucas and Johnnie, and when Billy Logan came out of the restroom, he was stunned to see his nemesis and the whore he adored sitting in a booth, looking into each other's eyes like they were deeply in love. His first thought was *How do I get out of this shit now?* All the talking he'd done was just talk. He had no desire to tangle with a ruffian like Lucas Matthews and take another severe beating.

Fuck it. I ain't takin' another ass whuppin' over no whore. I'm getting the fuck outta here while the gettin' is good.

Just as he made the decision to sneak out the back door, a cute girl he liked locked eyes with him. Now he couldn't leave. His pride was in the way. Lucas had kicked his ass and won Johnnie's heart in the process, so he couldn't let yet another girl he liked see his fear, especially after all the talking he'd done in her presence. He'd have to do something now. Besides, all the other students in Walter Brickman's heard his braggadocio's words too.

Filled with fear, Billy Logan fast-walked over to Johnnie and Lucas' table. The heels of his shoes were clicking in a quick cadence in the quiet restaurant.

Then, having made it over to their table, Billy, in a loud voice said, "I see you're still with this whore, huh? Her pussy must be as good as her mama's, huh? One day it'll be my turn to try it out and see if it's really that good. Ain't that right, sweet thang?"

Unable to believe his brazen attitude, Lucas shouted, "You must be tired of living!" He was about to get out of his seat when Billy Logan hit him with a right haymaker that stunned Lucas.

Then he hit him again and again and again, saying, "Yeah, muthafucka! I got yo' ass now!" and hitting him over and over again. "How does it feel, muthafucka? I'm kickin' yo' ass!" He kept hitting him.

The kids in Walter Brickman's quickly gathered around the table, making it impossible for Johnnie or anybody else to help Lucas, who was bleeding from the nose and mouth and swelling rapidly. In the meantime, the crowd cheered like they were in the Roman Coliseum watching the Carthaginians battle hardened gladiators to the death.

Suddenly, Walter Brickman, a behemoth of a man, pulled Billy off Lucas, who he was still pounding as if he were a speed bag. "That's enough, Logan!" Brickman shouted and tossed him into the crowd like he was a rag doll. "Get the hell outta here and don't ever come back! You're not welcome here anymore! You hear me? Get outta here!"

"I'll get out, old man," Billy shouted with venom. "I did what I said I was gon' do. I kicked his ass and everybody saw it." He looked down at Lucas, who was dazed but still attempting to get up. "Stay down, muthafucka! We even now." Then he looked back at the cute girl he had locked eyes with. She was looking at him like he was the man, and it made Billy feel powerful. He stretched out his arm, beckoning her, and she went to him. He put his arms around her and said, "Let's blow this joint!" Then they both swaggered out of Walter Brickman's.

Chapter 45

"Let me know when you're ready."

THE SWELLING had gone down considerably since Johnnie placed repeated ice packs on Lucas' face. Except for some residual bruises, he didn't look that bad. As a matter of fact, he looked pretty good considering the vicious blows he'd taken. His ego was more bruised than his face. Johnnie had seen him take a terrible beating, and he never even got a shot off. After the sucker punch he took while sitting in the booth, it was pretty much over. As he lay on Johnnie's bed, he relived the surprise assault over and over, wondering what he could have done differently.

Johnnie interrupted his thoughts by saying, "Remember the day we met?"

"I don't feel like talking now," Lucas barked. "I'm gonna kill Billy Logan when I catch him."

Johnnie ignored his embittered words and decided to tell him how he made her feel when they'd met that day Billy led the crowd that followed her home from school. "I remember it like it was yesterday."

Lucas looked at her incredulously. "So, you gon' tell me anyway, huh?"

She ignored him and continued on. "You came out of nowhere, as if by magic, like an angel from heaven; my angel, there to rescue me from the devil in the form of Billy Logan. I knew right off that I was going to love you for sticking up for me. Sometimes a girl just needs to know that someone cares. I mean really, really cares. And then you hit 'im and got 'im good. I knew no one would ever bother me again after that."

"Uh-huh? Well, his ass is mine when I catch up to 'im. This time it's gon' be worse."

"Can I make a suggestion?"

Lucas looked at her sternly. "Don't even bother trying to talk me out of it."

"No, I won't try that. I know you gotta get 'im. But you don't have to get him now, do you?"

"Hell yeah, I gotta get 'im now. I can't let this shit stand. I gotta find him and fuck his ass up. Everybody saw him sucker punch me."

"Okay, but what about the other business?"

"What about it?"

"Lucas, are you still going to do it? Are you still going to sell marijuana to your friends in college?"

"What does have to do with this?"

"You said you wanted to get out of New Orleans, didn't you?"

"Yeah, so?"

"Well, do you still need the money? If not, get him now. If you do need it, let's take care of business and take care of Billy Logan later. He's not going anywhere, right?"

"I can't let him get away with that. People will think I'm weak."

"Let 'em."

"Are you crazy? Why would I let them think I'm weak?"

"So that he'll relax and make it easy to get him later. What do you think he's doing right now?"

"Probably hidin' somewhere, wondering when I'm going to catch up to him."

"Exactly. And if you don't go looking for him, he'll think you're afraid and come outta hiding. Like I said, let's handle business, and then you can take care of Billy before we leave."

Lucas thought for a few seconds before saying, "What about my reputation? What about my collections job? People might not want to pay on time when they learn what happened."

"If they don't pay on time, what would you normally do?"

"Kick some ass."

"Do this instead. Tomorrow, when you make your rounds, kick some ass before even asking for what they owe. That way, they know you're still as tough as ever."

"Hmmm, yeah, yeah. I'll do that first thing tomorrow."

"Okay, now, do you want me to do that thing for you again? It might make you feel better."

Lucas frowned. "What thing?"

"You know what thing. Don't make me say it. The thing I did before that you like so much."

"You wanna do it again?"

"If you want me to. I'll do whatever you want to keep you away from Marla."

"Oh, yeah, I was supposed to tell you about what happened this morning."

"Okay, tell me while we get undressed."

"We gon' do it too?"

"Yep . . . every day, if that's what you want. I'm keeping you. I know that's what you want, so I'll do whatever I have to do to keep you, okay?"

"Okay, well, I'ma tell you the truth," he said and pulled his shirt over his head. "I went to my apartment this morning and—"

"After you agreed not to go without me?" Johnnie asked and unzipped her maid's uniform and let it fall to the floor, revealing her awesome body.

"Yeah, but hear me out," he said, unzipping his pants. "Marla was there waiting for me—naked."

"Did you fuck her again?" Johnnie asked, unable to believe he was that weak for her.

"No, I didn't. I swear to God I didn't."

"But you wanted to?" Johnnie asked, looking down at him, wearing only a pair of white panties and bra.

"Yes, I did want to. I ain't gon' lie. I did want to, okay, but I didn't, and that's what's important, right? And I learned a valuable lesson too." He lifted his rear end off the bed and slid his pants and underwear down to his ankles. "I learned that if I didn't want you to mess around, I shouldn't either."

"Really?" Johnnie said and finished taking off his pants and underwear, pulling them over his ankles and feet.

"Really. If I didn't do it with Marla, Napoleon wouldn't have been able to threaten you. I learned that I put you in that situation. It was all my fault."

Those last comments made Johnnie feel guilty because he was telling her the truth and she was still lying to him. Napoleon knew about Martin Winters, Johnnie's stockbroker before Sharon Trudeau took over for him. Napoleon was in her kitchen when he overheard Johnnie's conversation with Meredith Shamus, Earl Shamus' wife, when she told Johnnie she had put a stop to the sex-filled love triangle.

This was Napoleon's trump card; this was the truth he threatened to expose, which was why Johnnie was feeling incredibly guilty at the moment. But she promised herself she would make it up to Lucas, believing that if she sucked him real good and made good love to him, somehow that made up for her lies. She could live with her lies then because her acts of love would serve as atonement for her sins against him.

Johnnie reached around back and unhooked her bra, looking into Lucas' eyes while doing so. She loved the way he looked at her, like he wanted her, like he needed the thing that only she could provide. All women had the same equipment, but in her mind, she was the best at what she did to a man. After all, Earl Shamus, Martin Winters, and Napoleon Bentley were proof of this. And for that reason, if she gave Lucas all he wanted, if she made him feel real good, he would never have a reason to leave her. She slid out of her panties and continued looking down at Lucas, who was throbbing.

Johnnie got in bed and climbed on top of him. She began by kissing him long and hard, which turned her private place into a busted geyser. But when she closed her eyes, Napoleon Bentley invaded her mind again. She opened her eyes so she could make love to the man she loved instead of the man she desired. Before long, Napoleon disappeared and it was just Lucas.

After kissing every part of his body, she positioned him to enter her private place and slid all the way down until she had all of him and began a slow steady grind. Then she eased up his shaft until she neared the tip and pumped it, which drove Lucas crazy.

A few hours later, over dinner, Johnnie told Lucas about her "interesting" day with Katherine, and Eric and Ethel Beauregard, and they had a nice laugh.

Part Three

Miracles Never Cease

Chapter 46

"None of this will come back on us."

THE INFORMANT had just left John Stefano's mansion after boldly telling him of Marla and Lucas' affair. This same informant sat in his office a few weeks ago and told the Boss of New Orleans about Napoleon's relationship with Johnnie Wise, which was the reason Napoleon stepped in and sanctioned the murder of Klansmen, Richard Goode. When Stefano realized this action was what triggered the riot, which hurt his business, he called Chicago Sam for permission to kill Napoleon. But Sam said, "No."

Now, Stefano knew about Napoleon's wife's affair too. A nefarious grin crept across his face when he realized that not only was Marla having an affair with a nigger, but Napoleon knew about it and did nothing to stop it. In Stefano's mind, if Napoleon would kill a white man on a whim, why wouldn't he kill the nigger for fucking his wife? As a matter of fact, why wouldn't Napoleon pop them both and be done with it?

It has to be the nigger broad he's bangin'. She's turned his mind to mush. He's not fuckin' thinkin' straight, that guy! The fuckin' fool is in love with her. He has to be! Why else would he let another man fuck his wife and live? A nigger, at that!

John Stefano looked at his bodyguard, Salvatore Porcella, and said, "What did you think of Vincenzo Milano when he was here in this room with Sam?"

Porcella looked him directly in the eye and reduced his impression of Vinnie with one word. "Hungry."

"The Colored section was originally promised to Vinnie before he lost his mind in a fit of rage and murdered that guy in a Chicago suburban bar." He looked at Porcella intensely. "You think he still wants the Colored section? You think he's that hungry? Hungry enough to do my dirty work?"

"Why wouldn't he be? We're talkin' about three million dollars a year on the numbers racket alone. The niggers call it policy. You add in the drugs and we're talkin' about the pot of gold at the end of the fuckin' rainbow, John."

"The question is, does he have the stones to go against Sam?"

Porcella leaned forward. "I think Sam'll go along once the deed is done. Sam is a reasonable man. Once Vinnie kills Bentley and things settle down, he'll be okay with it."

"I want the three million, Salvatore. I say we get Vinnie to kill Bentley and then we kill him, but make it look like that big, black bastard Bentley has watching his back clipped Vinnie. Then we take what was once ours back because the contract is only good as long as Bentley is alive. When he dies, I get my territory back. Sam knows this. That's why he said I couldn't take Bentley out."

"Why did we give it to Sam in the first place, John? I mean, we're talkin' about a lotta fuckin' money."

"I got a guy in the government that I needed to stay alive. He serves this thing of ours very well. He fucked Sam over but good, okay? Stupid thing to do, but what are ya gonna do, eh? You protect your people when you can. Besides, the Colored section wasn't worth three million at the time. Bentley took it over and inside of six years, turned the place into a fuckin' gold mine. I want it back, but I can't go up against Sam. By all rights, that should be my goddamned money, not his. And Sam, that cocksucker is making a small fortune in my fuckin' territory."

"So, if we take down Bentley, we go up against Sam. If we get Vinnie to do it and kill him after the job, who's gonna complain because Sam told you, you couldn't kill Bentley. And then you get the Colored section back free and clear, and Sam gets no more of the three million dollars."

John Stefano couldn't help laughing when he thought of the prospect of this orchestration. It was so perfect, so flawless, so fucking clean, he thought. He leaned forward and opened his box of Cuban cigars and pulled out one. Salvatore Porcella stood up, went around the desk, and lit Stefano's cigar.

Stefano said, "I want you on the next plane to Chicago to handle this piece of business. You know what to do if Vinnie doesn't agree to do it, right?"

"I'll take care of everything, John. Don't worry. None of this will come back on us."

Chapter 47

"It's still warm."

SALVATORE PORCELLA'S plane landed at O'Hare International Airport at 9:30 P.M. He wanted to get a room at the Drake Hotel in downtown Chicago, where he normally stayed when he was in town, but he knew Sam had people working there, and decided to go to a hotel whose staff didn't know him. The Napoleon Bentley thing was more delicate than a woman's hymen and would prove far more bloody if he didn't handle Vincenzo Milano just right.

Salvatore Porcella didn't want to give Milano a chance to tell Sam about the plan to kill Bentley, which was why he didn't call him and set up a meeting. He knew Connie Giovanni, the woman Milano was currently bedding. It was no secret that he spent most of his nights in her bed. All Porcella had to do was wait for him to show up at Connie's.

Connie Giovanni was ahead of her time, believing that a woman's body was her own to do with as she pleased. She had an extensive list of mobbed-up celebrity lovers to prove it. Salvatore Porcella was just one of them. As much as he'd like to stop by Connie's apartment and have his way with her, he couldn't. No one could know he was in town. It was too big a risk.

Besides, Connie couldn't be trusted to keep her mouth shut about anything. Making conversation and telling other people's business was part of who she was. The best course of action, he thought, was to stakeout Connie's place. At some point, he knew Milano would eventually get the itch that only Connie could scratch.

Salvatore Porcella was parked outside of Connie's apartment, a few houses away from the entrance. He'd been there since midnight, hoping to see Milano enter the building. His plan, however, was to approach him when he left. If he tried talking to him before he went in, he might tell Connie about the deal. While this was something Mafiosi wouldn't normally do, it was known to happen from time to time.

Of course, Vinnie could still tell Connie or anyone else about the Bentley hit, but Porcella believed that if he talked to Milano, he could make sure he understood not to say anything to anyone. If Porcella believed at any point that Milano would tell what he knew, he'd pop him on the spot and get on the next plane back to New Orleans without anyone ever knowing he was in Chicago.

At about 2:30, Milano came out of the apartment building. Porcella got out of his car and approached him. "Paesan!" Porcella called out. "How's it hangin'?"

Milano immediately went for his piece while simultaneously squinting to see who it was.

"Relax, Vinnie. It's me. Porcella."

"Porcella?" He pulled out his .38 and pointed it at him. He looked to the left and then to the right, looking for Porcella's backup. "What are you doin' here?"

"We need to have a conversation."

"A conversation, huh? About what? For what reason?"

"I've got three million reasons that I know you want to hear."

After saying this, a window from the apartment building squeaked open. "Hey Vinnie," Connie shouted. "You forgot your wallet." She tossed it down to him. Milano caught the leather billfold. "Salvatore? Is that you down there?" Connie asked. She was surprised to see him. "Why didn't you tell me you were coming to Chicago?"

Suddenly Porcella realized that he and Milano were standing directly under a streetlight and could be clearly seen—a huge mistake on his part. "Connie Giovanni," Porcella said sweetly. "I wanted to surprise you. I was on my way up when this SOB comes outta the fuckin' building."

"Ya comin' up?" Connie asked. "It's still warm."

Porcella laughed. "Sure, doll face. I'll be up in a few minutes. Leave the door open, will ya?"

"Just come in. I'm gonna take a quick shower," she told him.

Chapter 48

"Hey . . . don't underestimate the Spaniard."

"John is beside himself with anger about the riots," Porcella offered persuasively. They were sitting in the front seat of Vinnie's car. "We lost a fuckin' bundle when the good citizens of New Orleans lost their fuckin' minds over the dead Klansman and attacked the moulies."

"What does that have to do with me?" Milano asked.

"We hear you've got a ten-year-old beef with Napoleon," Porcella offered and left his words hanging in the air, like he expected Milano to confirm the rumors.

"Yeah? Where'd ya hear that?"

"People say things, Vinnie. You know that."

"What people?"

"People that know you tried to have the Spaniard iced in prison ten years ago. We know that the Colored section was yours before that unfortunate incident at that bar in the suburbs."

Milano's suspicions hardened his eyes. "Why are you here, Porcella? What kinda cloak and dagger shit are you tryin' tuh pull?"

"New Orleans thinks you oughta have what's yours."

"What's in it for you guys? How many points we talkin'? What kinda bite are we talkin' about here?"

"Zero points. Zero bite."

"You're fuckin' kiddin' me! Are you telling me that New Orleans don't wanna cut?"

"Never said we didn't want a cut, but the truth is, John is in no position to make demands. Our hands have to be totally clean on this. You understand what I'm saying, Vinnie. Totally fuckin' clean. No mistakes or this shit could start an unnecessary war. And John would . . . let's say . . . lose a bit of juice with New York, Cleveland, Kansas City, and the rest of our friends."

"What about Sam?"

"We think Sam and the rest of our friends will go along if this thing is handled professionally. All you gotta do is take out Napoleon and claim what's yours. Sam owned it and gave it to Napoleon. All you're doing is taking what was originally yours to begin with. Who's gonna have a beef?"

"And I can run the Colored section without any interference from Stefano?"

"Hey, don't insult us, okay, Vinnie? If John kept his word to Sam and let a fuckin' Spaniard in his backyard, certainly he'll let a Paesan do as much. You're one of us, Vinnie. Come on. Get your head straight on this. Am I right or am I right?"

"When can I move on this, Porcella?"

"The National Guard is gone. Things are getting back to normal. Napoleon's smart, and he's gotta know there's gonna be repercussions."

"Why would he expect repercussions when Sam made it clear that nobody was gonna move on him? Sam already told him he's run outta favors, so he thinks it's all over."

"Hey, don't underestimate the Spaniard. I got a lotta respect for the man, considering what he's done with the Colored section. You'll only get one shot at this. And remember, the fuckin' moulies love him more than they love Abraham Lincoln. They'll do anything for 'im."

"Consider it done."

"Good. Now, if you don't mind, I'm gonna go and visit Connie for a while. You all right with that?"

"No problem. I'm not the only one fuckin' her, okay? I like Connie, but she's a fuckin' whore. There are two things that a whore could never do. You know what they are, Sal?"

"No, Vinnie. What are they?"

"The two things a whore can never do is keep her mouth shut and her legs closed." The two men laughed uproariously. "She can't do it, Sal. She's gotta fuck, and she's gotta run her goddamned mouth. Show me a woman that's fuckin' everybody, and I'll show you a woman that runs her fuckin' mouth." They continued laughing. "That's why I would never, never let myself fall in love with a whore. Don't get me wrong, Sal. I've got nothin' against whores, you understand? We all have our purpose on earth. But ya never try and turn a whore into a wife. It'll never happen, Sal. Never. So, you go on upstairs and do whatcha gotta do."

Porcella laughed a little more as he exited the car and said, “You’re a cruel man, Vinnie. Cruel.” He closed the door and walked into the apartment building.

Chapter 49

"Smart girl."

SALVATORE PORCELLA quickly climbed three flights of stairs, torn by what he knew he had to do. He'd made an unforgivable mistake, and now Connie Giovanni had to die for it. Just before he climbed the last flight, he stopped on the landing and pulled out his piece. Then he pulled out a long black silencer, screwed it on, tucked it in the back of his pants, and climbed the last flight of stairs.

Killin' Connie is gonna disappoint a lot of men. What a real ball breaker she is. She can suck a cock for hours—non-stop. How could I have been so fuckin' stupid? I should have followed him home and stopped him there. Now I gotta kill a good piece of ass so she won't run her fuckin' mouth. Oh well. No need in cryin' over spilled milk. Somebody would have killed her sooner or later over her mouth. Might as well be someone who cares about her like me. But I'll be damned if I don't get a piece first.

He walked up to apartment 301 and knocked on the door. He forgot he had asked her to leave it open for a second or two. Suddenly it came to him that the door was only closed, not locked. He turned the doorknob and walked in, closing it behind him.

He could hear the shower running in the bathroom. If this had been a regular hit, he would have walked into the bathroom, snatched the shower curtain open, and popped her. But this was Connie Giovanni, and she offered him a slice of the sweet heaven that marinated not far below her waistline.

His mind began to conjure up all sorts of naughty things he was going to do to Connie. He also pictured all the naughty things she was going to do to him, and began to throb as his heart rate increased signify-cantly. Yet he knew he was going to kill her before the sun rose.

He went into her bedroom and looked around at pictures of her family, who would no doubt miss the vivacious vixen. Connie had told him who each of the people were in the black and white photographs that sat on her mirrored dresser. He reached around back and pulled his piece out and put it on the chair next to the bed. Then he sat down on the bed and untied his shoes and removed them.

After removing his socks and tucking them inside his shoes, he took off his clothes and neatly folded them, then placed them on the chair, covering the silenced weapon he would use to kill an unsuspecting Connie. He pulled back the covers and looked at the black silk sheets. He saw a wet stain in the middle of the bed—remnants of Vincenzo Milano. *I guess she didn't have time to change the sheets. Fuck it! I'm not staying the night anyway.* He slid into the bed, careful not to touch Milano.

A half an hour later, Connie was still in the shower. Porcella lost his rock hard erection and had nearly fallen asleep waiting for her to get out of the shower. When he realized he was nodding, he called out to her. “Hey, doll face! How much longer are you gonna be?”

No response.

Porcella listened intensely, hearing only the constant splashing of water in the tub. “Connie,” he called out again. No response. “Fine, I’ll get it in there.” He laughed softly. “Ready or not, here I come!” he sang as he walked into the bathroom. “Connie?” No response. He looked at the black shower curtain. “Connie . . . you all right, honey?” He walked over to the shower and pulled the curtain, but Connie was not in the shower. Porcella laughed from his belly and then said, “Smart girl.”

Chapter 50

"What a fuckin' dimwit."

CONNIE GIOVANNI knew why Salvatore Porcella hadn't called her before coming to town. She also knew why he was in Chicago and what he was talking to Vinnie about. The moment she closed the window, she got dressed, grabbed the keys to her car, and ran down the backstairs. Unlike Porcella, she exercised extreme patience, waiting for them to finish talking, waiting for Salvatore to enter the apartment building, and waiting for Vinnie to pull off before she ran to her car and got in.

She looked in the rearview mirror and checked herself over. Even though her heart was pounding in her chest, her vanity demanded that she look in the mirror, check her make-up, and see if her blond hair was presentable. *Who knows? What if I meet a man on my way outta town?* If Salvatore figured out she had tricked him, he would be running out of the building in hot pursuit.

But Connie knew that wouldn't happen because she had offered him something no man had ever turned down in the thirty-three years she'd been alive—at least that's what she told herself. And she counted on it. She counted on Salvatore Porcella's lust to give her the precious minutes she needed to blow town until all the killing was done. But before she left town, she owed Napoleon Bentley a favor.

Connie Giovanni had pledged her undying allegiance to Napoleon years ago when he saved her life by killing her abusive husband—no charge. So, when Napoleon called her and asked for reports about Vincenzo Milano and whenever Salvatore Porcella came by to "visit," she agreed without hesitation. This, to Napoleon, would be a clear signal to prepare for a hit, he'd told her.

"What a fuckin' dimwit," Connie said after looking at her watch and seeing that her plan of escape had worked too well. A half an hour had passed and Salvatore was still waiting for her to come out of the bathroom. She laughed a little when she pictured a naked Porcella lying in bed, waiting. "Figure it out, Sal," Connie said.

As soon as she finished her sentence, Porcella came out of the building. He took his time walking to his car, which led Connie to believe he fell for everything. Porcella thought she was long gone. He would look for her later, but not tonight.

If Napoleon was right, Porcella would leave Chicago immediately and get back to New Orleans. Porcella started the car and pulled away from the curb.

Connie waited until he turned the corner and she could no longer see his taillights before starting her car. She followed him at a comfortable distance to a hotel, but didn't bother stopping, assuming he was staying there while he was in town. Everything was going according to plan. She had packed a suitcase weeks ago, just as Napoleon had told her to. And now, she was leaving Chicago and going to sunny Fort Lauderdale, Florida, where no one knew her.

Just before getting on Interstate 65 South, she pulled into a gasoline station and called Napoleon at his home. It was almost 4 A.M. She knew there was a possibility that he wouldn't be home, but she had to reach him. Her life depended on her being able to let him know that Salvatore Porcella was in Chicago.

Napoleon answered the phone. "Hello." His voice sounded like his mind was in a haze.

"Napoleon?"

"Who else would it be?"

"This is Connie Giovanni. Salvatore is here . . . in Chicago. I followed him to his hotel."

"Connie, don't take those kinds of chances. Just get outta town."

"Okay, I'm leaving right now. When can I expect the money you promised me for the job?"

"I'll send my man Bubbles with the money. It won't be long, okay?"

"Okay."

"Connie . . . be careful. They've got people everywhere. They may not figure it out, but if they do, you can bet they'll be looking for you. I don't want to read about you in the papers."

"I'll be careful," she said and hung up.

Chapter 51

"I know who you are."

SALVATORE PORCELLA sat in his hotel room, thinking about what happened, and how he might have blown the Bentley hit by being incredibly careless. *What the hell am I gonna tell Stefano? The truth? Why . . . so I can get whacked? Fuck no! Vinnie's on his own. I ain't sayin' shit. I should have called Connie just to cover my ass. Dammit! Now she's on the run, saying God knows what to the wrong fuckin' people.*

On the other hand, what is she going to tell people? That I didn't call her before coming to Chicago? And who gives a damn? The worst thing that could happen is that Sam finds out that I was in Chicago without his knowledge. So what? Big fuckin' deal! I came here to recruit Vincenzo Milano. I did that. I'm satisfied. And honestly, I'm glad Connie figured it out. I'm glad she got outta that apartment before I put a bullet in her brain. I'm gonna get some shut-eye and get on the first plane back to New Orleans.

But just to be sure, I'm gonna go back to Connie's apartment. Maybe she's dumb enough to come back, in which case I'll find out if she said anything to anybody. If she somehow knows something and talked, I'll have to pop a few people. Damn! This thing could get outta control. I've got less than twenty-four hours to clean up this mess; otherwise, Stefano will wonder what took so long to handle this piece of business.

After waiting in Connie's apartment until 7 P.M., Porcella gave up and decided to get back to New Orleans. He knew Connie was gone and to ask questions in Chicago would alert Sam's people to his presence. And if it got to Vinnie that Porcella was looking for Connie, he might change his mind and tell Sam, which would more than likely force John Stefano to have him whacked just to cover his own ass. *One phone call could have avoided this shit!*

His plane landed at Moisant Field at 11:59 P.M. He and other passengers grabbed their bags and made their way to the parking lot, where they left their cars. He had made up his mind to tell John Stefano nothing about the Connie Giovanni situation. There was no point. If it ever got out that he didn't take care of Connie, he would tell John that there was no way she could know their plan that quickly, since only he and John knew of it.

Porcella tossed his bag in the backseat and got behind the wheel. He started the car and pulled off, heading for US 61. He was so preoccupied with his thoughts about Connie that he was totally unaware that he was being followed by three cars. Not long after he had gotten away from Moisant Field, a squad car's siren blared. He looked at his speedometer to see if he was speeding.

Porcella was going a couple of miles over the speed limit, but he wasn't going fast enough to be stopped by the cops. He slowed down, pulled over and stopped his vehicle. Then he looked in his rearview and saw the cop get out of his car. Porcella pulled out his wallet, since he knew the cop would ask him to. The cop made his way over to the driver's side window.

"Nice night for a speed trap, huh, officer?" Porcella said sarcastically. Then he recoiled. His face twisted as he looked down the barrel of a Smith and Wesson .38 special. "Hey, wait a minute, pal. Do you know who I am?"

"Yeah, Sal," Bubbles said. "I know who you are. I also know why you were in Chicago, and so does Napoleon."

Salvatore Porcella's face drained of blood and went stone cold pale as fear polluted his mind. "You? Bentley sent you . . . to kill me?"

"That's right, Sal. Me!"

Then suddenly, Sal saw the last flash of light he would ever see. *POW! POW! POW! POW! POW! POW!*

Seconds later, a tow truck came and connected Porcella's car and towed it away from the scene with Sal still in it. Salvatore Porcella would disappear and never be seen again.

Chapter 52

"Right, and I'm the king."

"It's done," Bubbles said when he walked into Napoleon's office.

"Any problems?" Napoleon, who was reading the Bible, asked.

"Naw, no problems. It went off without a hitch. Sal was very surprised to see that I was his executioner and that you sent me."

"He was, huh?"

"Yeah."

"Your plan was beautiful," Napoleon said. "He never suspected a thing, did he?"

"Nope. Complete surprise. I saw it in his eyes."

"Good. At some point, Stefano will begin to worry about his number one man, but he won't be able to do anything about it. He won't be able to ask Sam about it because he wasn't supposed to be making any moves on me." He laughed. "How will he ever explain what Sal was doing in Chicago?"

"What about Vinnie? Do you think he's still coming?"

"Of course, and that's when it'll get dangerous for me."

"Yeah, I'll beef up security."

"No. Do not add any security, because that would tip them off that I'm on to them. And if I'm on to them, they'll know what happened to Sal. Let's continue doing business as usual."

"Well, how will we know when they're going to hit us?"

"When Vinnie visits John Stefano. He'll wanna check in and make sure everything is okay. He'll need to know that Sal wasn't running a private war. For that, he'll need to speak directly with Stefano, face to face. That's why he won't call first. He'll need to get Stefano's reaction. They'll talk about it here, in New Orleans, and decide to handle things without bringing Sam into it. They're figuring Sam'll go along once the deed is done. Alert all of our people, especially the maids, the butlers, the elevator operators, the shoeshines, everybody—cover the city so we'll know when he uses the can. They'll know who comes and goes."

"So . . . uh . . . you gettin' religion?" Bubbles asked, looking at the Bible Napoleon was reading.

"No, old friend. I'm doing some reconnaissance."

"Reconnaissance, huh?"

"Yeah, man. It's all a part of the game."

"The game, huh?"

"Yeah. But this is the game men and women play with each other, and the secret is in this book."

"What?"

"Yeah. All the answers are right here."

"And you understand it? I could never make heads or tails of it."

"Don't forget I'm Catholic."

"So, Catholics got a monopoly on understanding the Bible?"

"I wouldn't say that. But I was taught by the Jesuits. I know a few things the average Joe don't."

"For instance?"

"For instance, women are attracted to power, beauty, and knowledge. Those are the things the Serpent used as enticements. It's right here in the third chapter of the book of beginnings—Genesis. Old friend, I'm telling you any one of those three things can be used to get any woman today. If you know what you're doing, that is. And if you use any one of the three against her, she doesn't stand a chance against your wiles."

Bubbles laughed from his belly. "So, this is about Johnnie. I should have known."

"Of course it's about Johnnie. In her mind, she's a good Christian girl in spite of all the dirt she's done. The church is still in her, though her sins be as scarlet. And I'm gonna get her the same way the Serpent got Eve. Oooh, I'm so bad. I can hardly stand myself." He laughed. "It's all coming together, too. Lucas is on his way out. It's just a matter of time now. The trick, though, isn't getting him outta the way. His own greed will be his undoing. The trick is to win her over. That's the trick."

"You think he's gonna take the bait?"

"Of course. The temptation is too good to pass up. Actually, I admire him for looking to strike out on his own. He would have been good for us, but . . ."

"But you want his woman."

"Right! And I'm the king."

"And none of this bothers you? I mean, the kid doesn't deserve this."

"You goin' soft, Bubbles? C'mon, man. You're gonna make a fortune on this deal. A fuckin' fortune. So the kid'll get his heart broken? We're talkin' about millions, man."

"I guess you're right."

"You guess? C'mon, man. Are you with me on this or not?"

"Yeah, man, I'm with you. The shit just doesn't feel right, ya know?"

"Just think of the money and you'll be all right. Believe me. Money salves the conscience better than any medicine on the planet."

"Perhaps we shouldn't underestimate the kid. He's been kickin' a lotta ass since Billy Logan beat his ass in Walter Brickman's."

"Has he found Logan?"

"No."

"Find him. We might be able to use him."

Chapter 53

"Nobody deserves it more than that guy."

A WEEK LATER, John Stefano hadn't heard from Salvatore Porcella, and he was worried. In his heart, he knew Sal was dead, but what bothered him was that he couldn't do anything about it. Sal had been Stefano's protector for nearly twenty years. He was a third generation Mafia bodyguard, having taken the place of his father, Vito Porcella, who had taken the place of his father before him. And now, Sal's son, Vitorio, would one day stand by the Don's side and vow to give his life for the Boss of New Orleans.

As Stefano thought on these things, he reasoned that Sam had found out what was going on and had Sal clipped. If that was true, and he believed it was, he couldn't even ask about this, since Sam had refused to sanction the Bentley hit. Stefano had lost a good man for nothing, he thought, until Vincenzo Milano showed up at his door, asking for a sit-down.

With Sal missing and presumed dead, Stefano had to play it cool. For all he knew, Milano was the one who had killed Sal. Now he was in New Orleans, asking for a meeting with the Boss. Milano had been frisked and shown to Stefano's office, where the meeting was to take place. The two men greeted each other with a handshake, which turned into a hug, and then a kiss on the cheek. They sat down.

"What can I do for you, Vincenzo?"

"Where's Sal?"

Good move, Vincenzo. Play dumb. Ask about the man you killed. "Sal is doing something special for me. If you wanted to talk to him, why come to my home?"

"Well, Don Stefano, I actually came to talk to you. But—"

"Then talk to me, Vincenzo. What is it? Share your heart with me."

"I asked about Sal because he came to Chicago a week ago and said New Orleans wanted Bentley dead."

Stefano's eyes hardened. "Sal told you this?" He couldn't acknowledge the truth—not yet anyway. Stefano needed Milano to spill it all before he told him anything.

"Yeah. He said that if I took care of Bentley, I could get the Colored section back, which was supposed to be mine in the first place. He also told me that there would be no interference from you, and I would continue paying Sam the same thing Bentley was paying because you only wanted Bentley dead."

"And what did Sam think about all of this?" Stefano asked, baiting him, hoping he would say something, anything that would lead to what Sam knew, if anything at all.

"Sam doesn't know anything about this, Don Stefano. I thought you wanted it that way. Sal says that if I take care of the Spaniard, Sam'll go along. I agree with Sal, Don Stefano."

"Vincenzo, you sat in this office just a few weeks ago. You heard your Don. You heard him say he didn't want anything to happen to Bentley. Why would I violate our agreement and provoke a war that would hurt both our businesses?"

Milano realized what was going on. He now knew that Stefano was covering his ass because he thought he was there looking out for Sam's interests. Besides, Sal had told him that New Orleans had to be absolutely clean on the hit. And with Sal on some errand for Stefano, there was no way to get him to verify the conversation. "Don Stefano, let me assure you that Sam knows absolutely nothing about this. But I need to know if Sal had your permission to make the offer. Did he?"

"Are you telling me you're willing to take care of Bentley on your own?" Stefano asked, continuing to evade direct questions. He still wasn't sure what Vinnie and Sam were doing. It could all be a set-up, and they might be trying to kill him.

"Yes, Don Stefano. With your permission, of course."

"And you're telling me you thought of this on your own?"

Milano stared at him. *Jesus H. Christ! The fuckin' guy acts like I'm a fuckin' Fed or somethin'!* "Don Stefano, I swear on the lives of my two daughters that Sam knows nothing about this. All I need is your permission to whack Bentley."

"Seems to me that you would need Sam's permission, not mine."

"You let me worry about Sam," Vinnie said, realizing that Stefano was never going to implicate himself in the scheme to kill Bentley. But it was very clear that was what he wanted.

"Then this is a Chicago operation. New Orleans has nothing to do with whatever Chicago does with their own people."

"Thank you, Don Stefano."

"For what? I didn't do anything. I didn't say anything, and I don't know anything. But if I was involved, I'd wait a few months, then do the job."

"A few months?"

"Yes. A few months. The National Guard left not long ago, and the FBI is still taking everybody's picture. I'd wait and let absolutely everything get back to normal. I'd say around Thanksgiving. I'd give him an early Christmas present." A sinister laugh erupted from deep within.

"Yeah, an early Christmas present." Milano laughed along with Stefano. "Nobody deserves it more than that guy."

But John Stefano didn't know that his maid, Stephanie Roselle, gathered some clothes as a pretense to wash them in the basement, which was right under Stefano's office. The maid could hear every word and would report it all to Napoleon.

Chapter 54

"Good. I'll straighten it out."

"Thanksgiving, huh?" Napoleon repeated gleefully. He was sitting at his desk in the office. "I'm going to take real good care of you if this pans out. Keep listening and keep me informed. Come by the Bayou tonight and I'll give you an envelope and a table up front, okay?" He hung up the phone.

Seconds later, Bubbles walked in. "I found Billy Logan. He's waitin' in the hall. You wanna see him now?"

Napoleon smiled. "Yeah. Bring him in. We're going to talk to the lad."

Billy Logan walked in, scared to death that he was about to meet God before the night was over. Napoleon looked at him. He saw how nervous Billy was and decided to put him at ease.

"Relax, kid," Napoleon said. "You're gonna see another sunrise."

Billy Logan didn't know it, but the relief he suddenly felt was evident to everybody in the room. "Thank you, Mr. Bentley."

"Everybody, and I mean everybody, calls me Napoleon."

"Yes, Mr. Bent—I mean Napoleon."

"Okay. Now, tell me about this beef you've got with my boy."

"Who? Lucas?"

"Who else ya got a beef with, kid?"

"It's just kid stuff, Napoleon."

"Tell me about it. How did it start?"

"You mean last week? Or the first time we fought?"

Napoleon looked at Bubbles and smiled, knowing he could use this to help get rid of Lucas if necessary. "Where's Lucas?"

Bubbles looked at his watch. "He should be in any minute now."

"Good. We need to have a sit-down about this." He looked at Billy Logan. "So, what happened the first time you two fought? What was it about?"

"Well, we got into a fight."

Napoleon laughed. Now he understood the rest. "So, he kicked your ass, huh?"

Defiantly, Billy said, "I wouldn't say all that. He got the best that time. But now he knows what's what."

Bubbles snarled before saying, "So, you think if it came down to it, you could take Lucas?"

"Hey, I do what I gotta do . . . period. Somebody messes with me, I mess with them. It's that simple."

Bubbles and Napoleon eyed each other. They both knew this was perfect.

"How'd you like to work for me?" Napoleon asked. "I got an opening for a runner."

"What's the pay?"

Napoleon looked at Bubbles. "Ya gotta love this guy, huh?" He looked back at Billy. "Twenty-five dollars a week."

"A week? Hell yeah!"

"But there's a catch."

"What's the catch?"

"You'll be working under Lucas." Napoleon saw the hatred rise in his eyes. He knew that if he took the job, they would never be able to work together. "But I need to know how the first fight started. The one when he got the best of you."

"That was some bullshit, man."

"What happened?"

Billy frowned before saying, "Some whore started it. I wasn't gon' take no shit off no whore. I wasn't gon' take no shit off nobody."

"You mean Johnnie?" Bubbles asked.

"Yeah. She's a whore. I told her to her face. The bitch started the whole goddamned thing."

Napoleon smiled. "You liked her, huh?"

"Who me? Hell naw! Not at all."

Napoleon looked at Bubbles. They both smiled. Then he looked at Billy again. "So, can you handle working for my man or not?"

"For twenty-five dollars? Yeah, man. I can if he can."

"Good. I'll straighten it out."

Just then, they heard a knock at the door.

Chapter 55

"Sure . . . go ahead."

LUCAS MATTHEWS walked in after Bubbles opened the door. He saw the back of someone's head, but paid it no mind. Besides, he had a lot going on in his head, and wanted to give Napoleon all the envelopes he collected, so he could get over to Johnnie's place for dinner and some real good sex. They were having sex every day, and that was all he could think about. But tonight, he and Johnnie were going to the Sepia to see a play titled *No Way Out.*

The film version was originally released in 1950 and starred Sydney Poitier opposite Richard Widmark, Stephen McNally, and Linda Darnell. The play was opening tonight. Some people thought the content was too similar to the recent riots, but Walker Tresvant III knew the play would sell out for those very reasons and vetoed any notions of cancellation.

The next day, which was Saturday, Johnnie had the day off. She and Lucas were going to pick up another supply of marijuana and take it to Jackson and Grambling Universities. Things were going better than he expected, and they were already talking about expanding to other campuses. It was too easy, and Napoleon didn't suspect a thing.

"Here you go, Napoleon," Lucas said, still having no idea that his nemesis was sitting in the chair. "I gotta run, though. Me and my girl got a date tonight." He handed him the envelopes.

"Just a second, kid," Napoleon said. "You know this guy, don't you?"

Lucas looked at the man in the chair for the first time. "Billy Logan." The words kind of lingered in the air for a second. "You know you got a ass whuppin' comin', right?"

Billy said, "You and what army?"

Lucas took a couple of steps toward Billy, who was on his feet, ready for the fight to begin.

"Just a minute, kid," Napoleon said. "He's workin' for me now."

"You've gotta be kiddin' me. This muthafucka sucker punched me in front of the whole town. I can't let that shit go. He hit me when I was in the booth. I'ma fuck him up for that shit."

"I'll tell you what, Lucas," Napoleon began. "I'm gonna let you have your shot at him, but if you lose, you're fired. If you win, you get a new job and a significant raise in pay. But you've gotta train this guy and work with him. Can you do that?"

"After I kick his ass, yeah, no problem."

"You all right with that, Billy?" Napoleon asked.

"Yeah, but what do I get if I win?"

"Hmmm, I don't think you will win, Billy. You wanna fuck his girl and you sucker punched him in front of everybody. Stupid move. But on the off chance that you do win, you get the job and the pay I was going to give him. Is that fair?"

"Hell yeah," Billy Logan said. "And don't fire him. Let's have him work for me. That way I can kick his ass again and take his job. And Johnnie's next. I'ma take her too. It'll be sweet. I'll take his job first, and then fuck his girl."

"Let's stop talkin' and settle this shit right now," Lucas said and looked at his watch. "I've got some time. If it's okay with you, Napoleon, let me call Johnnie and tell her I'll be a little late."

"Sure . . . go ahead. But I'm telling both of you right now that this is the only time this shit happens. I'm only letting this happen now because you sucker punched my man and he has to have an opportunity to get even. Otherwise, it will happen later and one of you will end up dead. You two understand? One time and that's it."

"Yeah. One time," they said.

Lucas picked up the phone and dialed Johnnie's house. "Hey, I'ma be a little late. Yeah, we still goin' to the play tonight. Billy Logan is here. I'm about to put my foot knee-deep in his ass. I'll be there in about thirty minutes." He hung up.

Twenty minutes later, they had to pull Lucas off Billy before he killed him. It was that much of a mismatch. Billy never even got in a punch. But was it all settled?

Napoleon hoped it wasn't. In fact, he was hoping that it escalated into murder. He knew Lucas would beat Billy to a pulp again, and he was hoping Billy would be stupid enough to kill Lucas later, leaving Johnnie free and even more vulnerable to his wiles.

Chapter 56

"Don't shoot!"

POLICE SIRENS SCREAMED as Lucas' souped-up 1941 Chevy sped down the highway at speeds approaching 120 miles per hour. *How did the cops catch me?* He had been so careful, only dealing with people he knew personally. With the raise he'd gotten from Napoleon, Lucas invested heavily in his deal with Preston Leonard Truman, the gas station attendant he'd met when he and Marla went to Shreveport to get the new car.

Three months had passed since Lucas beat Billy Logan to a pulp for the second time. It was the day before Thanksgiving, Johnnie's birthday, and he wanted to make it a special night for her. Johnnie was now seventeen years old and Lucas was planning to take her shopping for an engagement ring. His marijuana business was booming and he had plenty of money to get her whichever ring she wanted. The marijuana business was doing well enough for him to invest $5,000 of his money with Sharon Trudeau, Johnnie's stockbroker. The business had grown so quickly that he made contacts with other gas station attendants, who joined his network.

But now the cops were on to him and they were in hot pursuit. As he fled, thoughts of Angola Prison, better known as The Farm, invaded his mind. He had been told as a child that he wouldn't amount to much and that he would end up at The Farm like so many other young Negro men did, as if The Farm were their only destiny. And now, here Lucas Matthews was, in a high speed chase, attempting to get away from the people who wanted to take him to the prison that seemed to have an open door policy for the Negro men it housed.

Lucas and Johnnie were looking forward to spending her birthday and their first Thanksgiving together. Before the cops somehow found out about his private enterprise, Lucas' life couldn't have been more perfect. Even Marla left him alone. She had called him several times and he wouldn't talk to her. She came by his apartment several times, too, and he wouldn't let her in. After a couple of months of this, she gave up. He'd gotten her out of his system. Now Johnnie Wise was the only woman who occupied his mind these days, but it looked as if it was all about to come crashing down.

"Oh, shit," Lucas said when he saw the roadblock up ahead.

More cops were waiting for him. They had shotguns aimed and ready to fire. He slammed on the brakes. The tires screamed as if they were being terrorized, and left their marks on the pavement as the

Chevy screeched to a halt. The cop cars that gave chase stopped right behind his car, boxing him in.

"Outta the car, Matthews," a cop shouted.

They know my name? Somebody talked, but who? Was it Preston? Did Preston turn me in? It must have been Preston. Was it Wendell Smalls? Herbert Shields? Who? And why? We're all making good money.

"Boy! Don't think for a moment we won't kill you in that car. Now, get out with your hands up, or by heaven, we'll open fire. Ya got thirty seconds!" the same cop shouted.

Lucas closed his eyes and shook his head. Then he put the stick-shift in neutral and turned off the ignition. "Don't shoot!" he yelled out the window. "I give up! I'm getting out of the car. Don't shoot!" He opened the door and slowly got out of the car.

The same cop yelled, "Put your hands behind your head and lace your fingers!"

Lucas complied.

"Cuff him," the cop yelled.

Chapter 57

"Do you know who I am?"

NATHANIEL BEAUREGARD sat in his wheelchair as Johnnie pushed him through the rose garden on the Beauregard mansion grounds. He responded to Johnnie because he recognized her. Even though the stroke had disabled his motor functions, his mind was still intact and cognizant. In Johnnie, he saw the woman of his youth, the woman who taught him how to love and how to make love, and the woman he had impregnated so many years ago. How could he not recognize her when she looked just like his former flame, Josephine Baptiste?

But he couldn't speak. He couldn't embrace her and tell her what he knew she was dying to know—that being, who her grandmother was. Nathaniel was deeply in love with Josephine. He bought her a house and visited her regularly. But not long after Marguerite was born, something happened between them. Nathaniel kicked Josephine out of the house he'd purchased and stopped supporting her and his daughter, but he never stopped loving her.

Seeing Johnnie that first day, when his son Eric brought him back to New Orleans, gave him the will to live again, if only long enough to tell his granddaughter that he knew she was his flesh and blood. If Nathaniel ever got the chance to speak again, he would tell her much more than that. He would tell her all about Josephine, what happened between them, and tell her where she could find Josephine's personal diary, which contained all kinds of secrets.

He struggled to speak each day, believing that one day soon, he would have a monumental breakthrough so he could tell her he was glad she'd come to see him. Now that his health had failed him, he felt guilty and wanted to make amends for the way he'd treated the daughter he'd had with Josephine. It was too late now; too late to make amends; too late to apologize; too late to embrace his flesh and blood. All Nathaniel could do now was look upon his granddaughter and see the image of his beloved Josephine.

Johnnie stopped pushing the wheelchair and looked around to see if anyone was near. Then she knelt in front of his wheelchair and looked him in the eyes. "Do you know who I am?" Nathaniel blinked one time, which was the signal for yes. To be sure he understood, she said, "Do you remember Josephine Baptiste?" Again, he blinked once. "She's my grandmother. Did you know that?" He smiled and blinked once. "Then you know you're my grandfather, right?" He blinked once.

While she knew not to, Johnnie couldn't help herself. She threw her arms around Nathaniel and hugged him for a long minute. When she realized what she was doing, she pulled away and looked around to see if anybody saw what she did. She didn't see anyone looking, and no one said anything to her about it. Then she wiped the tears that slid down her cheeks. That's when she knew it was time to return to her heavenly father. She was going to get back in church and serve the Lord again.

When she told him that today was her birthday, his heart broke a little, knowing he'd missed seventeen years of her life—not that he would ever acknowledge this truth in public. Nathaniel Beauregard had known where her mother, his daughter, Marguerite, lived and he didn't do anything to help them when he was the picture of health. However, the stroke, coupled with incredible guilt, changed his mind. He told himself that if he ever recovered, he'd do what he could to help her.

Chapter 58

"What happened, Johnnie?"

JOHNNIE COULDN'T have been happier now that she'd told her grandfather who she was. She was in her kitchen preparing the Thanksgiving feast and reminiscing about the things she told Nathaniel in the rose garden earlier that day. She was standing over the sink, occasionally looking out of the window at the neighborhood kids, watching them play tag as she removed the shells from the eggs she had boiled to make the potato salad. But in her mind's eye, she could see Nathaniel sitting in his wheelchair as she pushed him around the Beauregard grounds.

Johnnie came to herself when she heard the phone ring. Somehow she knew it was Lucas calling and believed he only wanted to let her know he'd been delayed by the marijuana run. "Hello."

"Johnnie . . . I hate to tell you this, but the cops picked me up. I'm in jail. Can you get me out?"

Rudely awakened from her pleasant memories, she said, “What? What happened?”

“Somebody talked. They knew who I was and everything. They had a roadblock set up, waiting for the other cops to chase me right to them.”

“Oh my God, Lucas! What are we gonna do?”

“I’m looking at some serious time, baby. Sell my stocks and get me a real good lawyer.” He sounded desperate. “They said I’m looking at fifteen years, baby.”

“Fifteen years!” Johnnie repeated. “Why didn’t you listen to me? I told you this was a bad idea, didn’t I?”

“Johnnie, please, just get me a good lawyer, okay? It stinks in here.”

Sadie opened the back door just as Johnnie hung up the phone. She’d heard enough of the conversation to know that something was seriously wrong. “What happened, Johnnie?”

Johnnie turned around and looked at Sadie with a shocked expression on her face. “The police caught Lucas and put him in jail.” Her eyes went blank and she fell to the floor, hitting her head on the table as she fell. Just before she hit the floor, Sadie tried to catch her, but it was too late.

Chapter 59

What else can go wrong?"

THE HOSPITAL BED was comfortable, but Johnnie was unsure what had happened. The last thing she remembered was telling Sadie that Lucas was in jail. She had no idea how long she'd been asleep. Suddenly, she was very thirsty. Her mouth felt like it was full of paste. She opened her eyes.

Sadie was looking at her, waiting for her best friend to regain consciousness, waiting for that precise moment to deliver more bad news. While Johnnie was asleep from the sedative the doctor had given her, occasionally she would talk in her sleep, saying, "I need to call Sharon Trudeau and cash in some stocks to get Lucas outta jail."

Sadie said, "How are you feeling, sweetie?"

In a raspy voice, Johnnie said, "I'm thirsty, Sadie. Can you get me a glass of water?"

"Sure, honey," Sadie said and grabbed the pitcher of water that was on the table. She poured some in a cup and handed it to Johnnie.

"How long have I been here?" Johnnie asked.

"All day and all night."

Johnnie poured some water into her dry mouth and swallowed. "What day is it?"

"It's Thursday, Thanksgiving, Johnnie. The doctor said he wants you to stay twenty-four hours for observation."

Johnnie remembered she was supposed to get a hold of Sharon Trudeau, her stockbroker at Glenn & Webster. Lucas was counting on her to get him out of jail by cashing in some of his stocks.

"I've gotta get in touch with Sharon, but it's too late. Glenn and Webster are closed for the holidays, and the bank won't open until Friday. How am I going to get Lucas out of jail?"

Sadie diverted her eyes when she heard Johnnie's words.

When Johnnie saw her look away, she said, "What's wrong, Sadie? What's going on?"

Still looking away, Sadie said, "I've got bad news, Johnnie. Bad, bad news, girl."

"What, Sadie?"

"Sharon Trudeau . . . your stockbroker . . . ran off with all your money."

"What?" Johnnie managed to say through dry lips. "She ran off with my money? She stole it?"

Sadie handed her a copy of the *Sentinel* newspaper. "Every penny. Lucas' money too. All her clients, in fact. Sharon Trudeau's disappearance with her clients' money was front page news."

Johnnie's mind raced as she read the shocking truth, frantically searching for answers to unasked questions as tears formed in her brown eyes. Twenty-four hours ago, it was her birthday; a birthday she didn't get the chance to celebrate. Twenty-four hours ago, her life was going in the right direction. She was even ready to go back to church. Now she was in the hospital, under a doctor's supervision, the man she loved was in jail, and she was broke again.

Suddenly, everything that she had been through to accumulate her wealth flashed before her eyes. She had willingly slept with Earl Shamus for money, let his wife, Meredith, think she wanted him and took $50,000 from her as a bribe to leave her husband alone. She manipulated men and had even been an accessory to murder. She thought she'd gotten away with it all. Now she knew differently.

Johnnie kind of laughed and said, "What else can go wrong?"

With a sober look on her face, Sadie said, "I hate to be the one to tell you this, but...you're pregnant."

Chapter 60

What the fuck am I gon' do now?

THE LOVE OF MONEY is the root of all evil—at least that's what Johnnie had learned in church. But now, looking back on it, looking at all of her own deeds, Johnnie understood the verse and knew it was true. The love of money had gotten her irreplaceable virginity sold to Earl Shamus on Christmas Eve almost two years ago. The love of money had gotten her mother brutally beaten and savagely murdered. The love of money made it easy to choose prostitution over Christianity and Evangelism. But the love of money had also gotten her an expensive house and lots of nice things, which was all she had left.

Some people defined it as having a sugar daddy; some people defined it as being a kept woman. However, changing the words didn't change the institution, nor did it justify it. It was selling sex for financial gain. Prostitution by any other name was still prostitution, Johnnie realized. This unanticipated revelation was truly an emotional burden that felt like the weight of a heavy locomotive had been foisted upon her slender shoulders.

Have I become my mother?

The loss of that same money angered Johnnie. Everything in her mind, everything in her heart, everything in her very soul told her she had earned every penny of that money; she had worked hard for every single dollar. Her young body had been entered and thrashed around in over and over and over again. The money was her only salvation, her only emancipation, her only real joy. Money was the only thing that gave her peace of mind.

The money had become God incarnate—tangibility—the money took the place of faith and could be depended upon. The money was something that would never fail her. It provided her the kind of freedom most women would never know. She was only seventeen and had known the bliss of financial independence. And now it was gone, like a puff of smoke, like a magician's illusion, never to be seen again.

Three months ago, she told Eric Beauregard that she would quit working for Ethel if he didn't show her some respect. With the kind of money she had, she didn't need to work for the white side of her family. She didn't need to work at all if she didn't want to. Now all of that was gone. Gone. Gone. Gone. She was broke. Busted. Destitute. She felt like a whore with no money—worthless, but good for one thing only.

Later, Thanksgiving night, back home now and in her own bed, she looked up at the ceiling and blamed God again for the choices she made. *It's all Your fault,* Johnnie thought. *This is the second time You've let me down. I made lemonade out of the lemons You served me. I did it! Me! Not You, me! The least You could have done is look out for my money! Shit! But You couldn't even do that for me, could You? What the fuck am I gonna do now?*

Suddenly, out of nowhere, in the quiet stillness of her bedroom, Reverend Staples' words ricocheted in her mind and rang like the Liberty Bell: *The heart is deceitful above all and desperately wicked. Some of us are so self-righteous that it's going to take a lifetime to discover the truth of this verse so that we might be truly saved.* The words were loud and they were very clear, but instead of liberating her, Reverend Staples' words angered her even more.

What more do You want of me, God? I'm a good girl! You know what? Fuck it! Fuck it! Fuck it! I'ma get my goddamned money back! You won't help me, fine. I know some people that will! I'm not going to end up like my mother—forty-four years old, broke, and dead with nothing to even live for in the first fuckin' place. This shit ain't fair! Now I can't quit. I gotta work for the Beauregards. I can't start over with no money. I haven't even graduated from high school!

I know what. I'll call Earl. I bet he would love to start things up again. I bet he'd love to get some more of this. I know he would. He couldn't keep his hands off me. But we would have to be real careful. Shit! I can't stand for him to touch me. Fuck that! I don't want to deal with Martin Winters again either. That leaves Napoleon. I wouldn't mind doing it with him, though. This is so fucked up! I promised Lucas I wouldn't do it with him or anyone else anymore, and here I am thinking about doing the same things my mother did. I've become my mother.

And how . . . how did I get pregnant!? I should have used rubbers every single time. Now I'm pregnant! Pregnant and seventeen goddamned years old. I don't even know whose baby it is. I can't take care of a baby now. I don't have any money. I'm stuck! The doctor says it's possible to get pregnant and still have my period. Three months pregnant. Three goddamned months! I'm not gon' cry. I'm not gon' cry. I'm not gon' cry!

Johnnie got out of bed and went to her adjacent bathroom, tears streaming down her face. She looked in the mirror and placed her hand on her stomach. "Stop cryin'! You too old to be cryin'!"

How can I be pregnant and still have a flat stomach? I'ma take a bath and go over to the Bayou. Napoleon will help me out. I know he will. I'll give him some if he helps me find Sharon so I can get my money back. And I don't care what he says. If I offer him some, he'll take it. They all want it. But first, I'ma talk to attorney Ryan. Robert will know what to do. If that doesn't work, then I'll do what I gotta do.

Chapter 61

"Did you hear me, girl?"

BUBBLES KNOCKED HARD before entering Napoleon's office. He knew Napoleon didn't want to be disturbed unless it was really important. If it was anybody other than Johnnie, there was no way he'd bother his friend now. However, since winning Johnnie over was a part of Napoleon's plan, she could see him. As a matter of fact, they expected her to come seeking help to secure Lucas' release.

Before going to the Bayou, Johnnie had brazenly interrupted Robert Ryan and his out of town guests on Thanksgiving evening to get Lucas out of jail. She had spent an hour trying to convince the attorney to help her, but Robert told her he knew all about Lucas' incarceration and that he was where he belonged. He went on to tell her that she needed to move on with her life, and how riffraff like Lucas would only bring her down. None of that discouraged Johnnie, though.

Ryan had justified her need to turn to Napoleon, who she knew could and would get things done.

After listening to Robert Ryan's lecture, she left his home more than a little frustrated, and willing to do just about anything. She didn't even bother telling Ryan about her money being stolen. She went directly to the city jail to visit Lucas, but they wouldn't let her in. They told her Lucas couldn't have any visitors before the arraignment, which was scheduled at 9 A.M. Monday. She wondered what Lucas was thinking. He was counting on her to get him out, and she couldn't even get in to see him.

Johnnie was standing outside Napoleon's door, waiting for Bubbles to return so she could plead her case to the only man in New Orleans who could get Lucas out of jail and find Sharon Trudeau. The door opened and Bubbles came out.

"Johnnie, listen, he's busy, all right?" Bubbles said softly. "Say what you gotta say and let him finish what he's doing, okay?"

"Okay, Bubbles. I appreciate this, hear?"

Bubbles kind of grunted an acknowledgement and opened the door for her. "Go on in. He's waitin' for you."

Johnnie walked through the open door and Bubbles closed it behind her. Napoleon was sitting at his desk, grimacing in a predictable cadence. He took a sip from a tall, thin glass of red wine and returned it to the table.

What's wrong with him? Did he get shot or something? As she approached him, she heard him groan. *Is that a head? Oh my God! It is a head! He's gettin' a blowjob—right now.* Johnnie stopped and turned around. She didn't want to see that.

"I . . . thought . . . you . . . wanted something," Napoleon managed between groans.

Without turning around, Johnnie said, "I can come back later."

"It's . . . now . . . or never," Napoleon offered. He wanted her to see what was happening. He wanted her to know that the sex she was about to offer him could not only be gotten, but gotten in her presence, making it very clear that sex with her was not what he wanted or needed. But the truth was, he wanted her obsessively, and if he had to play games with this young vixen, he would. Chasing her was great sport for him.

With her back still to him, she said, "I want to talk to you about Lucas and some other business."

"Show . . . me some . . . respect. Turn around." Johnnie complied. "Now . . . sit down. Talk to me."

Johnnie walked up to the desk and just before she sat down, she couldn't resist looking at the woman on her knees. It was one of the waitresses from the bar.

"Well?" Napoleon said and furrowed his brow.

Damn, you expect me to just tell you why I came in here while her head is bobbing like that? Then, out of nowhere, it came to her. *He doesn't want me no more. But he likes to be sucked. I'ma make him want me. That's what I'ma do.*

"Lucas is in jail and—"

"I don't give a fuck!"

"But—"

Napoleon looked down at the woman who was pleasuring him. "Hurry up. I got business to discuss." The woman's head bobbed at a quicker pace. Napoleon's eyes returned to Johnnie. "You were there when Bubbles . . . Oh, shit . . . told him . . . right?"

After he said those words, he closed his eyes and his lids fluttered as if he was in rapid eye movement sleep. Johnnie just sat there stunned by the whole display, watching Napoleon as he came without shame, right in front of her. She quieted herself and waited until he opened his eyes again, which would indicate that the orgasm was finished and probably fulfilling.

Napoleon finally opened his eyes after his blissful interlude was complete. Then he picked up the glass of wine and handed it to the waitress. She looked at Johnnie, took a sip, threw her head back, and swallowed. Then she stood up and walked out of the office.

Napoleon took a deep breath, raised his arms to the ceiling, and stretched. "Did you hear me, girl?" He called her a girl deliberately because he knew Johnnie considered herself a grown woman.

Chapter 62

"Make it a hundred and fifty dollars and I'll give it some serious thought."

"Yeah, I heard you," Johnnie said defiantly. "And I'm getting sick and tired of you calling me a girl." She thought for a split second. "If I'm such a little girl, does that make you, Mr. Gangster, a child molester?"

Napoleon leaned back in his chair, zipped and buttoned his pants, studying her the entire time, his eyes intense, his mind considering the truth of what Johnnie had just said. He found the power of her truth completely overwhelming at that moment. If it were possible, he found her even more attractive.

Ignoring the molestation question, he said, "Three months ago, Lucas was warned not to get involved with drugs of any kind, yes?"

"Yes."

"And you know that I gave him a promotion and a raise in pay as incentive to keep him away from the drugs, right?" He didn't bother mentioning the brand new car he'd given Lucas since that was supposedly his way of apologizing for bedding Johnnie. To bring it up now would bring up their dalliance, and now was not the time for that conversation.

"Yes, I know."

"Hmm, you know all of that, and you still come to me for help. Why?"

"How old was the waitress that just left?" Johnnie asked, ignoring the questions he asked, just as he had ignored hers.

"Thirty-two, why?"

"Hmpf! And you call me a girl?"

Napoleon frowned. "What does she have to do with this?"

"You call me a girl, and yet a thirty-two-year-old woman doesn't know what she's doing. She has no idea how to pleasure a man."

"She doesn't, huh?"

"Listen, anytime you have to give a grown woman instructions, she's a child."

"And you can do better?" Napoleon asked, his erection back with a vengeance. *Can you do better?*

"Can you get Lucas out?"

"One subject at a time—please."

"Okay, one subject at a time. Lucas, can you get him out?"

"Hey, I asked you first. Now, can you do better? Yes or no?"

"Who, me? A child? Hell no. If a thirty-two-year-old woman doesn't know what the hell she's doing, how would a seventeen-year-old girl know?" She stared unblinkingly into his dark eyes. Having titillated his curiosity, she moved on, knowing he wanted to know if she was capable of backing up her words. "Now, can you get him out? Yes or no? I don't have a lot of time to waste if you no longer have the power to get things done in New Orleans."

Napoleon leaned forward, staring into her eyes, and said, "So, what are you sayin'? If I get your brilliant boyfriend out of jail, you're going to show me what you can do?"

"No. I'm just a little girl. You need to find yo'self a grown woman to do that. Me? A child like me wouldn't know how to pleasure a demanding lover like you. You've made it clear that I was a lousy lover and you want no part of me. It was hard to hear at first, but I've accepted it now. Besides, I wouldn't want you to lie to me to spare my feelings like you did last time."

Napoleon leaned back in his chair a second time and swiveled back and forth to the left and to the right, keeping his eyes locked on hers the entire time, wanting to lock the door, rip her clothes off, and ravage the young beauty recklessly. He successfully hid his thoughts from her and changed the subject.

"What's your other reason for being here? You mentioned some other business. What's that about?"

"I've been robbed, Napoleon."

"Robbed?" he said angrily. "I'll find out who took your stuff by the end of the week. What'd they get? Your television? Some precious jewelry?"

"Nothing from my house. They stole my money!"

"From the bank?"

"No. You've heard of Glenn and Webster brokerage firm?"

"Yeah, I've heard of them."

"And I know you remember who Martin Winters is, right? My former stockbroker?"

"Yeah, of course I remember, and I kept my word, too, didn't I? I never said anything to anybody about it."

"Yeah, you kept your word. But a woman named Sharon Trudeau took over my stock portfolio when Mrs. Shamus told Martin's wife."

"Speaking of Shamus, have you heard from him or Martin since that day the Mrs. came by?"

"Not a word. I guess she got both of them in line. Earl always has been greedy. She must have laid down the law. She probably even told him about Martin Winters. Ya never know, but back to Sharon Trudeau. According to the *Sentinel*, the people at Glenn and Webster say that she stole money from all her clients, not just mine. Without that money, I'm broke, Napoleon. If you help me out, I'd be glad to pay you a handsome finder's fee."

"A finder's fee, huh?" he said, frowning. "I'll look into this money situation as a friend, but Lucas is on his own. He was warned and defied my instructions. He gets what he gets."

"And there's nothing this little girl can do to change your mind?"

"No. He's gotta learn. If I get him out now, he won't learn a thing. He's looking at fifteen years on federal charges because the stuff he was carrying was worth fifteen thousand dollars."

"It was only a little weed."

"They found smack in his trunk."

"Smack? What's that?"

"You know . . . skag, junk, heroin? The stuff musicians use? The stuff they shoot in their veins."

Johnnie looked away, attempting to hide her thoughts because she had no idea Lucas was selling hard drugs like that. He never told her because of the way she responded to the idea of selling marijuana in the first place. She looked at Napoleon and said, "What would it take to get him out?"

"Listen, Johnnie, I like the kid, okay? But this is bigger than him. This is about letting my other people know they can't sell drugs and escape its consequences. You read the Bible, and you know that a man's gotta reap what he sows."

Johnnie bowed her head. She knew Napoleon had a point. Lucas not only defied his orders, but he started selling the heroin without telling her. She didn't know how to defend him any further, but she had to give it a try.

As if she knew what she was talking about, having listened to attorney Robert Ryan's rant about Lucas being riffraff and legal terms, she said, "Even though it's a federal offense, I know you can get him out. I'll do anything you want. Anything."

Napoleon shook his head in exasperation. Johnnie didn't get it. Lucas had to pay. "Listen, he's gotta do some time. But if I get him out, if I call in big, big favors, he's gotta get out of town. Nobody can know he only did a few months. It would hurt business. What if I get him . . . let's say three months in Angola and a few years in the Army or something? I could probably sell that to a federal judge I know. What do you think?"

"A few years?"

"It's the best I can do, if I can even pull that off. You've gotta understand the charges are serious and the time is severe. Now, tell me, what do you want me to do?"

"Get him the best deal you can." She paused briefly. "And what do I have to do for you?"

Nothing at all." He paused and thought for a second. "Here's what you can do for me. Quit working for them crackers and go back to school. Educate yourself. You're a smart woman. If you need money, you can sing here at the Bayou. I'll pay you seventy-five dollars a week."

His first thought was to say $150 because now that Lucas was out of the way, he wanted her near him to make it easier to build a relationship with her and break down her defenses. But if he offered $150 right away, she might get suspicious. The offer had to be tempting without being an obvious attempt at seduction.

"Make it a hundred and fifty dollars and I'll give it some serious thought," she said, thinking, *I always wanted to sing on stage anyway. And the last time I sang here, it felt great. Plus, there's no guarantee I'll ever get my money back from Sharon. The money could be a fresh start. Trouble is, I'd have to stay in New Orleans longer than I planned.*

"A hundred and fifty? Hell no! I'll start you at a hundred dollars and we'll see how you do. And if you're really good, if the people at the Bayou love you, we'll talk about your price and much more. Deal?"

"I've got some things going on with the Beauregards, which won't take very long. Let me finish that and it's a deal. And thanks for not takin' advantage of me, knowing how desperate I am."

"Hey, we're friends," Napoleon offered sincerely. "Being there for people is what makes you a friend, not taking advantage of them when they're down."

Chapter 63

"I could tell he wanted her."

"How did it go?" Bubbles asked when he walked back into Napoleon's office.

"Like fuckin' clockwork. She's go no idea I set this whole thing up. No fuckin' idea. And you know what feels good, old friend?"

"What?"

"The kid did it to himself, like a goddamned Shakespearean tragedy. I'm almost innocent in this. The kid made his own decision. I love it. That puts me one step closer to making her mine. Now, how are things with our friend Vincenzo Milano? Is he on his way?"

"Yes. One of our people, a porter, spotted him and four of his crew on the train."

"The train, huh? John Stefano wants to be very clean on this. He's not even going to supply the weapons. They couldn't get them on a plane. But the security on a train is almost nonexistent."

Bubbles asked, "Why didn't they drive down here, do the hit, get back in their cars, and drive back to Chicago?"

"A hit, even a well planned hit, is a fluid situation. If something goes wrong, the hitters have to improvise, see? They have to wing it from there. If it becomes public, the cops are likely to set up roadblocks and whatnot, but if they don't know what you look like, and you don't have weapons, you can get on a train and ride in luxury all the way back to Chicago. No roadblocks, nothing." He paused briefly. "How long before the train gets here?"

"It's a thirty-six-hour ride from Chicago to New Orleans," Bubbles said.

"Get on the train and take care of him and his crew before they get here."

"The train has a four-hour layover in Oklahoma City. I'll get aboard the train there. That's where I'll do the job. It'll be done at 4 A.M. I'll take care of Vinnie and his people. I'll give you a call when it's done."

"Take care of Preston too. Make it look like somebody robbed the gas station. Just in case Lucas talks, he'll be telling on his own people. Hopefully, he'll leave the college boys out of it. They all have promising careers. He won't wanna fuck them over because he got caught. But to make sure, on your way to Oklahoma City, stop by the jail and have a talk with Lucas. Let him know we're workin' on getting him out."

"Yeah, I'll have a talk with the kid. I'll get him to tell me who Preston and everybody else is. He'll think he has to talk to get out of jail. Then I'll make sure he goes for the deal. It was smart to keep Johnnie away from him. She's a smart cookie. I'm surprised she didn't figure it all out."

"She's got a lot on her mind, old friend. Thanks to us."

***

"What happened, kid?" Bubbles asked Lucas, who was sitting on his cot. "What the hell were you thinkin'? Didn't we tell you not to get involved with this shit? Now look at you. You're behind bars, lookin' at fifteen fuckin' years."

"Can you get me out, man?" Lucas asked, avoiding the question.

Softening his tone, Bubbles said, "You gotta do some time, man. Ain't no way around it. Now, how much time you do depends on you."

"What do you mean?"

"I mean, who's your connection? One of our people here in New Orleans?"

Bubbles was playing his part to the hilt. He had to convince Lucas that he and Napoleon were totally in the dark on this thing. That way, whenever he talked to Johnnie, which wouldn't be before the arraignment on Monday morning, thanks to Napoleon's connections, he could only tell her what Bubbles told him and make it look like they were looking out for him. All of this was necessary, in Napoleon's mind, to win favor with Johnnie.

"You mean I gotta squeal?" Lucas asked.

"Look, kid," Bubbles said, raising his voice. "We'll find the muthafucka on our own. And you can do the whole fifteen. It's up to you. I can't believe you would even do this shit, man. Didn't we take care of you?"

"Yeah, man," Lucas said reluctantly.

"If you cooperate, we might be able to get you three months."

When Lucas heard that, a smile lit up his previously dull face. "Three months! They said fifteen years! All right! Hell yeah! Three months! Shit yeah!"

"There's a catch, though, kid."

Lucas' smile vanished. "What catch?"

"Ya gotta remember that these are federal charges. Since this is your first offense, we can try and get them to drop the federal charges and just deal with the weed charges. That's where the three months come in, and ain't no way around that shit either. You gon' do that time at The Farm. You earned that shit, didn't you?"

"Okay, man," Lucas said, lowering his head. "What's the catch?"

"In order for the deal to go through, they want you to go into the Army for three or four years. They say you need some discipline. What do you think? Can you give Uncle Sam three years of your life?"

Lucas remained quiet, still looking at the floor. He walked around in the cell, mulling over the fifteen-year sentence he was looking at. After a minute or two, he looked at Bubbles and said, "I fucked up, man. I guess I'll do what I gotta do."

"Ain't no room for guessing, man. None at all. If we can get you this deal, when the judge asks you if you agree with this deal, you have to agree without hesitation. Otherwise, it may mean a trial and a fifteen-year sentence. They caught you with the damn drugs. You cold busted! It only makes sense to take this deal—that is, if we can even get it. Think long and think hard, kid.

"You're in the South, driving around in a brand new car, living better than crackers. What do you think the prosecutor and the judge are going to say? They gon' say, 'Make an example outta that nigga!' And then it's bye-bye Lucas Matthews. Fifteen goddamned years at The Farm. I've done hard time, and even I wouldn't wanna do time at The Farm. Damn! Oh, and don't forget, them crackers are still pissed off about the fuckin' riot, and they started the muthafucka! Yeah, they gon' fuck you over, kid, but good."

He paused and watched the wheels turn in Lucas' mind. Bubbles knew what he was thinking about. It wasn't the three years that Uncle Sam wanted that bothered him. It was leaving Johnnie for such a long period of time, and who would be bedding her while he was gone. He was wondering if she would wait for him. She was such a pretty girl. Grown men couldn't leave the teenager alone when he was in town. The thought of leaving her alone horrified him. But what could he do, take the fifteen years? Napoleon had put him in an impossible position. Lucas was through and he knew it.

"The Army will be good for you, man. You can learn a trade or something. Make good use of your time. Travel overseas or something. And listen . . . I know you're worried about your girlfriend. But take it from me; there will be plenty of girls where you're going. If you're lucky, you might get orders to go to the Presidio in San Francisco or something."

Excited, Lucas said, "San Francisco? Hmm, that might work out. Johnnie's brother lives there."

Bubbles already knew Lucas' chances of getting the Presidio were remote, but he had to give him something to hope and pray for in his time of need.

Napoleon wanted Johnnie, and he was just inches from having her. And so far, no one blamed him for anything he'd done. It was a well planned and well executed strategy. Soon, Lucas would do a short stretch at The Farm, and then he'd be on a train to wherever the Army trained their new recruits. And that would be that. Check and mate! Game over! In three months or so, it was going to be bye-bye Lucas Matthews, the unwitting stooge, who was unlucky enough to fall in love with a beautiful girl that another, more powerful man wanted; a man who would stop at nothing, including murder, to have her. Lucas never even had a chance. That night, three months ago in the Bayou, sealed his doom the moment Napoleon Bentley laid eyes on Johnnie Wise.

"So, who's your connection?"

"Huh?"

"Who got you started? Who's your supplier?"

"Preston Leonard Truman. He's a gas station attendant at exit 55 on I-49. Met him on the way to Shreveport a few months back." He paused and thought. "I wonder if he was the one who told on me. Yeah, yeah, it must have been him. I saw the way he was looking at Johnnie when we went to get my getaway car. I could tell he wanted her. So, I gave him a shot to the stomach so he could get his mind right, but I never thought he'd do something like this."

Hook, line, and sinker!

"We'll take care of Truman. Don't even worry about that. He jammed up my best man. I'll make damn sure he pays for it too."

Chapter 64

"Thirty minutes. No longer."

OKLAHOMA CITY was quiet at 3:45 A.M. The streets were wet and shinning from a late evening drizzle. So far, the hit was going according to plan, no surprises. The train was right where it was supposed to be. Bubbles could see it from the car. According to the porter who called from Chicago, 4 A.M. would be the best time to slip aboard the train, do the job and get back off before anyone knew what was going on.

Nearly everyone would be asleep, including the conductor. There would only be a few workers awake, loading supplies, preparing for the morning breakfast, but they would be far from where the passengers slept. All Bubbles would need is the master key, which the porter would give him when he boarded the train.

Bubbles looked at his new squeeze, Lee Shepard, who he needed just in case something went wrong on the train. If he was spotted and someone told the police they had seen a suspicious-looking black man leaving the train, they would be looking for a single male, not a couple. They were both sharply dressed and looked like they could pass for college professors. Staring into her eyes intensely, he said, "I'll be right back. Keep the engine running." He kissed her on the mouth—short and sweet.

Lee Shepard had no idea Bubbles was about to kill five men and she didn't want to know. Bubbles brought a bit more excitement than Dennis Edwards, the man she was committing adultery with. Besides, sex with Dennis wasn't what it used to be once Dennis' wife found out and confronted him. Now sex with him seemed like a wifely duty, boring, methodical, and terribly predictable. She was glad George, as she called him, rescued her after Marguerite's funeral at the reception.

"How long will you be, George?" Lee asked.

"As long as it takes," Bubbles said gruffly. "You just keep the engine runnin' and your mouth shut. You got that?"

"Got it, baby," Lee said, looking at him with wanton eyes. She loved it when he talked mean to her. It caused her juices to flow and made her feel alive.

"If the cops happen by while I'm on the train, what are you gonna tell 'em?"

"I'm gonna tell 'em my man had to use the restroom and will be right out and we'll be on our way."

"Good. Now, stick to the story and don't get creative. They'll buy that story and move on."

Bubbles opened the door and got out of the car, closing it behind him. Then he made his way to the train depot. He was wearing an expensive dark suit and tie. A black-and-white silk handkerchief that matched his cufflinks was in his upper left pocket.

Just before he entered the depot, he pulled his weapon from its holster strap and screwed on the silencer. He entered the empty station and looked around. Through the window in the back of the train station, he saw the porter returning his gaze. The porter raised his hand, summoning him. Bubbles looked to the left and to the right before moving toward the train.

The porter said, "Bubbles?"

He nodded.

The porter handed him the key and said, "You've got thirty minutes, no more. The conductor rises at 5 A.M. sharp. You take longer than thirty minutes and we're all looking at some serious time."

Bubbles handed the porter the payoff money. Napoleon, the snake that he was, knew that part of the Negro community's loyalty to him was not because he treated them fairly, but because he always paid well for information.

Bubbles said, "You're going to take care of the others, right?"

"Right," the porter said.

"Cabin numbers?"

"They've got 325, 326, and 327. Mr. Milano is in 325 by himself. Be careful. He sleeps with a gun under his pillow. The other four men are sharing cabins." The porter pulled out a pocked watch and opened it. "It's four A.M. Thirty minutes. No longer."

Chapter 65

I can be famous one day, who knows?

PREGNANT AT SEVENTEEN and having no idea who the father was, was keeping Johnnie up all night long, tossing and turning, wondering how she was going to get out of the mess she had made of her life. Without her money, she felt so powerless, so very vulnerable to the devices of men and the evil the world offered. Her mind drifted to a time when her mother was alive and remembered the story she had told her about Johnny Wise, her father.

Marguerite and Johnnie were in bathing suits, sitting by the pool at the famed Savoy Hotel, when Johnnie asked about her father. After much prodding and threatening, Marguerite told Johnnie a riveting emotional tale of love and betrayal. But later, Johnnie found out that it was all an elaborate lie. Johnny Wise was a good man and had been run out of town by Marguerite's lover, Sheriff Paul Tate, because Johnny Wise wouldn't sit by idly while his wife prostituted herself.

Maybe I should move to East St. Louis with my daddy and his wife. They'd love to have me there. I could sell my house and get the hell outta New Orleans for good. Then images of the movie she'd seen with Lucas entered her mind. It was called *A Street Car Named Desire.* The film had a profound effect on her. *Am I the real life Blanche Dubois? Am I? If not, is that how I'm going to end up, broke and used up?*

Johnnie quieted her mind and thought intensely about her dilemma. Decision time. Leave New Orleans broke and pregnant, or find someone who could get rid of the infant growing in her uterus.

But how can I kill my baby and live with myself? How? What other choice do I have? Have the baby? And then what? Work for the Beauregards the rest of my life? End up like Sadie? Disappoint her? Become the kind of woman she had warned me about? Life is so complicated! Life can be so fucked up! Well, I'm not gon' be broke! Fuck that! I'ma get my goddamned money back! The first thing I'ma do is quit workin' for the Beauregards. I'm through with that. I've met my grandfather and the rest of my folks, and that's enough for me.

They seem all right, I guess. Now I see why we're all whores. But I won't fuck up their family. They'll never know who I was as long as Grandpa doesn't say anything. If he ever regains his voice and tells them, what does it matter? They'll just deny it anyway. As a matter of fact, I shouldn't even go in tomorrow. Fuck 'em!

Naw, I'ma go in. I'ma tell Grandpa good-bye and that'll be that.

With Lucas going away, I'ma take Napoleon up on his offer to sing in the Bayou. After all, that's what I've always wanted to do. That time when I sang on Amateur Night was fabulous. I was on stage and the audience loved me. Napoleon said he would pay me $150 a week or more if they loved me. But I bet I can get more out of him than that. Hell, I can sing, play the piano, and write my own songs. Yeah, yeah—I can be famous one day, who knows?

The phone rang. Johnnie looked at the clock on her nightstand: 4 A.M. Still prostrate, Johnnie reached for the phone and said, "Hello."

"Hey, little sister. It's your big brother, Benny. I'm in trouble."

Johnnie shook her head, thinking, *what now?* "What's going on, Benny? Do you need money or something?"

"No. Nothing like that. Are you still friends with that Bentley guy?"

"Kinda. Why?"

"I had some Chicago gangsters tell me that if I didn't throw my fight next month, they would break both my hands so that I would never fight again."

"What?"

"Yeah. They meant business. Can you help me out? I'm undefeated and I'm destined to be the middleweight champion of the world someday. If I take a dive and it gets out, my career is over. Do you think Bentley knows somebody in Chicago that could take the heat off?"

"Benny, I just asked him to help me with another matter."

"You in a jam too, huh?"

"Yeah. My stockbroker ran off with all my money."

"Damn. When it rains, it pours, huh?"

Johnnie thought about telling him the rest of the bad news, but what good would it do? Instead, she said, "Yeah, and it's raining cats and dogs down here in New Orleans."

"I know I'm asking a lot, but can you talk to the guy? They want me to take a dive on some powder-puff-hittin' guy that I can whip blindfolded. Everybody'll know I threw the fight."

"Yeah, Benny. I'll talk to him, okay?"

"You think he'll take care of it?"

"If he can, he will."

"Thank you, little sister. Goodnight."

"Goodnight, Benny."

Chapter 66

"By we you mean you and Stefano, right?"

VINCENZO MILANO felt something nudging the back of his head. He was in such a deep sleep that at first he didn't feel anything. Milano was facing the wall, making the back of his head an easy target. But Bubbles, who was looking down at the sleeping Capo, seeing him clearly in the moonlit cabin, applied more pressure with the silenced weapon he wielded.

For a few brief moments, Bubbles' mind reverted to an earlier period in his life when he was in Claiborne Prison, doing time for three counts of armed robbery. He remembered the day that he saw a white inmate with a homemade knife approaching Napoleon Bentley as he stood in line in the prison cafeteria. He smiled when he thought of the irony of it all.

There he was, minding his own business, about to eat his dinner, when he saw what was about to happen to a white man who treated him with respect. It was Thanksgiving then too, almost eleven short years ago. Bubbles put down his fork and grabbed the white inmate. When he did, all hell broke loose. A race riot ensued and several prisoners were murdered, including the man who was attempting to kill Napoleon.

Now, here Bubbles was, about to kill the man who had set up the prison hit in the first place. He put the gun right next to Milano's ear and cocked it. "Vinnie, you're in the wrong business, man." Then he took a few steps backward, still pointing the gun at him.

Milano opened his eyes when he heard the cocking of a gun near his ear. Subtly, almost unnoticeably, he slid his hand under his pillow, reaching for his trusted revolver. Having it in his firm grip, he whirled around and attempted to point in the direction of the silhouette he saw.

Bubbles anticipated this and waited for the precise moment and kicked the gun out of his hand. It clumped to the floor and slid up against the wall. Then he said, "You have to be a light sleeper to last long in this business."

"Who's there?" Milano asked the voice. Bubbles stepped into the moonlight so he could be seen. "Bubbles?"

"In the flesh."

"That fuckin' bastard sent a nigger to take me out? I don't fuckin' believe it."

"Believe it, Vinnie. It's all over. Before you go, tell me a few things. If you talk, I'll do it quick. You won't feel a thing. I swear."

"I ain't gonna tell you shit, nigger, so do what you gotta do."

"Ahh, c'mon, Vinnie," Bubbles said, shaking his head. "I just wanna know if Sam is in on it."

"That's it?"

"That's it."

"Fuck you, nigger!"

Bubbles took a deep breath, shook his head, and said, "Nobody's coming to save you, Vinnie. They're all dead. I popped them first—execution style. They didn't feel a thing. Now, be reasonable, man."

A look of sheer terror crept across Milano's face when he realized he had no back-up. "What do you wanna know?"

"So, when you met with John Stefano three months ago, you were doing it for the three million in policy and collections, right? It wasn't personal, right? Just like when you set up the hit in Claiborne, it was about the money . . . not personal."

"Yeah, yeah. It wasn't because I hate Napoleon. He's all right for a Spaniard, I guess. But the Colored section was mine. I earned it."

"You may have earned it, but Napoleon did your time for the murder you committed in that bar. I think he earned it too. There's no harder time than the time we did in Claiborne, except for The Farm. You can believe that shit."

Suddenly, Milano frowned as the whole thing started to make sense to him. "How did you know about John and me? How did you find out? Who talked?"

"The maid was listening to every word, Vinnie. Every word."

"How did you know I was on this train?"

"We've got people all over. They tell us everything. In this case, it was the porter. When you came to New Orleans three months ago, it was—"

"Connie Giovanni," Milano said, finishing his sentence. "Where is she? I looked all over the place for that broad."

"We've got her stashed in Florida." Bubbles paused for brief moment. "Last question, Vinnie. Does Sam know about this or not?"

"No. Sam knows nothing. We figured he'd go along when we iced Bentley."

"By *we* you mean you and Stefano, right? No one else, right? Not the Commission, nobody, right?"

Milano nodded.

Bubbles' weapon hissed one time and a bullet entered Milano's head, exiting through the back, splashing gray matter against the wall. Then he left the cabin, making sure it was unlocked so the porter wouldn't be implicated when the bodies were found. If nobody talked, the cops, in all likelihood, would think another passenger entered the cabins and did the shootings when they looked at the passenger manifest. With the number of people getting on and off the train, anyone could have committed the crime—at least that's what Bubbles and Napoleon were hoping they would think.

Bubbles made his way back down the aisle and out the door and then down the stairs, where the porter waited for him. He gave him the key and went back to his car the same way he'd come. The car was still idling when he returned, and Lee Shepard was still there waiting for him. He put the car in gear and pulled off. He was going to take care of Preston Leonard Truman next.

Chapter 67

"The Fortuneteller."

"Sadie," Johnnie said in a low, almost inaudible tone. Unable to look her best friend in the eyes, she looked at the table. They were having breakfast in Johnnie's kitchen as usual. "I have something to tell you. I . . . I . . . I don't know how to say it."

Sadie stopped eating and looked at her, wondering what was going on in her young friend's mind. "Take your time. Is it about the Beauregards?"

"In a way. I'm quitting today."

Sadie started eating again, knowing that this day was inevitable. In her mind, Johnnie had plenty of ambition. Having her money stolen would only make her more ambitious, not less. There was no way she was going to be anybody's maid for very long. "I knew a girl like you wouldn't be there long."

Slightly offended, Johnnie said, "What do you mean by that?"

When Sadie saw the look on Johnnie's face and realized that she had inadvertently insulted her, she said, "You've got a lot of big plans for your life, Johnnie; plans that don't include being a maid. And I, for one, am happy for you. What's your next move?"

"Well, I need your help with something."

Sadie drank some of her orange juice before saying, "Just say it. You know you can tell me anything." She paused and waited for her to answer, but Johnnie remained quiet. Then it occurred to Sadie that Johnnie hadn't mentioned anything about her pregnancy. "Oh, I know. It's about you being pregnant, right?"

Johnnie's eyes welled and tears fell, which let Sadie know that whatever was bothering her, it had crushed her spirit. Sadie set her orange juice on the table, stood up, and went over to Johnnie. She embraced her, knowing full well what it felt like for an unwed woman to know she's pregnant for the first time. She knew all too well the range of emotions she was experiencing. She also knew that, even though Johnnie was a Christian, abortion was clinging to her mind like glue.

"I can't have this baby, Sadie," Johnnie said in utter desperation. "Do you know anybody that can help me get rid of it?"

"Are you absolutely sure you don't want to keep it?"

"I don't even know who the father is, Sadie. How can I have a baby when I don't know whose baby it is? And if I did have it, I would only end up like my mother, broke, and wishing I had done things differently. Do you know anybody who can do it for me?"

Sadie was quiet for a long minute before saying, "The Fortuneteller."

Chapter 68

"If she's a whore, yes!"

THE BEAUREGARDS were having breakfast in the dining room when Johnnie entered for the second time, bringing in more food and drink for her uncle, her aunt, and her first cousins, who were discussing the riot that took place three months earlier. The Shreveport Beauregards were in town too, but Beau didn't bring his wife and children. They had gone to her parents' home instead, and had taken Blue's children with them.

The problem the Beauregards seemed to be having was that the Negroes had started a riot for no reason, killed white men, women, and children, and no one had been arrested. They thought three months was more than sufficient time to find the killers. They were in favor of arresting any Negro they saw, just to get some kind of justice. Right or wrong, the Negroes had to pay.

When Johnnie walked in, nearly everyone at the table looked at her with accusing eyes. They had all read the stories about Marguerite being murdered. The papers had even printed stories about Marguerite and Richard Goode's supposed relationship. According to the August papers, Goode's murder was a revenge killing for Marguerite's murder, which was what angered Whites in the first place and sent them into a fiery rage.

"You know we're all in danger, don't you?" Eric threw out to his family. "Once a nigger kills a white man, he's gotta be put down. Otherwise, he'll kill again. He's like an animal and deserves the death of a dog—a bullet right between the eyes. That's what we used to do in the old days when they'd try to organize and kill good white Christians who paid good money for 'em. Then we'd cut off their ploys. If we don't do this, if we don't take care of these animals, they'll rape our women and our little girls!"

Beau, the son who was making love to Piper, his brother's wife, in the library when Johnnie walked in, said, "I don't know, Pop. It's been three months and the Negroes haven't killed anyone else. Besides, how do we know they started it?"

Eric looked at his favorite son for a moment or two. If Blue had said the same thing, Eric would have gotten angry with him. Blue had become a preacher, and Eric never forgave him. Eric didn't like preachers because he thought they were scam artists, getting rich off ignorant people who needed to believe in something other than themselves.

But since Beau made the remark, he ignored it, just like he ignored Beau's ongoing affair with Piper.

Eric looked at Johnnie and said, "Let's ask our new maid what she thinks about all this."

"Yeah, let's," Beau said.

Johnnie placed the orange juice and the milk on the table, and was about to leave the room when Eric said, "Are you any relation to the woman that was killed? Your last name is Wise, isn't it?"

"She was my mother, Mr. Beauregard."

"Your mother?"

"Yes, my mother," Johnnie said firmly and looked at Nathaniel, who was smiling.

"I suppose you approve of niggers killing white men, don't you?"

Johnnie didn't respond.

"It's okay," Eric prodded. "Tell us what you think, Johnnie."

Again, Johnnie didn't respond.

"You're glad the niggers killed Whites, aren't you? Admit it. There's no shame in wishing your mother's killers get what she got."

Johnnie looked unflinchingly into Eric's eyes before saying, "Do you really want me to answer your questions, Mr. Beauregard?"

"Of course I do. I want you to admit what we all know is the truth. The papers said Marguerite was a prostitute. Is that right? You, being her daughter, would know, wouldn't you?"

"Yes, sir, that's right."

"So, then . . . your mother was a whore that got what she deserved, right?"

"I'm not sure I follow you, Mr. Beauregard. Are you saying that any woman that does what my mother did should be beaten like an animal, shot in the head, and left to die on a lonely, dark road?"

"If she's a whore, yes! Whores are not people; they're things. Don't get me wrong. They serve a purpose, but when it comes to killin' 'em, well, they get what they get."

Chapter 69

The Miracle

FULL OF RAGE yet remaining calm in a very tense situation, Johnnie thought about her current situation—the pregnancy, the loss of wealth, mobsters threatening her brother, Benny, and the incarceration of Lucas. It had all happened at the same time. After all of that, after hitting rock bottom all of a sudden, she felt like she didn't have anything else to lose.

Having nothing to lose empowered her, providing the gumption she needed at that moment. She felt liberated from the fear of losing everything, especially since Napoleon had promised to help her. She was confident he would. She had a job singing at the Bayou and no longer needed to work for the Beauregards. Besides all of that, in her mind, Marguerite didn't deserve to be bad-mouthed by her own brother.

Johnnie nonchalantly said, "So, the same thing should happen to Piper, right? I mean, she is fuckin'

Beau. She was fuckin' him in the library on the table my first day here."

With the exception of Beau, every mouth in the room fell open. Beau looked at his brother and doubled over with laughter. "What can I say, Blue? I told you she was a whore before you married her. Now you know the truth!" Beau continued laughing.

It was one thing for the Negro maid to make a wild accusation, and quite another for Beau to not only confirm the accusation, but call her the whore she knew she was in front of the family. It was too much to bear. Totally embarrassed, Piper stood up and ran out of the room and up the stairs.

Blue left the dining room seconds later, calling her name. "Piper! Piper! Piper!"

"Now, just a minute," Ethel finally said. "There's no cause to use that kinda language."

"You told me you had changed!" Blue screamed. "You told me you would never do this again!"

"You knew how I was when you met me!" Piper screamed. "Don't play dumb now!"

Then the screaming became unintelligible, but everyone could hear Blue and Piper upstairs screaming at each other, even though they were still in the dining room.

Meanwhile, Johnnie, who was looking at Ethel incredulously, said, "Is that all you can think about, Ethel? What kind of language I used? Your son is having relations with your other son's wife. Is that better?"

Ethel quickly composed herself, being the lady that she was, completely ignored Beau's confession, and said, "Johnnie, we're not going to sit here and listen to your lies about this fine Southern family. And if you want to stay employed, you had better apologize for your slanderous outbursts."

Johnnie looked at Ethel and shook her head. "Ethel, three months ago, you told me you didn't know why Betty Jean left, but you knew all along what was going on, didn't you?"

"Why, whatever do you mean?" Ethel asked, pretending like she didn't know where this conversation was going.

"You didn't know Eric was constantly touching her, begging her for her sweet nectar?"

"No! That's not true! Eric would never do anything like that," Ethel shouted.

When Katherine heard what was being said, she walked into the dining room and yelled, "Johnnie! Don't!" She knew what was about to happen, and Katherine didn't want the truth to come out.

"Speaking of whores," Johnnie began again, relishing every moment of all the revelations, especially after Eric pretty much told her that Marguerite deserved to be murdered. "Are you going to tell me that you didn't know about your husband and Katherine?"

"What on earth are you talking about, Johnnie?" Ethel asked, continuing the shameless farce.

"Johnnie, please . . . please don't do this!" Katherine begged.

Johnnie looked at Katherine briefly, rolled her eyes then continued. "Oh, come on! The way I hear it, Beau used to have his way with her too. I guess it's Eric's turn now, huh? You can pretend all you want, but I saw the look in your eyes when I was coming back to the house. And I remember how you ran up the stairs when you saw Eric returning to the house after he'd gotten his brown sugar. Can you deny it?"

"All right!" Eric shouted. "That's enough! You're fired! Get out! Now!"

Johnnie laughed hard and from her belly. "Fired? Me? Please. I quit!"

The idea of being fired on the day she was going to quit was hilarious. At first she didn't know how to tell them that she was leaving, but Eric made it easy by reducing Marguerite to something less than human status. Even though Johnnie herself was glad her mother was dead, having been treated so badly by her, Eric had no right to say what he said about her. Now was as good a time as any to drop the final bomb on them. She wasn't going to ever tell them, but Eric forced her to tell it all.

"Eric, I'll gladly leave this tomb you call a family, but before I go, let me tell you one last thing. The whore that you say deserved to die was your sister." She paused for a second and let her words flood their minds. "Yeah, that's right! That makes me your niece!"

"Why, that's a goddamned lie!" Eric retorted angrily. "No fuckin' way I'd have a nigger for a sister. No fuckin' way!"

"The truth hurts, doesn't it?" Johnnie said, looking at Ethel. "Did I say that well enough for you?" she said to Ethel, and then turned her attention back to Eric. "It's the truth. Your father had a Negro mistress named Josephine Baptiste, and they had a daughter named Marguerite, the whore that you said deserved what she got." She turned her attention to Ethel again. "Remember my first day here? Remember when I wanted to see your library? Remember when I wanted to see the men in your family? I was looking for

Nathaniel. And only then did I accept the job, remember?"

Ethel, still trying to maintain her composure and a measure of dignity, was reliving it all in her compartmentalized mind, and when she put it all together, she put her hands to her face and wept, not because she was hurt by the revelation, but because of the coming scandal. This was going to be big. It was going to set tongues on fire with gossip, and Ethel couldn't bear the thought of it.

All of a sudden, Nathaniel stood up from his wheelchair. They were all stunned by this and stared in silenced awe as they witnessed a bona fide miracle. Although his voice was weak, he was able to speak clearly and distinctly and could be understood by them all.

"It's true, Eric," Nathaniel confirmed. "She is your niece." And with that, he fell forward into his breakfast and died.

Chapter 70

The Second Miracle

"Grandpa!" Beau screamed and hurried to his aid, but it was too late. He was gone.

After a moment or two, in a state of shock, Beau walked toward the kitchen like he was a zombie. Just as he was leaving the room, a butcher's knife appeared out of nowhere, it seemed, and plunged deep into his heart, all the way to the hilt. Beau gasped! His eyes bulged out of his head as he staggered around the room, knocking over precious crystal, trying desperately to dislodge the sharp blade from his heart.

Upon seeing this, Katherine fled.

Blue, who had wielded the knife, stepped into the dining room and watched as his brother futilely pulled at the knife. He had a gun at his side, but no one saw it. Instead, they focused on the look of pure evil that covered his face. His eyes were the conduit that transmitted satisfaction impulses to his brain, letting him know that his brother would die any moment now. He had already strangled Piper upstairs, and she too wore the same shocked look as her soon-to-die lover. Finally, Beau fell on the table and died right next to Nathaniel.

Blue walked over to his deceased brother and looked into the vacant eyes that were still bulging out of his head, staring at the ceiling, still surprised by the sudden, sharp pain. He screamed, "You shouldn't have done it, Beau! You shouldn't have fucked my wife! She was my wife, and I loved her!" Then he put the gun to his own head, blew his brains out, and fell on top of his slain brother.

Johnnie stood there, stone-faced, unable to move, watching it all in complete horror. It had all happened incredibly fast. No one could have predicted this. She didn't mean for any of this to happen. She just wanted to get back at Eric for what he'd said about her mother. And now, three men were dead. Three of her white relatives were gone just that quickly, seconds, it seemed, after revealing the family secret.

Suddenly, Johnnie felt hands around her throat. Powerful hands were squeezing and she couldn't breathe. She grabbed and pulled at the hands, but couldn't free herself.

Eric, who had lost his mind, was in a fit of rage. In his mind, Johnnie had killed his father and his favorite son, Beau. For that, she had to die, just like them—on the same day, in fact. He would see to it.

"You fucking nigger bitch," Eric screamed. "You killed my boy! You killed my boy! You killed Beau! I'm gonna kill you!"

As he applied more pressure, as he watched her gasp for air, as she weakened, and life began to evaporate from Johnnie's body, Eric saw his blood sprayed into Johnnie's face.

A gunshot registered in Johnnie's mind. Her eyes were closed. The sound was piercing and made her ears ring. She even smelled the sulfur. It happened that close to her. She felt the blood on her face and wiped it. She opened her eyes just in time to watch Eric fall on the table with the rest of the Beauregard men—dead and gone, just that quick. She looked at Ethel, who was now pointing the gun at her. Johnnie closed her eyes again. She knew it was all over.

While Eric was choking the life out of Johnnie, Ethel picked up the gun that Blue once held and fired a single shot into the back of her husband's head. Then she pointed the gun at Johnnie, saying, "You ruined the Beauregard reputation. For that, I'm going to kill you where you stand."

"Nooooo!" Morgan, the butler, shouted and grabbed Ethel. The gun fired just before he grabbed her.

Johnnie heard the bullet whistling as it came directly at her forehead. Something inside her frightened mind told her to open her eyes and turn around. She opened her eyes but she couldn't move, believing she was a corpse like the other men who had died suddenly. The voice told her again to turn around. This time she obeyed, but it felt like an out of body experience, like she was looking at it all from the ceiling, seeing Morgan grab Ethel, hearing the gun fire. Everything was moving in slow motion.

Then she saw it. The bullet in the wall was right where her head had been. In her heart, Johnnie knew God had performed a second miracle. She deduced that somehow the bullet that Ethel fired at her had disappeared before entering her head and reappeared behind her head and entered the wall. She looked toward the heavens and wept uncontrollably.

Morgan took the gun out of Ethel's hand. Fortunately, when Blue stabbed Beau, Katherine ran and got Morgan. By the time they returned to the dining room, Ethel had shot Eric and was ready to shoot Johnnie too.

The scandal would have been too much to bear, so Ethel killed her husband and had every intention of killing the woman who had caused it all—Johnnie Wise, her niece by marriage. Later, however, when she had time to think about it, she told the police that shooting Eric was the only way to keep him from strangling Johnnie. No one contradicted her story. There would still be a scandal, but Ethel would be seen as somewhat of a heroine for saving a defenseless Negro woman from certain death.

But Johnnie knew that later, after the funerals, she could get money for her silence. In her mind, she was entitled to it anyway. After all, she was a Beauregard, wasn't she? She believed Ethel would pay her because the thought of going to prison for murdering her husband was far too daunting to contemplate.

Part Four

Armed & Dangerous

Chapter 71

Suspicion

OKLAHOMA CITY MASSACRE was splashed across the evening edition of the *Chicago Tribune*. The featured article said that Vincenzo Milano was a well-known hood who worked for the Chicago Mob. They found numerous guns and ammunition in the cabin of the dead mobsters. The article went on to say that it appeared that the Chicago Mob was moving in on the New Orleans Syndicate. They based this on the mode of travel, the guns and ammo found at the scene, and the ticket stubs found in the cabins.

When Sam read this, he nearly flew into a rage. Every radio and television station was talking about the massacre. Sam began to wonder what the Commission was thinking about the massacre. This was the kind of thing that could start a war, and a war was bad for business—so was this kind of news coverage. There would be pressure for the FBI to get involved.

Sam had no idea what was going on, but because of the news reports, he believed John Stefano would think he was coming after him. He had to call John Stefano and make sure he understood that Chicago had no intention of moving in on him. He picked up the phone and called New Orleans.

John Stefano's wife answered the phone and told him he had an important call from Chicago. "What can I do for you, Sam?" Stefano said without emotion.

"I have no idea why he was headed your way. My guy was acting on his own, John," Sam said cryptically. "This was a solo show, ya know what I mean?"

Stefano remained quiet as he thought about what he'd heard Sam say. "I think we need to have a sit-down, Sam."

"Fine. Where?"

"Vegas. There's a fight there next month. We can meet at the usual place, if that's okay with you."

"Fine with me, John, but why so long? I'd like to have the sit down . . . say . . . this weekend."

"Let's let things settle down, Sam. Ya know what I mean?" He paused for a moment. "Let's wait and see what they do," he said, referring to a pending FBI investigation.

"Vegas then. The usual place."

Stefano didn't know if Sam thought he killed Vinnie or not, but he wasn't about to take a chance. As far as he was concerned, Sam could be in it too—up to his neck. Vinnie could have told Sam everything when he returned to Chicago three months ago. Sam may have played it cool with Vinnie, pretended to go along, and had his own people pop Vinnie for going against orders. He may have made Salvatore disappear too.

Stefano also considered the alternative. It was possible that Sam didn't know anything about the Bentley hit just as he had said. But Stefano didn't know, and one mobster could never trust another, which is why the situation was so dangerous. Once the killing started, there were two ways to end it. One was an all-out war until one Boss killed the other. The other way to end a war would be to sit down with the Commission, the ruling body of mobsters that made the final decisions on family disputes. After carefully considering all the options, John Stefano called New York.

Sam didn't trust Stefano either. He had no idea Vinnie had left Chicago. Since he was going to New Orleans with four of his best guys, he knew he was going to kill Bentley. Two questions coursed through Sam's mind. Did Stefano sanction the Bentley hit? If he did, that meant Stefano had broken his word. The other question that plagued his mind was, did Stefano find out that Vinnie was going to take out Bentley, take over the Colored section, and then move in on him? If that's what Stefano believed, he may have taken Vinnie out first. And he was smart enough to do it far from his own territory. However, Sam thought there was another alternative. Napoleon Bentley could be involved too.

Sam quickly dismissed the notion, because there was no way Bentley would know Vinnie was on that particular train. There was no way Vinnie was going to tell Bentley he was coming to kill him. And even if he did, he wouldn't tell him when, where, and what time he'd be coming to New Orleans. For those reasons, Sam believed it had to be Stefano.

He further reasoned that Stefano had to let Bentley live, in order to make it appear that Sam had taken out his own man because he could never admit that he was going to move in on Stefano, just as Stefano could never admit that he had broken his word and ordered the Bentley hit. To kill Bentley now would make it obvious that Stefano had popped Vinnie. That's when Sam called New York.

Chapter 72

"Leave now. Tonight."

"It's done," Bubbles said when he walked into Napoleon's office. "The shit'll be hittin' the fan any time now."

"Did you take care of Preston?" Napoleon asked and continued rocking in his chair, slow and steady.

"Yeah," Bubbles said. "I almost felt sorry for 'im. But with the money we're gonna make on this deal, we'll be set for life."

"Uh-huh. What did he say?"

Bubbles reached into his pocket and pulled out a thick wad of money. He pulled the rubber band off, found a five-dollar bill, and handed it to Napoleon. "He said just what you said he'd say. He asked why was I going to kill him since he followed orders and recruited Lucas just like you asked him to."

"And you made it look like a robbery?"

"Yeah."

"How much did you get?"

"Three hundred dollars. You wanna slice?"

"Nah, keep it. We've got bigger fish to fry now, though. You read the papers this morning?"

"Sho' did. What's their next move?"

Napoleon leaned forward, put both elbows on the table, and made a steeple formation with his hands. "George, my man, it's all coming together. Sam and John are probably on the phone as we speak, making plans for a sit-down with the Commission because they can't trust each other." He smiled. "That's why the plan will work. Mobsters are greedy and they know they can't trust each other, so they don't communicate. They can't afford to say much of anything about what they know and what they suspect, see?"

Bubbles nodded and sat in the leather chair in front of Napoleon's desk and relaxed. "And you don't think they'll suspect you?"

"Of course they'll suspect me. That's why I told you not to beef up security. They think I'm weak and we want them to continue believing that. I'm sure John knows all about Lucas and Marla. He knows I know about it and haven't done a damn thing about it. If I won't kill Lucas and Marla for fuckin' each other, which shows them how weak I am, they won't believe I have the balls to kill Vinnie and Sal. Then they'll suspect each other more. So, yeah, old friend, they'll suspect me, but they'll suspect each other more."

The phone rang and Napoleon answered. "Yeah, what is it?" He listened for about five seconds. Then the devilish grin he was famous for emerged and lit up his whole face. "Thanks. Come by the Bayou tonight and I'll take care of you . . . yeah, I'll get you a seat by the stage . . . yeah, you and your husband." He hung up and looked at Bubbles and said, "Vegas in a couple weeks. But Stefano called New York. You know what that means, right?"

"Yeah, they'll have a sit-down with the Commission and straighten out their problems. They'll figure you did it all and decide to come after you."

"Exactly. But when and where, I'll decide."

"How are you going to do that?"

"There's a fight in Vegas around the same time they'll be there. That's where they'll try to take me out."

"How do you know that?"

"I don't, but I just got a call from Stefano's maid. Sam called, and they're going to Vegas."

"But what about the sit-down with the Commission? Why would they wait until the fight? Why not come up in here and blow your brains right outta yo' head?"

"Because these guys don't work that way. They'll get together and talk and plan it all out. These guys like to use finesse when they kill you. The trick is to kill the guy when he thinks he's safe."

"Okay, but why Vegas? How do they even know you'll be there?"

"The informant will tell 'em. Make sure all of our people know about us going to the fight. Make sure absolutely everybody knows and everybody is talking about it. The informant'll run right to Stefano, and he'll think the hit fell right in his lap."

"When are you going to tell me who this informant is, man? Don't you think I should know?"

"No. Not now. It'll all become crystal clear to everyone soon. Hold on a second." He picked up the phone and asked the operator to make a long distance call to Fort Lauderdale. "Vegas . . . the Sands . . . yeah, both of you. Leave now. Tonight. One other thing: make sure the stuff is where it's supposed to be. My man is leaving tonight and he'll need it." He hung up the phone and looked at Bubbles. "We're all set."

Bubbles frowned before saying, "Who was that?"

"Some people I know." Napoleon paused. "Listen, let me pull your coat on something now, okay?"

"Okay," Bubbles said and leaned forward.

"For this thing to work, I've gotta bring in some of my people from Chicago and some outside sources nobody in the Syndicate knows about—the kind of people they would never deal with or suspect. It's going to be fuckin' beautiful. But don't worry, you've got the Colored section just like I said. The Italians won't allow Negroes in their thing, okay? You know I don't give a fuck about race. They do. The fuckin' dagos!"

"I know, man. Don't worry about it. Three million dollars a year is enough for me."

"A lot of things are going to change once we take out Stefano. I won't be able to come down here as much as I do now. Don't take that shit personally. It's self-preservation. That's all, okay, my man?"

The two men stood up and embraced.

"Listen, George. I need you to get to Florida and take care of Connie and that other thing we discussed. We just got a few loose ends to tie up and we're home, my friend."

"I'll get a plane tonight. Where are we with Lucas?"

"It's all set. Three months and he's in the Army, and then Johnnie is mine. I've got another move or two left if I need them."

Chapter 73

"Mama, you were right."

THE GUN FIRED and the bullet was coming right at her head, Johnnie remembered. She could see it in her mind's eye as she stood in her shower, washing Eric's blood and brain fragments from her face and hair while simultaneously reliving the briefest, yet most terrifying moment in her young life. *POW!* The sound of the gun exploded in her mind, the smell of sulfur filled her nostrils, but the bullet missed her. This visual filled her mind like a thirty-second horror flick stuck in a perpetual loop, playing the whole incident in her mind, stopping, rewinding, and playing again and again. But as the incident played, everything was moving in slow motion.

"Johnnie!" Sadie yelled through the bathroom door. She had driven a severely shaken Johnnie home and escorted her up the stairs to the bathroom, undressed her, and helped her get in the shower, promising to return after she changed clothes. "I'll be downstairs, okay? I'll put on some coffee, okay?"

"Okay," Johnnie managed to say.

"You all right?"

"No, Sadie, I'm not," Johnnie mumbled. "I can't get it out of my head. It just keeps replaying in my mind all by itself."

Sadie felt the pain Johnnie was experiencing as she listened to the emotion in her words, but she also felt powerless. If she had been cut, Sadie could have cleaned her wound, put some alcohol on it, bandaged it, and given her some aspirins for the pain. But what could she do for the mind? How could she ease the pain Johnnie felt?

On the way home, Johnnie retold the entire story, describing the deaths of her grandfather, Beau, Blue, and then finally Eric Beauregard in chilling, spine-tingling detail, while repeating the arguments that brought the situation to a head. As she listened, Sadie felt as if she were actually in the Beauregard home, as if she were in the room, listening, watching, yet powerless to change the terrible events taking place.

With tears in her eyes, Sadie said, "I'll wait for you downstairs."

Johnnie didn't respond. A few minutes later, she turned off the water, pulled back the shower curtain, and stepped onto a thick, black rug. Like an automaton, she grabbed a lavender beach towel, dried herself, and then wrapped it around her body. She grabbed another towel and dried her shoulder-length, naturally wavy hair. When she finished, she wiped the steamed mirror so she could see herself.

She took a deep breath and exhaled. Then she looked at her hair to make sure there were no more brain fragments in it. She closed her eyes, and aloud she said, "Thank You, God, for saving my life." Almost immediately after saying this, she began to blame God for everything that happened, including the murders.

In her mind, there were a number of opportunities for God to step in and do something, but He didn't. Sure, He had performed a miracle and saved her life, but Johnnie thought that the only reason He saved her life was to make sure she suffered some more. Still looking in the mirror, she placed her hand on her belly, as if checking for yet another miracle, but she knew instinctively that she was still carrying a new life—somebody's baby. She still had to see The Fortuneteller.

Then she said, "Why didn't You make this baby disappear like You made that bullet disappear? *If* You made it disappear. Ethel probably just missed. Yeah, that's what happened. Ethel missed, and that's all there is to it!" She quieted herself for a moment, still looking at herself in the mirror. "Mama, you were right. Nobody's going to help me but me. I've gotta be tough. I've gotta be strong. And I will be. I will be strong. I will be strong. I . . . will . . . be . . . strong!"

Somehow, she began to believe her own words. The perpetual horror flick stopped playing, and she didn't feel weak anymore. She grabbed her robe, put it on, and went downstairs, still repeating the words that empowered her. "I will be strong!"

Chapter 74

"You know what I mean, Sadie?"

"How are you feeling?" Sadie asked when Johnnie entered the kitchen.

"Much better," Johnnie replied and sat down at the table.

"Well, you look almost relieved," Sadie said after going over to the stove and grabbing the coffee pot. As she poured, she asked, "What happened?"

Johnnie poured some cream into her coffee, put in a couple of teaspoons of sugar, and stirred. "Nothing happed. I just remembered something my mother told me at the Savoy before Richard Goode killed her."

Sadie sat down and sipped her coffee. She knew her friend was feeling vulnerable and weak no matter what she said. She knew she had to choose her words carefully. "What did she tell you, Johnnie?"

Johnnie looked into Sadie's eyes and said, "I've gotta be tough. And I'm glad she did."

"Well, I hope you don't think you're over this thing already, because you're not. You're still in shock, the way I see it."

"Whether I'm in shock or not, I don't know. What I do know is I've gotta press on. I've still got somebody's baby in me, and I want it out. We need to see The Fortuneteller as soon as possible. Tomorrow, if she can do it. I've gotta take control of my life. No one else is going to do it for me. I'ma start by gettin' rid of this baby."

"Are you sure you want to do this?"

"I'm three months as it is, Sadie," Johnnie said, unaware of her harsh tone. "Life is short. I think what happened today proves that, don't you?"

"Okay, Johnnie," Sadie said with resignation. "I'll call her and see if I can set it up for tonight, if you're sure you're up to it."

"No, not tonight, Sadie. See if she'll take me tomorrow. Tonight I have some business to take care of."

"What business?"

"My brother's in trouble."

"Benny?" Sadie questioned. The thought of him excited her as memories of the one night they had together at the Savoy hotel invaded her mind, and evoked a momentary lust-filled vision of that past experience. "What kind of trouble?"

"Some Chicago mobsters want him to throw the fight next month in Las Vegas."

"What?"

"Yep. They told him if he didn't throw the fight, he'd never fight again, or something like that."

"So, he wants you to talk to Napoleon?"

"Yeah. I told him I'd do what I could."

"Um."

"Um, what?"

"Nothing.

"I'm not going to do it with him if that's what you're worried about. Napoleon's got plenty of women to screw. He doesn't need me."

"Didn't he try to rape you last time you went to his office?"

Johnnie remembered the lied she'd told her friend. "Last time I went there, he had one of the waitresses between his legs when I walked into his office. Her head was bobbin' up and down and he was groanin'. So, there you have it."

"When was this?"

"Yesterday."

Puzzled, Sadie asked, "What were you doing there?"

"I needed a favor. He's the man to see when you need a favor around these parts." She paused and questioned whether she should tell it all, and decided she would.

"The whole truth of it is that I wanted him to track down Sharon Trudeau and get me my money, Sadie. There's no feeling like the feeling of being broke. When you don't have money, you don't have power. I know that now. Being broke limits my choices. I know that now too. A few months ago, I told Eric if he didn't show me some respect, I'd quit. That's power. When you don't need their jobs, you run things, not them.

"Then you tell me Sharon stole my money and I can't quit. Just like that, I'm in the goddamned poor house—broke as hell." As she spoke, Johnnie didn't realize it, but her face had twisted into an angry scowl.

She looked angry enough to kill. "I don't like that shit either." Johnnie continued her tirade. "You don't know how you're going to pay bills or nothin'.

"Next thing you know, you're willing to sell yourself. And you think of ways to justify that shit too. You tell yourself there's no other way, when in fact, you could work like everybody else. But you don't want to do that. You want to live carefree with no money worries. It disgusts me to even think about this shit!"

When Johnnie heard herself say this, the story her mother had told her about Benny's father, Michael, came to mind. Marguerite and Michael were in love and ran away to Chicago together. One thing led to another, and she ended up pregnant, on her own, and broke. Selling herself was her only means of generating some income, and she believed she had to submit to the humiliation. Marguerite bought a bus ticket back home to New Orleans, where she had to listen to Josephine's "I told you so" speech the moment she walked into the house.

Johnnie had judged her mother harshly for this and now, even though she had been smarter, planned better, and made more money than Marguerite ever dreamed of having, she was almost in the same position, having to choose the poor-house or selling herself. It was quite sobering.

"When I thought about it, Sadie, I had made up my mind that if Napoleon wanted to fuck me again, I would let him. If that's what I had to do to get my money, I would have. It's strange that when you get older, when you experience more and more evil, you understand the evil that people do."

Sadie sipped her coffee and listened because she had made those same choices years ago. She regretted it, but at the same time, she didn't. Her bills were being paid, she had plenty of food in her refrigerator, she lived in an affluent Colored neighborhood, but she had no freedom. She didn't even have a real man.

All she had was Santino Mancini, her part-time lover and the father of her children. While Sadie would never admit to it, she knew that she, like many other women in her position, had chosen a life of prostitution because it was much easier than making a living on her own in a world that stacked the deck against those of the female persuasion.

"You know what I mean, Sadie?"

"Yeah, Johnnie . . . believe me, I know."

Chapter 75

"Okay. I'll let Benny know."

NAPOLEON BENTLEY saw Johnnie enter the Bayou the moment she walked in. She was looking good—too good for someone of Lucas Matthews' caliber. As he watched her from across the room, erotic visions of their naked bodies entwined in a secluded retreat made him hard. She was close to giving him everything he wanted; anything he wanted, in fact—sex, more sex, oral sex, kinky sex, if he wanted it.

He knew this because for the third day in a row, she had come to his domain, looking for him, seeking his help, just as he knew she would. He took a sip of his drink, continued staring at her, shook his head in wanton desire, and smiled. *It's going to feel so damned good when she finally gives it up. I can hardly wait.*

When he saw her making her way over to his table, he went to his office so they could be alone. Less than a minute later, he heard a knock at the door.

"Come in," he called out.

The door opened and Johnnie walked in. Everything was red. Her dress, her pumps, her nails and her thick, kissable lips, all were red. He wanted her. He wanted her badly, but knew there was no way he could show her his true feelings.

"Johnnie, we have to stop meeting like this. Three days in a row? With Lucas in jail, people will talk."

"People always talk, Napoleon. That's all they know how to do. But when it comes to solving problems, I go wherever I need to go to get what I need done."

"Ah, so you need something again? What is it this time?"

"You haven't heard about what happened today?"

"Yeah, I heard. I hear everything. You seem okay, though. Most people would be in bed, contemplating suicide. But not you. You're a tougher woman than most," he said, flattering her. "Have a seat."

Johnnie sat down and looked at his dark, penetrating eyes, saying, "If you knew what happened, why didn't you come and check on me and make sure I was okay? That's what friends do. If something like that happened to you, I would care enough to make sure you were okay."

"You would, huh? And why is that?" Napoleon asked, loving all of this. It couldn't be going any better.

"Well, I thought we were friends. Are we?"

"Friends, huh?" Napoleon said with a harsh tone, but it was all a part of his game. "You only come to the Bayou when you want something. Friends don't use friends and then cast them away once they've gotten what they want. So, let's just cut to the chase. What do you need this time, Johnnie?"

"You remember my brother, Benny, don't you?"

"Vaguely. Why?"

"He called me late last night from San Francisco. Some men from Chicago threatened to hurt him if he doesn't throw the fight in Las Vegas next month."

Napoleon leaned back in his chair, put his feet up on the desk, and slowly rocked back and forth. "So, it's your brother fighting, huh?"

"So, you know about this?"

"I knew about a fight in Vegas, yes. There's a big meeting being held there also, so I'll be going to Vegas. I guess I'll see the fight too. Perhaps you should come to Vegas with us. No strings attached. That way you can see your brother fight."

"If you find Sharon Trudeau, I could pay my own way. Have your people found her yet?"

"Not yet, but we have an idea where she is."

"Where?"

"It's better you don't know the details."

"Okay, but can you help my brother?"

"Listen, if Chicago is involved, there's only so much I can do. I can't tell other Bosses what to do. If the Chicago people made a move on your brother, it could get very sticky. If I ask them to call off their people, I'll owe them. And these people usually demand big favors."

"Well, when you find Sharon, I'll be glad to pay them."

Napoleon laughed. "These people don't accept money as payment. They want favors. Big favors. I don't know that I wanna put myself in that kinda position. You never want to owe these guys anything. I think I've spoiled you by doing things for free."

"I appreciated you being a gentleman, Napoleon, and helping me out like this in my time of need."

"The only thing I can promise you is that I'll look into it, okay?"

"Okay. I'll let Benny know."

"When do you think you'll be ready to sing for us here at the Bayou?"

"After what happened today, I need to take some time off. I still see it all in my mind from time to time. I'm doing a good job controlling the images right now, but it was difficult to be in a room where people are dying all around you. You know what I mean?"

"Yeah, it's gotta be hard on you. If you ever want to talk about it, I'm here for you . . . now, if you like."

Chapter 76

"Two hundred fifty thousand and some change."

THE PLANE LANDED in Fort Lauderdale at 8:25 P.M. and Bubbles went directly to locker number 1619, where a loaded pistol and a silencer sat in a briefcase. There was an envelope with instructions inside, along with two keys, and pictures with names on the back. One key was for the car he would be using, and the other was his motel key. The instructions gave him the location for the car and the motel. After locating the vehicle, he got in and drove to the motel he would be staying in. He placed his suitcase inside the room, closed the door and left.

Fifteen minutes later, he entered the lobby of the Fort Lauderdale Hilton, where he would be making the first of two payoffs that night. The lobby was bustling with people who were there for some sort of convention. There were so many people that they barely even noticed him. Those who did probably thought he worked there as a bellhop or something, as he was dressed in a black suit with thin pinstripes, and a white shirt, no tie. The top three buttons were open, as it was hot and sticky. The air conditioned hotel was a welcomed relief.

He picked up a hotel courtesy phone and asked for room 721. He didn't want to startle the woman and attract attention. This was supposed to be a quick payoff. In and out. So, he called first to let her know he was coming up—no surprises.

"Hello," the woman on the other end said.

"George Grant. Napoleon sent me."

"Yes. Come on up."

"I'll be right up."

Bubbles hung up the phone and made his way over to the stairs. The elevator would have been quicker, but he didn't want to be seen by guests who might have been riding. It was one thing to walk through a crowded lobby, and quite another being on an elevator with a limited number of people, who would probably remember seeing a well dressed Negro male. If anything went wrong, he could be easily identified, and that was the last thing he wanted. Besides, it was only seven floors.

The sound of his shoes colliding with metal echoed in the empty stairwell as he took his time climbing the stairs, ascending floor after floor until he reached the seventh. Prior to opening the door, he set down the bag with Connie Giovanni's money, and screwed on the silencer. Then he looked through the glass window to see if he spotted anyone. No one was there. He put the weapon in the small of his back for easy access when he needed it, picked up Connie's money, and went to room 721. He knocked on the door. A few seconds later, the door opened.

"Sharon Trudeau?" Bubbles asked, pretending that he hadn't seen the picture of her in the locker at the airport.

"Yes. Come in," she said. "Would you like a quick drink? My plane leaves for Switzerland in an hour and a half. I've gotta get going soon."

Sharon was a redhead, about five feet tall in heels, and okay to look at—nothing to get excited about, Bubbles thought.

"Sure, I've got time for a quick drink," he said then entered the hotel room and closed the door. "Take my advice and don't tell people where you're going, okay?"

"I've got bourbon. I hope that's okay."

"That's fine. Where do you want the money?"

"Just put it on the bed, will you?"

"Do you want to count it?" He went over to the bed and tossed the money on it. Then he looked in the bathroom to make sure they were alone.

"No. No need. I trust Napoleon," she said and poured the bourbon into a glass. "Tell me something, George. Why did he want me to steal Johnnie's money if he was going to give it right back to her? Don't get me wrong. I'm glad to give it back to her, considering that Napoleon matched what I stole from her. And I get to keep the other four million. A nice take for very little work. So tell me, why did he want me to steal her money, only to give it right back to her?"

"He wants her."

Sharon frowned. "That's a lot of trouble to go through to get a woman, don't you think? I mean I'm happy with my end, but why not use seduction?"

"It's a long story, to be honest, Sharon."

Sharon handed him his drink and said, "It's been my experience that a long story is usually a short, complicated story. Let's hear it."

"Let's finish our business first," he said and waited for her to drink her bourbon first. "Where's Johnnie's money?"

"I'll get it for you." Sharon walked over to the closet and pulled out one of four large suitcases. She grunted a little when she pulled it out. "Can you help me with this? I had a bellhop bring it into the room for me."

Bubbles set down his drink and went over to the closet. At six-four, 260 pounds, the suitcase was easy for him to pick up. He carried it to the bed and tried to open it, but it was locked. He looked at Sharon. "Keys?"

Sharon tossed a key to him and sipped her bourbon.

Shocked at what he saw, without thinking, he said, "All of this is Johnnie's?"

"Yep," she said as she went back to the bar. Then she continued, saying, "Two hundred fifty thousand and some change. Tell her it's going to cost more to buy back into the companies because the stock went up. I have a complete list of companies if she wants to buy back in, and a list of investment opportunities she should take a serious look at. And tell her I'm very sorry that I had to—"

Sharon never finished her sentenced. The last thing she would ever hear was the hissing sound the pistol made when Bubbles squeezed the trigger. She dropped the glass and fell to the floor, dead.

He returned the gun back to the small of his back, closed the suitcase and locked it, grabbed Connie

Giovanni's money, and was about to leave when he heard someone knock at the door.

"Bellhop, Miss Trudeau. I'm here to take your luggage downstairs. Your cab is here."

Bubbles kept his cool. He knew something like this could happen, no matter how well you plan out a hit. You do the best you can to get in and out as quickly as you can without being seen. This was unexpected, but he'd deal with it. He set down the money, went to the door, and looked through the peephole. He saw the bellhop and opened the door so the first thing the bellhop would see was the luggage.

The bellhop walked in and *hiss, hiss*—two in the back of the head. He was dead too. Bubbles then grabbed the money and quickly made his way down the stairs and out the back door of the hotel. It was time to pay off Connie Giovanni next, but he wasn't going to kill her. She was going to live.

Chapter 77

A Meeting Foretold

THE FORTUNETELLER felt a familiar tingle in her spine when she heard rapid knocking on her front door, which indicated that the special customer she had been expecting had come to her secluded domicile. From the moment she got the phone call from Sadie Lane, The Fortuneteller knew something was different about Johnnie Wise. She didn't fully understand why she felt this way, but she knew the fog that clouded her ability to *see* would be lifted the moment she laid eyes on the young woman.

Jupiter DeMille was The Fortuneteller's name, and she was a fifth generation soothsayer in the DeMille lineage, which made her ability to see, that is, to look upon an individual and know what is unknown, legendary. Some fortunetellers needed to touch their customers; some needed a personal possession; some needed to visit the home of their customers. But not Jupiter DeMille. Like Johnnie Wise, the customer standing on the other side of her door, she was special too.

Jupiter had gotten her name in 1653, three hundred years earlier, when her great great grandmother, Afeni, received a vision that would come to pass in 1893, the year Jupiter was born. She was sixty years old, still a virgin, and didn't look a day over thirty-five. Men found her attractive, but none dared approach her doorsteps, fearing that she would put a curse on them. They were right.

The women in the DeMille clan never married before they reached the age of sixty. Sex before then would cause them to lose their sight before the time, making it necessary to rely on tarot cards and the like. The DeMille women remained fertile for one year after their sixtieth birthday, which was when they took a man for the first time, conceiving almost immediately.

Jupiter DeMille knew that every life had a story and a purpose; both of which led to understanding. She also knew that life itself was about an individual's story, the choices they made, and the results of those choices. She further knew that far too often, the history of a woman was too painful for the woman to deal with. Rather than working through the pain that her story produced, she suppressed it, hid it, denied it, so that she could have a semblance of the happiness that constantly eluded her, only to have her story resurface again and again, experiencing an even more intensified pain that could never be medicated.

Chapter 78

You will never amount to anything.

THE DOOR WAS OPENING, and it was dark in the quiet, thickly wooded area near Bayou Cane, Louisiana. Badly in need of oil, the door whined sour notes, the kind of creaking that promised terror and foreboding expectations that made a person's blood run cold. And run cold it did as Johnnie stood there, inches away from sprinting to her car and beating the wind back to Baroque Parish and her Ashland Estates home.

If Sadie wasn't thinking those same thoughts, if she was more than two seconds behind Johnnie when the time came to make a run for it, Sadie would have been on her own because Johnnie's prevailing thoughts were to get away from whatever was behind the door, which was taking forever to open, creaking louder and louder as it swung.

Johnnie looked at Sadie and Sadie returned her fearful gaze. At that moment, it didn't matter that they had driven over an hour to find this backwoods fortuneteller. It didn't matter that if she left now, she would more than likely keep the baby that was becoming more real with each passing day. All that mattered to Johnnie and Sadie was that they were both terrified at that moment.

Just as they turned to run, a voice called out to them from inside the house, saying, "Do not go. Stay."

The voice was female and husky, yet unmistakably sexy. The door was still opening, still creaking, and they could see inside, but they could not see the woman behind the voice. Curiosity got the better of them and they felt compelled to stay, if for no other reason than to see what The Fortuneteller looked like before they made a quick dash for the car.

Then, finally, the door was fully open and they could see The Fortuneteller. Her gorgeous, shoulder-length black hair was hidden in a multicolored wrap that matched the sleeveless dress she was wearing, which was long enough to reach her ankles, showing her bronzed bare feet and black painted toenails. Her eyes were light brown and eerily penetrating.

When Johnnie Wise and Jupiter DeMille made eye contact, the fog was lifted from Jupiter's mind—her sight was clear instantly, knowing important parts of Johnnie's future and much of her past. The two women stood perfectly still, staring at each other in a hypnotic gaze so gripping that they seemed to be in a trance as information flooded Jupiter's mind.

But as Johnnie stood there, transfixed, unable to move, she could hear a voice inside her head that was crystal clear, imploring her to look away from the woman before her, and run to the car. *Run! Now!* The voice thundered in her mind, but she was also being drawn, pulled magnetically, it seemed, by this beautiful Negress.

"Let's get outta here, Johnnie!" Sadie shouted and started for the car.

"If you leave now," Jupiter said evenly, "you will never know what your future holds. My time draws nigh, and my sight will be no more."

The voice in Johnnie's head shouted one last time. *Flee this place and never return!* This time, Johnnie turned to leave, choosing to obey the voice in her head.

But Jupiter DeMille said, "If you leave now, you will have the baby you're carrying and you will never amount to anything."

After hearing that, after hearing she would be destined to failure—that was Johnnie's interpretation anyway—her mind went back to the neighborhood she was reared in. She remembered the night she was sold, and everything that happened after that; the murder of her mother, meeting Lucas Matthews, Napoleon, Sheriff Tate, Bubbles, Sadie, the Beauregards, and their Shakespearean-styled deaths, and singing that night at the Bayou. All of it came back in a single moment. But what stopped her from leaving were the words The Fortuneteller had spoken. *You will never amount to anything.*

Chapter 79

"I don't need them."

"No, Sadie," Johnnie said to her friend. "We're staying."

And with that declaration, the voice inside her head silenced itself and spoke no more. Having decided to ignore the voice, Johnnie turned back to The Fortuneteller and entered her house—Sadie too.

"I am Madame DeMille," she said with a French accent. "Please . . . come into my parlor and I will tell you the things you want to know." She turned and led the way. Johnnie and Sadie followed her. Without turning around, she said, "This is for the pregnant one only. Where we go, you cannot follow. You may wait here. Please have a seat and wait until the time."

"Do you want me to go in there with you?" Sadie asked defiantly.

“Wait out here, Sadie,” Johnnie said as she was pulled into the parlor by The Fortuneteller’s powerful aura.

Johnnie had been taught spiritual things in a Holiness church and knew the Old Testament spoke against the soothsayer, but ignored her training and continued on. She had to know what her future held because the alternative, having the baby and amounting to nothing, was just too unthinkable. Johnnie wanted to be rich; she wanted to be somebody. She had promised herself that she would never end up like her mother. If what The Fortuneteller had to say led to riches, she had to listen and know her story before the time.

They entered the parlor and sat at an empty table—no crystal ball, no tarot cards, nothing at all that would lead Johnnie to believe that she was in the parlor of a bona fide soothsayer. But still, her curiosity demanded that she listen to the woman who introduced herself as Madame DeMille. She offered the woman her palm as if she knew how the future was prognosticated.

“I don’t need them,” Madame DeMille said.

“Huh?”

“You’re wondering where my crystal ball is, right?” Johnnie nodded and pulled her hand back, placing it in her lap. “I don’t need them for you. Do you believe that?”

“I don’t know what I believe anymore, Madame DeMille,” Johnnie said without hesitation, yet still full of fear.

The Fortuneteller laughed. “I don’t blame you. Shall I begin?” Johnnie nodded. “The child you carry was not conceived by your boyfriend. He sits in the city jail tonight. He loves you, but the child is not his."

After hearing that, Johnnie believed Madame DeMille was authentic. "Whose child is it?" Johnnie blurted out, desperately needing to know.

"You have had three other lovers besides the boy—white men. But of the three, the powerful one is the father. He is a dangerous and devious man . . . capable of anything. These things draw you to him, do they not?"

Johnnie lowered her head, ashamed of the truth. The truth was that she was a Christian who had always found herself attracted to evil things and evil men, even before the auctioning of her treasured virginity. Blinded by her desire for Napoleon, she would never say that he was evil; the things he did were. Completely oblivious to her love for money, she never understood how it led to evil deeds, even though it was staring her right in the face.

She herself had committed evil deed after evil deed, which made her financially secure, until Sharon Trudeau ran off with her money. She had even been an accessory to the murder of Richard Goode, the Grand Wizard of the Klu Klux Klan. Somehow, she was able to twist it in her mind so that she could deny her own complicity in the murder and the sordid affair which led to it.

"The money that was stolen from you has been found," Madame DeMille continued.

Madame DeMille continued talking for forty-five minutes, never asking Johnnie questions, because she didn't need to. She was providing the answers. When she finished saying all she had to say, she warned Johnnie never to divulge what was said to anyone, or there would be terrible, unpredictable consequences. DeMille told her that if she ever said anything, what she had experienced the last two years would pale in comparison to what would befall her in the future. After the clear warning she had given her, Madame DeMille, Johnnie, and Sadie went into the basement, where the abortion was successfully performed.

Chapter 80

"I'm flying out to Las Vegas. . . ."

THE MURDER OF SHARON TRUDEAU was in the *Sentinel* newspaper that Sadie brought to Johnnie along with her breakfast, as she was weak from the abortion and the loss of blood, and needed to be looked after until she regained her strength. As she read the front page story, which ripped the former stockbroker to shreds, a wide, gleeful smile defined her.

The way the story read, no one at the *Sentinel* was sorry Sharon Trudeau was dead. A number of their staff writers had lost a bundle too, the story claimed. Several large suitcases full of cash were found in Sharon's hotel room, along with an unsuspecting bellhop with two bullet wounds in the back of his head, who happened to be in the wrong place at the wrong time. When Johnnie read about the death of the bellhop, she kind of shrugged her shoulders as if to say, "Oh well," and continued reading the riveting story.

After listening to Jupiter DeMille the previous night, Johnnie made up her mind to go back to school. For the second time, she felt like she had control over her life, and she was going to walk back into the school with her head held high, just as The Fortuneteller had instructed, right after the new year, January, 1954.

Richard Goode was dead. Sharon Trudeau was dead. Everyone knew she was behind Goode's murder, and Johnnie thought she was the real power behind Sharon's murder. For those reasons, she decided she wouldn't put up with the schoolgirls who called her those awful names on that terrible, yet wonderful day she met Lucas. She was going to stand up to them, and if necessary, fight them.

Johnnie heard someone knocking on her front door. Sadie was in the kitchen washing dishes, Johnnie knew, and she would see who was at her door. Moments later, she heard someone coming up the stairs. Whoever it was, it wasn't Sadie. The footsteps were too heavy. It was a man—Napoleon, she thought, happy he cared enough to come and see her while she was *ill*. She smiled.

"You decent?"

The voice definitely belonged to Bubbles. Johnnie respected Bubbles and she was happy he came to see her, but she wished it was Napoleon.

"Yes, I'm decent. Come on in."

He walked in with the suitcase he had taken from Sharon Trudeau in Fort Lauderdale. "What's wrong, little lady? Why are you in bed on a gorgeous day like today?"

"I'm not feeling good, Bubbles. Tell me something," she said as if it were an afterthought. "What's your real name?"

"My real name? Why?"

"I think I should know, don't you?"

"I guess. But if I tell you, are you going to use it?"

"I might."

He grunted gruffly and then said, "George Grant. There . . . you happy now?"

"Happy? No, but I do feel privileged to know whatcha mama named you." They both smiled. "Is that my money?"

"Yeah, you wanna count it?"

"Yep."

Bubbles placed the large suitcase next to Johnnie, and noticed the winged angels with long trumpets in their mouths that were carved into the headboard of her bed. He shook his head, but Johnnie didn't notice. Bubbles, like all of Baroque Parish knew what Marguerite and Earl Shamus had done to the girl who was once a good Christian, and he felt a pang in his conscience again. He wondered how it would all turn out now that she had been knowingly and unknowingly involved in not one, but two murders.

Bubbles watched Johnnie's eyes light up when she saw all the money. While she counted it, he allowed his conscience to come alive, and it began to prick his heart as he thought about Lucas Matthews, who had been set up by his boss because he wanted his woman.

The kid doesn't deserve what he's about to get in Angola. The place is a meat grinder. Is three million dollars worth all of this? Then his mind began to justify his actions. *Angola will toughen the kid up. He thinks he's tough now, but three months in that sweat shop will harden him. When he leaves and enters the Army, boot camp will seem like a vacation in comparison.*

Besides, Johnnie would have left him sooner or later anyway. She's too much woman for him. As much as I love her, the truth is, she's a conniving whore just like her mother and her mother's mother before her. She'll stop at nothing to get what she wants—even murder. She'd only end up hurting the kid anyway. This way, it's clean, and I get the Colored rackets that I helped build in the first place.

"What's wrong, George?" Johnnie said gleefully, still counting her money as if she were a teller in a bank. "I like it. George. It fits you."

"You think so, huh?"

"Uh-huh."

Sadie walked into the bedroom and saw Johnnie counting the money. In the recesses of her mind, she knew murdering Sharon Trudeau was wrong, even though she had stolen a lot of people's money. But she would never say anything to Johnnie about it because she had been through too much to be seventeen years old. A part of her was glad Johnnie got her money back. She just wished the police had found Sharon before Bubbles had.

"Do you need anything before I go to the library to get those books we discussed?" Sadie asked.

"No, I'm fine, Sadie. I appreciate everything you've done for me. Everything."

"That's what friends are for," Sadie said. "I'll be back in an hour or so, okay?"

"Okay," Johnnie said. "Maybe George here will keep me company while you're gone."

"Is that his name? George? It fits him."

Johnnie smiled. "That's what I said, Sadie."

"Okay, I'll be back," she said and left.

Bubbles sat on the bed. "Johnnie, you can call your brother and tell him he doesn't have to take a dive next month. It's all settled."

"I know," she said confidently. I already told him. He was very happy. He says he's going to win easily. I'm flying out to Las Vegas to watch the fight now that I got my money back.

"How did you know?"

Johnnie thought of Jupiter DeMille and smiled. "Sometimes a woman just knows things, George."

Chapter 81

"I need a fuckin' name, John!"

THE MAFIA LEADERSHIP, better known as the Commission, was having a very important meeting in a high-rise boardroom somewhere in Midtown Manhattan. They were there to discuss the public massacre of Vincenzo Milano and his crew on a train in Oklahoma City. The bloodbath made headlines across the country and brought more unwanted attention to their gambling and vice operations. Mobsters from as far away as Los Angeles, Kansas City, Florida, Cleveland, Chicago, New Orleans, and various other parts of the United States were seated at a long table full of catered Italian food, delicious garlic bread, and vintage wine. The Bosses engaged in small talk and rambunctious laughter while they ate, until Chicago Sam walked in. He wasn't smiling.

"Vincenzo Milano is dead, and one of you did it," Sam said forcefully.

The room was suddenly graveyard quiet.

"Who would do such a thing, Sam?" Frank De Luca, the Boss of Kansas City, asked. "I swear on my children that I had nothing to do with the death of your friend, Vinnie."

Then one by one, all the Bosses swore the same thing.

Joe Russo, the Boss of New York, said, "There's a bigger problem, Sam, and everybody here knows it. So, you tell us, Sam. What was Vinnie doing on a train to New Orleans with four of his guys in the first fuckin' place? Tell us that."

"I have no idea, Joe," Sam said.

"Now's a good time to tell everybody what you told me," Russo said to John Stefano.

Stefano said, "I think Sam sent Vinnie Milano to New Orleans to kill me. And I think he wanted this meeting to hide this fact."

"Fact my ass, you fat sonofabitch!" Sam shouted. "Why would I kill my own guy? Tell me that."

Before Stefano could answer, Russo said, "What about Bentley? Could he have done this?"

Without thinking, Stefano said, "There's no way he'd know."

Sam said, "Know what, John?"

"Nothing," Stefano said, realizing he had just implicated himself.

Frank De Luca said, "Out with it, John. It's too late now. We know you know something."

"Yeah, John," Russo said, "Let's put an end to this. Tell us what was going on."

Reluctantly, John Stefano said, "It was all his idea."

"Whose idea?" Sam asked.

"Vinnie's. He came back to New Orleans after you left, Sam. He said the Colored section was his and he wanted to make sure he had my permission to whack Bentley. I asked him if you were in on it and he said no. But I couldn't take a chance, and told him I didn't want to have nothin' to do with it. Vinnie tells me you'll go along if he does the job himself, which led me to believe you must have been in on it, but you didn't want me to know, because if Vinnie kills Bentley and takes over, you get the whole shebang, right? Not just a taste. We're talkin' about three million dollars here."

"If he was going to get rid of Napoleon against my orders, why kill him, John? Did you think he was coming to kill you instead of Napoleon?"

"For the last fuckin' time . . . I didn't kill Vinnie," Stefano screamed after leaping out of his chair. "But to answer your question, Sam, there are two ways to look at it. You could have killed Vinnie to make it look like I did it, then later make a move on me, and take over New Orleans altogether. Murdering Vinnie the way you did gives you an excuse. You popped him on the train, and then called this fuckin' meetin' to blame me. That's why you whacked my guy first—Salvatore Porcella."

Surprised by this new revelation, after putting his hand over his heart, Sam said, "I had no idea Sal was dead. I swear."

Russo stood up and said, "Gentlemen, we're here to settle our differences. So, please," he said, gesturing his steeple hands as if he was making a supplication to God, "let us reason together."

Chicago Sam and John Stefano quieted themselves and sat down.

Russo continued. "Now, let's assume, for the sake of argument, that neither of you had anything to do with Sal's or Vinnie's deaths. Who do you think would do something like this to your families?"

Stefano spoke first. "Napoleon Bentley. But I don't get how he'd know."

Russo asked, "What makes you so sure Bentley didn't hit both your guys, knowing you'd blame each other?"

"Because I've got a believable informant in his organization, that's how. Besides, if he did something like this, he would have extra security around him, even among the niggers. That's how I know."

Sam asked, "Who is this informant? And how do you know you can trust him, since he works for Bentley? It could all be a set-up."

"Believe me, the informant is solid," Stefano replied.

"I need a fuckin' name, John!" Sam said, on the verge of exploding again.

"We all need a name, John," Russo said.

Chapter 82

"What about Vinnie, Sam?"

JOHN STEFANO pulled a Cuban cigar from his inside breast pocket, smelled it, moistened it with his tongue, put it in his mouth, then lit it. He puffed several times until the Cuban could sustain its own fire, and blew out the residual smoke. "Bentley's wife, Marla. But I don't want anything to happen to her. I gave her my word."

"It's too thin, John," Sam said with rancor. "Don't you see this is a set-up?"

"I don't think so, Sam," John said. "The wife was fuckin' the black broad's boyfriend—a nigger—while Bentley was fuckin' the broad. You tell me, what Italian woman would admit to such a thing unless it was true?"

A cacophony of murmuring filled the room when this information was revealed, as the Mafia leaders began giving this bombshell serious contemplation. Russo pick up his spoon and struck his crystal wine glass, which rang out like a small chime. The men quieted themselves again and listened.

Russo began, "It's clear to me that Bentley outwitted you, John. You wanted the Colored section and he knew it. Tell us now. Were you in cahoots with Vinnie to kill Bentley?"

"He came to me and I listened to him. Then I sent Sal to Chicago to meet with Vinnie. He never returned. I thought Sam had found out and whacked Sal. What could I do about it? Like I said, if it had worked, we believed Sam would go along."

"Are you sure Sal's dead? Do you have a body?" Russo asked.

"All I know is that I sent him to Chicago three months ago and he never returned. The next thing I know, Vinnie's in my office asking for permission to hit Bentley. He needed to make sure Sal was telling the truth before he popped Bentley."

Sam said, "For all we know, Sal could be behind all of this, waiting to whack you, John."

"No fuckin' way. Sal was a stand-up guy."

"So was Vinnie, but he went against my orders, didn't he, John? Sal could have done the same thing."

Russo interrupted. "Fine then. We assume Sal's dead, John. But since you went after Bentley, it's up to you to finish it."

Stefano looked at Sam and said, "I say we do the hit in Vegas. He'll be there, and he doesn't know we figured it all out."

"I'll be in Vegas for the fight, John," Sam replied, "but now that we all know you started this mess, you're on your own. You handle Bentley and it's over. If he handles you, we're not going to war over your bullshit."

The men murmured loudly in agreement, since no one wanted bloodshed.

"What about Vinnie, Sam?" John asked. "Don't you want to settle the score?"

"Hey, I loved Vinnie, okay, but he fucked up. He was fuckin' greedy and he went against my orders. He got what he got. As far as I'm concerned, Napoleon had every right to defend his territory. And I dare any one of you to say you would have done differently." There was a long silence. "Now, that's it."

"So be it," John said. "I'll kill the bastard in Vegas and bury him in the fuckin' dunes."

Chapter 83

"You gotta be strong."

DEPUTIES ESCORTED LUCAS into the courtroom. The chains rattled loudly with each step he took, soliciting long, unwanted stares and incredible embarrassment, especially when he saw Johnnie, who was sitting on the first bench, near the defendant's table. When they made eye contact, their hearts broke at the same time, and their eyes watered as if on cue.

Are you crazy? The words had been ringing in Lucas' head the entire weekend. Johnnie had said them to him immediately after he'd told her about his plan to sell marijuana. Even then, he knew she was right, but in his mind, he needed to have his own money. Now, looking at her in that beautiful peach skirt and matching bonnet, he was filled with regret. Just as a tear from his left eye began a slow slide down his face, he turned away so that she couldn't see him cry.

Full of guilt, Johnnie wept too. She felt guilty because in her heart, she knew this day would come, but hoped it never would. Knowing this was going to happen, she knew she should have tried harder to convince him to give up his foolish plans. But because it was his chance to make some money and he had allowed her to make hers by prostituting herself, she didn't give her best effort to deter him from the life he was choosing for himself. Nevertheless, a battle waged in her mind when she thought on these things.

If I could convince him to accept my relationship with Earl Shamus, if I could convince him that Napoleon was a terrible lover and that I didn't enjoy any of it, I could have convinced him not to sell drugs.

Lucas was sitting at the defendant's table with his court-appointed lawyer when he heard Johnnie say, "I love you. You gotta be strong. You hear me, be strong." Lucas heard her, but he couldn't bring himself to turn around. He loved her too, but he believed that a pretty girl like Johnnie wouldn't wait for him. She would have all kinds of men after her, and he would be in jail, imagining it all. The thought of her being with another man shattered his heart into a thousand pieces.

"They found Sharon, Lucas," Johnnie continued. "You'll get your money back at least."

Lucas wiped his eyes and composed himself. He couldn't let her see him cry. He was a man, he told himself—whatever that meant. Finally, he turned around and looked into Johnnie's eyes, saying, "Take care of my cars until I get out, okay?"

"It's only three months," Johnnie offered as consolation. "I'll be here for you. I promise."

"No," Lucas said firmly. "Move on with your life. I done fucked mine up. I should have listened to you. You tried to tell me and I wouldn't listen. I had to do things my way, and now I'm about to get what's comin' to me." He kind of laughed. "I'm lucky they're letting me in the Army so I don't have to do the whole stretch. So, waiting for me is not going to change anything. I gotta go into the Army right after I do the three months. Good thing the Korean War is over. I'm sure they'd want to send me over there. But I hear that since the French lost in Vietnam, America might get involved, and if they do—"

"Don't talk like that, baby. Don't even think like that. You've got three months. Then you've got four years in the Army. Take advantage of your time and learn a trade so we can be together when you get out, okay?"

"I've already thought about it, Johnnie. I'm going to better myself, but don't bother waiting. I couldn't take it if you weren't here when I get out of the Army."

Johnnie wanted to tell him that Bubbles had gotten her money back and she could pack up any time she wanted and go wherever he was because she was rich again. But she couldn't say anything in open court, so she kept her mouth shut.

"All rise!" the bailiff shouted.

Chapter 84

"Sure, Sam."

"I don't wanna read some book about some Uncle Tom," Johnnie had said to Sadie when she brought her Harriet Beecher Stowe's classic novel, which many believed to be the catalyst for the Civil War.

But when Sadie asked Johnnie how the term "Uncle Tom" came to mean what it means today, Johnnie had no answer. That's when she decided she would read the 1852 bestseller on the way to Las Vegas.

This would be Johnnie's first time on an airplane. It was very exciting for her. They met Napoleon and Bubbles at the airport and boarded the plane together, but sat in different sections of the aircraft. As soon as the plane leveled off, Johnnie whipped out the book and began reading it, saying "Hmm" every now and then as she read, which made Sadie, who was reading a book too, smile. The novel fascinated Johnnie and she continued reading as they rode in a taxi over to the Sands Hotel and Casino.

Sadie could tell that her friend was beginning to understand why she wanted her to start reading because when Johnnie came to a word she didn't understand, she'd pull out the dictionary she'd purchased on Main Street in Baroque Parrish at Cambridge Books before the riot, and looked up words—she was growing.

The taxi stopped in front of the Sands. They got out and walked to the entrance, amidst disapproving Whites who stared at them unrelentingly. They were stopped by the doorman, who said to Napoleon with a sincere smile, "You can come in, but we don't accept their kind." The doorman turned to Johnnie, Sadie, and Bubbles, and said, "The Moulin Rouge Hotel is where Coloreds stay when they come to town."

"Look, mister doorman," Napoleon began evenly, "we have reservations here. We're with Chicago Sam and John Stefano. And this pretty lady here is the sister of Benny Wise, the man fighting in your courtyard tonight."

"I'm sorry, sir," the doorman offered. "I still don't think they'll let them in. Go to the front desk and maybe they'll make an exception. I'm not even supposed to let them through the front door. Even the colored entertainers enter through the back door."

"Napoleon," Bubbles said, I'm not waiting outside in all that fuckin' heat, man."

"Come on," Napoleon said, and pushed his way past the doorman.

As they made their way over to the front desk, Johnnie and Sadie stopped at the marquee in the lobby. They saw a poster of Benny, who was wearing a pair of white trunks trimmed in black. His hands were on his hips, covered in black boxing gloves, and he was facing his opponent, Paul "Sweetwater" Smith, who was a Negro too.

When Johnnie looked at Sadie, who was quietly studying Benny, she saw a woman who was looking at a man that she had made up her mind to bed. Johnnie smiled to herself, thinking that Benny must have really put it on her the way Sadie was looking at the poster.

"It's a good thing Brenda didn't come to Las Vegas, huh, Sadie?"

Snapping out of her hypnotic gaze, Sadie smiled and said, "Huh? Uh, yeah. It's a good thing."

"I don't give a fuck," they heard Napoleon scream in the crowded lobby in response to the clerk, who obviously confirmed what the doorman had told them.

There was a long line of well-dressed guests waiting to check in, but Napoleon and Bubbles brazenly cut the line and demanded their rooms. The manager heard the screaming and came to rescue the desk clerk.

Johnnie and Sadie stopped looking at the poster and focused their attention on what was going on at the front desk. They saw two white men behind the desk. They were wearing blue sport jackets with Sands Hotel in gold lettering sewn into the fabric above the left breast pocket.

One of the men was saying, "It's hotel policy, sir."

Napoleon grabbed the man who was speaking by the collar, snatched him off his feet, pulled him over the counter, and slapped him mercilessly about eight times. The man's head turned left and right and left and right, becoming more flushed after each stinging blow.

"Now, you've got rooms for me and my friends, right?" Napoleon said to the manager.

"I'll see what I can do," the manager replied and attempted to walk past Napoleon and go through the swinging door to get back to the other side of the desk.

"Where you goin'?" Napoleon asked him.

"Sir, I have to get on the other side of the desk to find your registration."

"Crawl over."

"Excuse me?"

"You heard me the first time. Crawl your ass over the goddamned desk. You humiliated my friends, now you get to see how they feel. Now, crawl your sorry ass over the desk before I toss you over it.

When the manager stood there, looking at him incredulously, Napoleon slapped him again for moving too slow. Then he grabbed him by the collar and threw him over the counter. "Hurry up!"

"Yes, sir," the manager said and handed him four keys.

Seeing this ostentatious display of power and authority triggered something in Johnnie's private place, and she began to marinate. She realized that power turned her on. She now had the same look in her eyes that Sadie had when she looked at Benny.

"We want something on the top floor," Napoleon snapped when he looked at the keys.

"I'm sorry, sir," the manager began, "the entire seventh floor has been reserved for our Chicago guests."

"That's right," Sam said, after walking up to the counter.

Napoleon turned around when he heard Sam's voice, and changed his tune quickly. "Hey, Sam, I didn't know."

Sam was sharply dressed, sporting his typical fedora, dark shades, with a cigar in his mouth. There was a beautiful brunette with him, who Napoleon recognized as a famous singer, but he couldn't remember her name.

"It's all right, Napoleon. We're having a party after the fight. If you like, stop by and have a drink. Bring your friends with you."

When Sam said that, Napoleon knew they were going to try to kill him before the fight.

"Sure, Sam. We'll be there, right after the fight," Napoleon said confidently.

Chapter 85

"And you couldn't afford me."

TWO HITTERS entered the Sands Hotel through an unlocked stairwell door in the back of the building and stealthily made their way up the stairs, silenced pistols in hand. It was an hour before fight time, and the team had to get in the hotel, pop a few people, and get back out without being seen. When they reached the target's floor, they looked at each other—their way of acknowledging that they were ready to enter the hallway.

Seconds later, one of the hitters knocked on the target's door. One hitter had his back against the wall while the other stood in front of the door, so that one of the targets could look through the peephole and see someone there. The hitter who was standing in front of the door was looking at the space between the carpet and bottom of the door to know when someone was looking through the peephole.

When the hitter standing at the door saw the light under the door darken, she smiled, knowing that the man behind the door would let her in.

The man opened the door and said with a hearty smile, "I think you got the wrong room, sweetheart."

The woman was stunning. Her features were distinctly Asian, and she was about five feet seven inches tall, with raven hair that was pulled back in a tight ponytail. Although she was slender, she was well put together. She was wearing a black skirt/white blouse combination. Her erect nipples were poking through the white sheer silk covering them. She had her hands behind her back, but the man was paying attention to her breasts and not to her hands, just as she knew he would be.

"Who is it?" a male voice called from inside the room.

The man said, "I think we got Ms. Hong Kong here." He laughed. "What's your name, honey? And what's your price?"

She pulled the pistol from behind her back. Her weapon hissed twice. The man fell to the carpet. She had put two side-by-side bullet holes in his chest. The man with her ran into the room and shot another man.

The woman closed the door and went to where the man she had shot had fallen. He was still breathing, and blood was starting to cover his white tuxedo shirt. She looked down at him and said, "My name is Tia Nimburu." *Hiss!* She shot him the eye. "I'm Japanese." *Hiss!* She shot him in the other eye. "I'm from Singapore." *Hiss!* She shot him in the groin. "And you couldn't afford me." Then she kicked him in the face.

By the time Tia finished with the man who had opened the door, Khiro, her husband, had his pistol on the man they came to kill.

"Call him and tell him we have his man," Khiro said to Tia.

Chapter 86

"First round."

JOHNNIE AND SADIE were talking to Benny while he hit the gloves of his trainer in the portable dressing rooms, which were at a diagonal on either side of the ring. The blows sounded off. *Bam! Bam!—Bam!—Bam! Bam! Bam!* There was a menacing scowl on his otherwise handsome face, and he delivered the powerful blows in a smooth cadence that begged to be admired.

"I'ma kill that muthafucka!" Benny said with conviction. *Bam! Bam! Bam!—Bam! Bam! Bam!* "This'll be his last fight! I'ma torture that muthafucka!" *Bam! Bam!* "It ain't gon' be quick, either." He threw a hook. *Bam!*

"How many rounds, champ?" his trainer asked.

"How many rounds is the fight?" Benny asked.

"Since it's not a championship bout, this one'll go twelve rounds."

"Then I get twelve rounds to beat his ass. Thirty-six minutes worth of ass whuppin'!"

"Why don't you knock him out early so you can save your strength for other things?" Sadie asked.

Benny stopped punching and said, "What do you have in mind, girl?"

"Use your imagination," she said with a licentious grin.

"You name the round, baby, and I'll drop 'im just for you."

"First round."

"No. He's gotta earn some of the money he's makin' tonight. Besides, Sweetwater is supposed to be tough. We don't want the people thinkin' he took a dive, do we?"

"Okay, six rounds."

"Sixth round it is."

Johnnie smiled unnoticeably because she was glad Sadie would be busy, since she planned to be busy too—with Napoleon. She wasn't going to take no for an answer, either.

Chapter 87

"I'm ready."

TIA AND KHIRO heard someone knocking on the door. They looked at each other. Khiro tilted his head toward the door, and Tia went to see who it was. Khiro kept his gun on the man they had come to kill. Tia, having made it to the door, looked through the peephole and saw the man who was paying them. She put her weapon behind her back, ready for anything, just in case there was a double cross. Then she opened the door.

The man walked in and looked down at the dead man. He recognized him, but didn't say anything, and continued on to the dining room, where he saw another man at the table. He had a hole dead-center in his head. The man recognized him too. He kept walking until he reached the private bedroom where the man he was there to kill was being held.

"Napoleon Bentley," John Stefano said. "I should have known it was you."

Napoleon pulled up a chair and sat down while Tia and Khiro kept their weapons on Stefano.

"John, you should have known not to come after me. And you definitely should have picked better hitters than those two bums."

"How did you know?" Stefano asked.

Napoleon took a deep breath and exhaled as he reveled in the moment of his greatest triumph.

"Should I tell him, guys?" Napoleon asked the husband and wife hit-man team.

"You're askin' the chinks?"

Khiro raised his gun, and was about to hit Stefano in the head with it.

"No," Napoleon said before Khiro brought the weapon crashing down on Stefano's head. "I don't want his wife to see bruises on him."

"Do me this one favor before I go," Stefano pleaded. "I gotta know."

"It was the maid you employ," Napoleon said.

"Stephanie Roselle?" Stefano said, shocked at the revelation. "You've gotta be fuckin' kiddin' me. I knew her from the time she was a fuckin' baby."

"I know," Napoleon said. "You shouldn't have killed her father and fucked her mother."

"But how did she know?" Stefano said, neither confirming nor denying the accusation, though it was true. "You can't trust anybody these days."

"Your office is right above the laundry room, and she could hear every word. Don't be so hard on yourself. I'm good at this—real good."

"Did you do Sal too?"

Napoleon nodded.

"The Oklahoma City thing too?"

Napoleon nodded.

"Is Sam in on this?"

"No. It's just me and you, John. That's all it's ever been. Me and you. But you never stood a chance, John."

"How did you know what train he'd be on?"

"The colored porters have a grapevine like you wouldn't believe. Not only do they know each other, but they know the shoeshines, the cabbies, the washroom men, the cooks, everybody. And they are all loyal to me. See, you fuckin' dagos think too little of the Coloreds. They are invaluable if you treat 'em with respect. They'll do anything for me." He paused briefly. "Any more questions, John?"

Stefano shook his head and then he crossed himself and said, "I'm ready."

Hiss! Hiss! Khiro's gun discharged twice.

Chapter 88

"It's just me and you."

"In this corner, wearing black trunks, hailing from Odessa, Texas, weighing an even one hundred and sixty pounds, ranked number ten by the World Boxing Association, Paul 'Sweetwater' Smith!" Napoleon heard the ring announcer say when he sat next to Sam, who was sitting next to the famous singer.

Sam said, "That's Stefano's seat." He could barely hear himself over all the cheers for Sweetwater Smith.

"He won't be coming, Sam," Napoleon said. "He had an appointment with his maker."

Sam kind of laughed and shook his head. "Well done." Then he put his cigar in his mouth, puffed a few times, and blew out smoke.

"And in this corner, wearing white trunks, hailing from San Francisco by way of the Crescent City, New Orleans, Louisiana, ranked number twelve by the World Boxing Association, the Bay City Terror, Benny, 'The Body Snatcher' Wise!"

The two combatants met in the center of the ring and glared at each other as the referee gave them their final instructions. Seconds later, the bell rang and they met in the center of the ring again.

Benny hit Sweetwater with a wicked left hook that knocked him off balance. In an attempt to offset the power of the blow and regain his balance, Sweetwater appeared to be running backwards. The ropes caught him and flung him forward into another hook that dazed him. And thus began the beating Sweetwater would take. When Benny saw that Sweetwater was out on his feet, he clenched and walked him around the ring until he was cognizant again.

While in the clench, he said, "Yeah, muthafucka!" *Bam! Bam!* "I'ma beat yo' ass like you stole somethin'!" *Bam! Bam! Bam!* "Ya mobster friends can't help you in the ring."

Sweetwater didn't know what Benny was talking about. He wasn't in league with the Mafia. Napoleon had sent the men that threatened Benny, knowing Johnnie would ask for his help again.

"It's just me and you." *Bam!—Bam!—Bam! Bam! Bam!—Bam!—Bam!—Bam! Bam! Bam!* Clench. "Unt-uh, muthafucka. Stand yo' ass up and take this ass whuppin'!"

The fight went on and on like that for nearly six rounds, when Benny ended it with a left hook. As the referee counted Sweetwater out, Benny looked at Sadie, who was ringside, and winked. She winked back.

Chapter 89

"I'm a good girl."

NAPOLEON WAS SURPRISED to see Johnnie when he opened the door to his suite. Her hair was up, showing the diamonds in her ears. She wore elbow-length gloves that matched her elegant black gown, which showed off her divine curves. Normally, she didn't wear any makeup, but tonight was different. She saw Sadie put on a touch of ruby red lipstick before she left to meet Benny and thought she'd try some for the first time in her young life.

Johnnie didn't wait to be asked; she just walked in like she owned the place. Lucas had told her not to wait for him, and she used his words as a means to justify her wanton sexual desire for a man she had wanted to bed again anyway—even if it was only one more time. To further cement the justification in her mind, she told herself that Lucas had bedded Marla over and over again. He had admitted as much the night she bathed him and told him that lie about Napoleon having his orgasm thirty seconds after the interlude began. Besides, what Lucas didn't know wouldn't hurt him, she told herself just before leaving her suite.

"There's some wine at the wet bar," Napoleon said. "Pour yourself a drink. I have to go to the bathroom."

Less than two minutes later, Napoleon came out of the bathroom and found Johnnie completely naked and lying on his bed. He stiffened as he gazed at her voluptuous body. His mouth watered and he swallowed hard.

Johnnie watched Napoleon's lust grow. "Stop playing games. Come and get it," she whispered in a breathy tone. "You know you want it. I'm the crème de la crème."

Napoleon took his time getting to the bed. He kicked off his shoes and sat next to her. "You said I wouldn't have to tell a real woman how to do it. Show me what you meant by that."

That's all Johnnie needed to hear. She was finally going to show him she was a woman. Without hesitation, she stood to her feet and began to undress him. When he was totally nude, she ran her moist tongue all over his body, which made him twitch. Then she took him into her mouth, and Napoleon moaned loudly. And he went on moaning for over an hour.

Then she slid a prophylactic on his thick tool. She straddled him and rode him the rest of the night, using her strong muscles to keep him hard. When she had put him to sleep, when she was sure that she was a sensual, skilled sex goddess, she went back to her suite, satisfied that she had proven she was a real woman, at least to herself anyway. As for her satisfaction, it was good, but nothing like it was the first time. She thought about this long and hard and realized that what had blown her mind before was the oral sex Napoleon provided prior to entering her. Without that weapon, he was putty in her hands, like any other man.

And with that knowledge, she knew she didn't really want him, she wanted cunnilingus. That was what she enjoyed, and that was why she knew to keep control over herself where Napoleon was concerned. She couldn't let him lap at her private place ever again because he was too good at it and it made her weak. She had to be strong, she thought.

Her thoughts shifted to the only man she ever loved, Lucas Matthews, who was in Angola Prison, probably dreaming about her that very night. For a moment or two, she felt guilty for betraying Lucas, but she quickly reminded herself that he had given her permission to move on with her life. Besides, she had resisted long enough.

Then out of nowhere, Reverend Staples' words rang in her ears: *The heart is deceitful above all and desperately wicked. Some of us are so self-righteous that it's going to take a lifetime to discover the truth of this verse so that we might be truly saved.*

After hearing this again, Johnnie said, "I'm not self-righteous. I'm a good girl." And with that, she went to sleep.

Chapter 90

The Letter

Dear Lucas,

It's been so long since I've seen your handsome face. Saying I miss you terribly somehow doesn't express the longing in my soul to be near you, to have you wrap your powerful arms around me, to make incredible love all night long. I often wonder if you miss me, and I want to see you, but you know why I can't come to visit you, right? I promise to visit you when you get your first Army furlough, if you want to see me. Please say you do.

Is Angola as rough as they say? Are you being strong? Do you need anything, like soap or toothpaste? I will do some shopping for you and send it in a package with some oatmeal raisin cookies. I'll bake them myself. I know how you love my cooking. I only wish I could cook you a nice meal and bring it to the prison, so we could have a picnic or something.

I don't know if you have time to read, but I'll buy you a few books and send them with the other things. Please read them. I hope you won't find them boring. I think I'll start with Up from Slavery. *It's Booker T. Washington's autobiography. It's about overcoming obstacles. It was written over fifty years ago, but I think you'll find it is still relevant in 1953. You'll need a dictionary. I'll put one in the package, okay?*

I guess that's all for now. Oh, when you write, please note the return address is in Chicago. I'm leaving Napoleon as soon as he returns from Las Vegas. Take care of yourself.

Love,
Marla

When Lucas finished the letter, he smiled for the first since he arrived at The Farm. He had gotten a letter from Marla before he'd gotten one from Johnnie. *I guess she took my advice and moved on with her life. I will have to move on with mine too.* As he folded the letter and put it back into the envelope it came in, he began to consider her offer of seeing him when he got his first furlough. He hadn't had any sex in weeks. The withdrawal was very difficult, since he and Johnnie had been doing it nearly every day.

He hadn't seen her in three months, yet she cared enough to write. That touched him, but he had to get through three months in Angola first. After that, he'd see where he and Johnnie stood. *If it's over between me and Johnnie, I might see Marla again, since she's finally leaving Napoleon. But next time, it'll be far away from New Orleans.*

Chapter 91

"I hope it turns out the way you planned."

MARLA BENTLEY finished packing her suitcase, closed it, and went downstairs to the living room to wait for Napoleon, who had just gotten in from his Las Vegas jaunt. It was time for their conversation; the conversation that would make her free of him—forever, she hoped. Marla considered leaving him while he was in Vegas, but she needed closure. She needed him to know that it was completely over and that there was absolutely no chance to reconcile. This could only be done face to face.

Marla violated her conscience when she agreed to set Lucas and Johnnie up for Napoleon's gain, but it was the only way she could leave a man she no longer loved. She felt bad about what she had done, but somehow reasoned that Napoleon was going to have his way whether she helped him or not. If she helped him get Lucas out of the way, he would allow her to leave with lots of money in her purse—enough money to be set for the remainder of her life.

Marla had known about the countless affairs for years. Napoleon had broken her heart too many times to count. After a while, he abandoned the pretense of fidelity and continued his philandering ways in the open. The first time he hurt her by sleeping with another woman, a part of her love for him died and would never be resurrected. Little by little, hurt after hurt, any love she had for him evaporated like water in Death Valley—nowhere to be found.

Marla would never let him into her inner sanctum again, that most tender and vulnerable part of her heart, that place where she once dreamed of forever, because to do so would invite the stinging pang of betrayal again. She had to protect her heart; she had to protect her mind, and she did. She tried to go on with the marriage. She even thought she'd forgiven him, but she hadn't. She couldn't forgive him because not only had Napoleon violated his vows before God, he had flagrantly violated her trust, which was sacred, and did so openly. She didn't realize she hadn't forgiven Napoleon until he pointed it out.

Napoleon told Marla that if she had really forgiven him, she wouldn't bring it up again. He went on to tell her that not only did she bring it up, she constantly harped on a past indiscretion that was over, which gave him the right to see other women—in his mind, anyway. And when he was caught again, a little more of her love for him died. By the time he was caught the seventh time, she didn't love him at all, but he was a good provider, and so she stayed for her children's sake.

Marla had played her role in the sordid play that Napoleon directed. Even the chance meeting at the Mobil filling station was orchestrated. If Lucas hadn't stopped to get gas at that particular station, Marla would have told him to pull in so she could use the restroom to give Preston Leonard Truman a chance to speak to Lucas alone and pitch the drug deal to him. She liked Lucas, but she knew Napoleon was going to have Johnnie no matter what, even if he had to kill Lucas to have her. Marla convinced herself that she was saving Lucas' life, securing her freedom from her loveless marriage, and getting some much-needed sex with a young, strong, virile male.

And now she was ready to move on. There was nothing left in New Orleans for her. Both of her children were grown and in college. She had done her duty. In fact, she had gone above and beyond her duty, but before she left Napoleon, she wanted to be compensated for all of her years of self-sacrifice. The day Napoleon ripped her to shreds in front of Lucas when they were in the swimming pool together was the day she decided she'd had enough. When he came home after Amateur Night at the Bayou, the night he met Johnnie Wise, she told him she wanted a divorce.

For the first time in a long time, they talked all night long, and she told him everything. When Napoleon asked her about the swimming pool antics he had seen, she admitted to being attracted to Lucas, which gave him the idea of how he could use that to take over New Orleans. Napoleon had given her permission to seduce Lucas and to blow his mind, if she could. He even told her he planned to get rid of Lucas and take Johnnie from him.

Marla didn't want to do it at first, but he promised her he would let her go and give her enough money to do whatever she wanted. He knew their marriage was over too, but he thought he could use her relationship with Lucas to fool John Stefano into believing he was weak.

Napoleon walked into the house and saw her bags. He looked at her and felt a slight sting in his heart that only Marla would notice. They had been together for nearly two decades. It was a difficult moment for them both. He forced himself to smile and asked, "Do you want me to take you to the airport?"

"I called a cab."

Napoleon said, "Okay, well, I guess this is it then, huh?"

With tears in her eyes, Marla could only nod in response. With trembling lips, she said, "I hope you'll finally be happy. I tried to love you the best I knew how, but it wasn't enough for you."

"I know," he said. "You're going back to Chicago? With your mom?"

"For a little while, yes," Marla replied. "What about you? When do you go before the Commission?"

"Tomorrow."

"I hope it turns out the way you planned," she said. A horn blew. "That's my cab," she said and stood up to leave.

"Do you want me to carry your bag to the car for you?"

"No. the cabby'll get it."

"Okay, then. Take care of yourself, Marla, and thanks for helping me take control of New Orleans."

"You take care of yourself too."

And with that, Marla Bentley left Napoleon.

Chapter 92

The Commission

NAPOLEON BENTLEY was in Manhattan to meet with the Commission. He was standing right outside the door, waiting to be announced. While he didn't show it, he was afraid because he knew he might be carried out of the boardroom, hacked to pieces with a butcher's knife, and never seen again. Nevertheless, he had to go in and meet with all the Bosses because if they wanted to kill him, they could do so easily. The tentacles of the Mafia stretched around the globe. If they wanted to kill someone, there was no place to hide from them.

Napoleon believed that it would be better to die on his feet, looking in the faces of the men who had killed him rather than waiting and wondering when they would be coming after him. Of course, that was the worst case scenario. On the other hand, he could be offered a prestigious seat on the Commission, which is what he was hoping for.

Napoleon believed he had earned the right to sit down with the big Bosses. He was smart, ruthless, and a good earner. In his mind, taking out John Stefano was nothing less than brilliant and he deserved New Orleans, because if he was right, the Bosses knew Stefano was seeking to take him out first. While the Bosses were killers, they were all reasonable men. The moment he explained what happened and why he killed Stefano, they'd either kill him or allow him to have the territory that he had every right to.

The door opened and one of the guards said, "Go on in. They're ready for you."

Napoleon took a deep breath, blew it out, and walked into the boardroom. Nervous and yet exhilarated, he saw all the Bosses standing, watching him as he approached the long table where they dined. At the head of the table he saw Don Russo, the Boss of New York, whom he'd heard about, but had never met. He saw an empty chair at the end of the table, opposite Don Russo. One of the Bosses gestured for him to take that seat, and he did. Once he was seated, the Bosses sat in their chairs.

After introducing everyone and himself, Don Russo said, "Napoleon Bentley, do you know why you're here?"

"Well, you're either gonna kill me or make me the Boss of New Orleans. I don't know which, but I'm ready for either one."

Sam said, "Some stones this guy has, huh?"

"The Boss of New Orleans?" Russo questioned. "Why would we do that?"

"Don Russo," Napoleon said with humility, "John Stefano was going to have me hit in Las Vegas. I found out about it and hit him first. It was either him or me.

Now, if you gentlemen think I was wrong for defending myself, kill me now. But before you do, ask yourself this question: If you knew a man was going to kill you because he wanted territory you worked your ass off to build and turn into a goldmine, would you kill him first? Or would you stand still like a deer caught in headlights and let him kill you instead?" He paused for a moment and let them think about it. "Now, do what you will. I'm unarmed. I won't run and I won't resist."

Don Russo said, "You're a Spaniard, and we only allow Italians in La Cosa Nostra."

"My family is from Europe, Spain to be exact, but my father was an Italian. He and my mother never married, but I thought this might come up, so I brought my birth certificate." Napoleon pulled out the important document and handed it to the Boss on his right.

The Boss he handed it to quickly and thoroughly examined it. The certificate was old and crinkled, which added to its authenticity. Then he nodded his head, handed the certificate to the Boss next to him, grabbed a plate, and began filling it with food. Each Boss examined the document and nodded.

Finally Don Russo examined it, and he too nodded. "Are there any objections to accepting Napoleon into our brotherhood?"

"Yes," one of the Bosses said. "What about his niggers? He's gotta separate himself from them. This is an Italian thing."

"Are you agreeable to this, Napoleon?" Russo asked evenly.

"Yes, Don Russo," Napoleon said. "I've already taken steps toward that end. It will not be a problem, I assure you."

"Any more objections?" Russo asked again.

The room fell silent for a few moments as the Bosses looked at each other. Then Don Russo stood up, picked up his glass of wine, and said, "To Napoleon Bentley, the Boss of New Orleans."

All the Bosses stood and said, "Salut."

Chapter 93

"This'll be the best Christmas they ever had!"

SOMEONE WAS KNOCKING on Johnnie's front door. It was Christmas Eve, and she was still wrapping the last minute gifts she had purchased, putting them under her Christmas tree. Most of the presents were for Sadie and her kids, who were coming over for dinner. They planned to sing Christmas carols, drink eggnog, and spend the night.

This would be her first Christmas without her mother, who she now had mixed feelings about. Marguerite was right about a lot of things, Johnnie realized, given all that she had been through. She understood, and missed her terribly now that she was gone. If it weren't for Sadie, it would have been a very lonely holiday season, with Lucas still 135 miles away at The Farm in Angola.

As she walked to the front door, Johnnie wondered why Sadie and her children hadn't come to the back door as usual. She opened the door, and her mouth fell open when she saw Earl Shamus standing there. Madame DeMille had told her he would arrive when least expected. Ironically, it was two years to the day that he had stripped her of her virginity.

The fulfillment of another prediction scared Johnnie. Her heart was pounding in her chest as anxiety saturated her mind. There she was, looking at the man who had defiled her, the man who had taken her innocence, the man who had snatched her youth and turned her into a woman long before her time.

Madame DeMille said I had to confront him, and I will. I guess it's time for me to take care of this shit now. She told me I would experience many hardships and obstacles, but I would triumph over all my enemies because my hardships would open my eyes. I wonder what that last part means.

Johnnie opened the screen door. "Long time no see."

"Can I come in?" Earl asked respectfully.

"I'm expecting company. How long is this going to take?" she asked, having made up her mind to make every effort to speak proper English from now on. She looked at her watch.

"You expecting that boyfriend you deceived me with? Or are you expecting Martin Winters, my former friend?"

"Come on in, Earl. I see we've got some things to say to each other."

Earl walked in and closed the door. "So, you don't deny sleeping with Martin?"

"I only did what you and my mother taught me to do. Are you really going to stand there and blame me for what *you* did?"

"What did I do besides get you this wonderful house and put beautiful clothes on your back? What did I do besides get you stock in a company that was flourishing? What did I do besides love you the best way I knew how? And how did you repay me? By fucking my friend!"

"How dare you come to me, blaming me for some shit *you* did?" Johnnie shouted. "I was fifteen god-damned years old, Earl! Fifteen! Don't come into my house yelling about all the shit you did for me. You should have done that and more. As a matter of fact, they should lock your ass up for raping a minor! What you did is called statutory rape, Earl!"

"But I—"

"Shut up! I don't wanna hear your bullshit! You're not getting out of this! You came over here! You came to *my* house!" She folded her arms. "So, I'm going to tell you the truth about you, Earl! The truth is you didn't just want some pussy, did you? You wanted to fuck a child, didn't you? How would you like it if somebody fucked all three of your daughters, huh? Would it be okay if a sex-crazed insurance man fucked Janet or Stacy or Marjorie? Oh, and on Christmas Eve, at that! Do you even remember what you did two years ago today; that you fucked me in my mother's bed? Do you remember me saying the Lord's Prayer while you pumped me?

"So, yeah, I got what I could get out of you. Yeah, you bought me this house. You bought me just about everything I own. But guess what? None of it, and I mean none of it, can replace what you took from me!"

"I'm sorry, Johnnie," Earl offered without contrition, which was indicative of a conscience that had long since been abandoned.

"I'm not finished, Earl! You know you're partially responsibly for my mother's death, don't you?"

"What? How can you possibly blame me for that? I had nothing to do with that, Johnnie. You're being totally unfair to me."

"I can, and I do blame you, Earl, because you gave me a taste of the good life."

"You've gotta be fucking kidding me! I took you out of a rat trap Marguerite called a house and you blame me?"

"You're too blind to see your own bullshit," Johnnie said, calming down. "My mother was trying to blackmail Richard Goode because you had given me so much. Don't you see? A mother's jealousy often overshadows her love. By doing all you did, by giving me all you gave me, by helping me make some real money, my mother saw her own failure as a whore. Like you, she was blind to her own bullshit too. Now she's dead, Earl . . . dead and gone, all because you wanted to fuck a child."

"What can I do to make it up to you?" Earl said sincerely, finally coming to grips with what he'd done.

Johnnie shook her head in disbelief and said compassionately, "Do you really think you can make it up to me, Earl? Do you really? People are dead because of you—lots of them."

"You mean the riot? You're blaming me for that too?"

Enraged again by his need to deny his complicity in the murders, Johnnie screamed, "You goddamned right I blame *you* for the riot! But I don't just blame you for that. I blame you for the death of my white uncle and his two sons. See, *your* sin has spread through the whole damned town. You corrupted me, and now lots of people are dead." She stopped short of telling him about Sharon Trudeau's murder. Tears formed and dropped. "I watched my cousin, Blue, kill his brother, Beau, in a fit of rage. Then I watched Blue put a gun to his head and blow his brains out.

"After that, my uncle tried to choke the life out of me, and my aunt, Ethel Beauregard, shot him in the back of the head and blew his brains and blood all over me. All of this because my uncle Eric didn't know he was calling his half-sister, Marguerite, a whore who got what she deserved. When he called my mother that, when he talked about her like she wasn't even a human being, I told him about the whores in his own family, and that's when the killing began. So yes, you caused their deaths too."

Crying now, Earl asked, "What can I do? How can I make this right?"

Calm again, Johnnie said, "Go home, Earl. Go home to Meredith. She loves you, and only God knows why. Don't ever come here again. If you return to this place, I won't be responsible for what happens to you. If you see me on the streets, act as if we are total strangers. And in time, perhaps I can forgive you for all that you've caused because you didn't have enough self-control to keep from fucking a defenseless child, a fifteen-year-old, church-going, Bible-believing Christian girl."

She walked past a whimpering Earl Shamus, who she had completely dismantled with her truth, and opened the door. "Get out," Johnnie said in a genteel voice that would otherwise be soothing. "You can cry out there if have to, but this is Christmas Eve, and I won't let you ruin another one for me."

Earl walked out. He stopped in his tracks and turned around to say something, but Johnnie slammed the door in his face. Feeling good in her soul for the first time in a very long time, she walked over to the sofa, sat down, picked up the phone, and called her best friend, Sadie Lane, saying cheerfully, "Everything's all set. Bring your kids over. This'll be the best Christmas they ever had!"

After she hung up, Johnnie realized it was time to visit Marguerite in her mausoleum. She had a number of things to say to her too. Earl Shamus was wrong, but so was her mother. The things she had to say to her mother could wait. Christmas Eve was supposed to be fun, and when Sadie and her children came over, fun was what they were going to have.

Book Club Discussion Questions

1) Should Johnnie feel guilty about Richard Goode's murder? Why or why not?

2) Why do you think Johnnie is strongly attracted to Napoleon?

3) If you were Lucas, would you have given Johnnie another chance? Why or why not?

4) Lucas and Johnnie had other relationships while claiming to love each other. Is it possible to be in love, yet have an affair? Why or why not?

5) Johnnie is a descendant of the aristocratic Beauregard family. Given the behavior of Nathaniel and Josephine, Eric and Marguerite, and Beau and Johnnie, in your opinion, can promiscuity be passed along from generation to generation? Why or why not?

6) Johnnie is a Christian who made decisions that went against her beliefs. Do non-Christians do the same things? Do they say one thing and do another?

7) If so, is hypocrisy applicable to all? Or does it only apply to religious groups?

8) When Johnnie learned the reason Lucas found it difficult to leave Marla completely, and decided to do what Marla was doing, why did she pretend that it was her first time performing fellatio?

9) Why didn't she do for Lucas what she did for Napoleon, since it was the same act?

10) Two years have passed since Marguerite sold Johnnie to Earl Shamus. In your opinion, what has Johnnie learned?

11) Johnnie blames God for all the evil that happens to her. Is she justified? Why or why not?

12) Napoleon is obsessed with Johnnie, and willing to commit multiple murders to have her. While *Little Black Girl Lost I & II* are works of fiction, do you think sex can make a person that obsessive in the real world?

13) Ethel Beauregard, at point blank range, fired a pistol in Johnnie's face. The bullet hit the wall. Was this an act of God? Why or why not?

14) When Johnnie went to see The Fortuneteller, the voice warned her, telling her to run. Why didn't she?

15) In real life, do you think people ignore the voice in their heads? If so, why?

16) Johnnie Wise can be very persuasive when she wants to be. Why didn't she persuade Lucas to stay away from the drug trade?

17) After all she's done, Johnnie still considers herself a good girl. Give your opinion as to why she feels this way.

18) Do you agree with Johnnie's behavior in the two novels I've written about her? Why or why not?

19) Discuss Johnnie's virtues and her shortcomings.

20) In the final chapter, Earl Shamus visits Johnnie. She accuses him of being responsible for the riot and all the murders, including Marguerite, Sharon Trudeau, the bellhop, and all the Beauregard men. Is her accusation accurate? Why or why not?

IN STORES NOW

1-893196-37-2

1-893196-41-0

1-893196-23-2

1-893196-28-3

shoulda, woulda, coulda

1-893196-25-9

0-9747025-9-5

1-893196-27-5

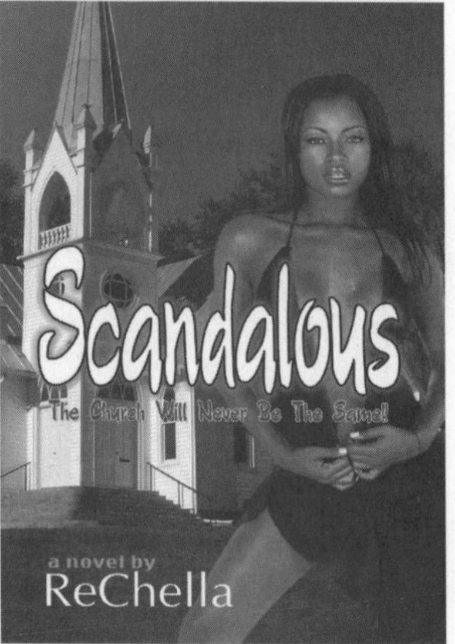

1893196-30-5

MARCH 2006
1-893196-32-1

MARCH 2006
1-893196-33-X

APRIL 2006
1-893196-40-2

APRIL 2006
1-893196-34-8

OTHER URBAN BOOKS TITLES

Title	Author	Quantity	Cost
Drama Queen	LaJill Hunt		$14.95
No More Drama	LaJill Hunt		$14.95
Shoulda Woulda Coulda	LaJill Hunt		$14.95
Is It A Crime	Roy Glenn		$14.95
MOB	Roy Glenn		$14.95
Drug Related	Roy Glenn		$14.95
Lovin' You Is Wrong	Alisha Yvonne		$14.95
Bulletproof Soul	Michelle Buckley		$14.95
You Wrong For That	Toschia		$14.95
A Gangster's girl	Chunichi		$14.95
Married To The Game	Chunichi		$14.95
Sex In The Hood	White Chocolate		$14.95
Little Black Girl Lost	Keith Lee Johnson		$14.95
Sister Girls	Angel M. Hunter		$14.95
Driven	KaShamba Williams		$14.95
Street Life	Jihad		$14.95
Baby Girl	Jihad		$14.95
A Thug's Life	Thomas Long		$14.95
Cash Rules	Thomas Long		$14.95
The Womanizers	Dwayne S. Joseph		$14.95
Never Say Never	Dwayne S. Joseph		$14.95
She's Got Issues	Stephanie Johnson		$14.95
Rockin' Robin	Stephanie Johnson		$14.95
Sins Of The Father	Felicia Madlock		$14.95
Back On The Block	Felicia Madlock		$14.95
Chasin' It	Tony Lindsey		$14.95
Street Possession	Tony Lindsey		$14.95
Around The Way Girls	LaJill Hunt		$14.95
Around The Way Girls 2	LaJill Hunt		[illegible]
Girls From Da Hood	Nikki Turner		$14.95

Girls from Da Hood 2	Nikki Turner		$14.95
Dirty Money	Ashley JaQuavis		$14.95
Mixed Messages	LaTonya Y. Williams		$14.95
Don't Hate The Player	Brandie		$14.95
Payback	Roy Glenn		$14.95
Scandalous	ReChella		$14.95
Urban Affair	Tony Lindsey		$14.95
Harlem Confidential	Cole Riley		$14.95

Urban Books
74 Andrews Ave.
Wheatley Heights, NY 11798

Subtotal: ______________

Postage:_______________ Calculate postage and handling as follows: Add $2.50 for the first item and $1.25 for each additional item

Total: _________________

Name: ____________________________

Address:____
____

City: ____________________ State: _________ Zip: ____________________

Telephone: ( ) _______________

Type of Payment (Check: ___ Money Order: ___)

All orders must be prepaid by check or money order drawn on an American bank.

Books may sometimes be out of stock. In that instance, please select your alternate choices below.

Alternate Choices:

1.______________________________

2.______________________________

PLEASE ALLOW 4-6 WEEKS FOR SHIPPING